# TOMORROW'S CHILD

## Jim Garrison

*For Bob & Dawn*
*Hope you enjoy*
*Thanks,*
*Jim R Garrison*

AmErica House
Baltimore

© 2001 by Jim Garrison.

First printing

ISBN: 1-58851-342-4
PUBLISHED BY AMERICA HOUSE BOOK PUBLISHERS
www.publishamerica.com
Baltimore

Printed in the United States of America

This book is for Nancy, who means all the world to me, and without whom it could not have been written.

With special thanks to Susan. She read the first draft and offered much appreciated advice and encouragement.

*My plan, my only dream, was to stop pollution and bring the earth back to what it once was. By attempting to correct all the wrongs done to it, I may have destroyed the very thing I was trying to save. In creating this new life, I have unleashed a monster, but the monster still has not yet fully awakened.*

From the journal of Jason Harding
December 17, 1997

# Before the Storm

The 1961 Ford F-10 pickup bounced along a dirt road that was barely more than a path through the woods. Each turn of the tires seemed to find another pothole or deep rut in the baked earth. A cloud of dust billowed out from beneath the rear of the dented, rusted truck and obscured the road behind them.

Jason sat next to the door with his arm hanging out and Robert, his best friend, sat in the middle straddling the gearshift in the floor. School had let out for the summer and Earl, Jason's father, had promised the two ten-year-old boys he would take them to the family cabin at Shaver's Lake for a long weekend. Shaver's Lake was a large body of water deep in the West Virginia Mountains, and the tiny primitive log cabin was perched on a small knoll several hundred yards from the water. Earl typically referred to this place as West Virginia's best-kept secret, unspoiled by man and industry. He still prided himself on the deal he had gotten when he purchased the place back in 1962. It was a real steal, he was always bragging, and he should feel guilty for taking advantage of the fellow who sold it to him, but he couldn't blame himself for the guy's ignorance.

Unfortunately, Jason's mother didn't feel the same way about the place and had been up here only once. He once overheard them arguing about it. His mother wanted to get rid of the place. She said it was costing them too much in taxes and maintenance. Earl was stubborn though. He wouldn't even consider selling it. He came up here often, usually by himself, sometimes bringing friends from work, and sometimes taking Jason and Robert. He told them he liked to fish, but Jason had a feeling he just liked to get away.

Jason leaned forward and grinned at his father.

"What?" Earl laughed.

"Are we almost there, Dad?"

"Why? You in a hurry?"

"I thought maybe we'd be in time to go swimming."

"Well, don't you worry. We'll be there before it gets dark. This old girl doesn't like the dark any more than I do." He patted the metal dash.

Earl Harding always referred to the truck as an old girl, and he took care of her as if she were a real person. He said she might be held together with duct tape and a prayer, but she would always get you where you were going. He was always quick to point out that you couldn't say the same for that little imported job Marie liked to drive. Jason knew his mother wouldn't be caught dead riding in this old thing. She was even embarrassed to have it parked in the driveway and made his father park it behind their neat two-story house so the neighbors wouldn't see it. She might be embarrassed by it, but his father hadn't been wrong yet.

"Look!" Robert pointed.

Jason saw the great bald eagle gliding above the trees even as Robert was pointing. Earl had seen it also.

"He's a magnificent creature." Earl said. "I've heard they are almost extinct."

"Why is that, Mr. Harding?" Robert asked.

"People. People and their damn machines," he answered. "Destroying the environment. Polluting the streams and the air. It's a miracle we all don't become extinct."

"Can't we do something about it?" Jason asked.

"I wish we could, son. I really do. But until everyone starts caring about the environment, things are just going to keep on getting worse."

Jason looked at the eagle again. The great bird suddenly dived below the treetops.

"Where did he go?"

"Probably the lake or Shaver's Creek. Eagle's are born fishers."

"We almost there, then?"

"Just over that hill." He laughed and nodded. "Didn't I say you'd have plenty of time to go swimming?"

"Maybe we'll get lucky and see him catch something," Robert said.

"Maybe we will." Earl smiled. "There's the cabin now."

As they crested the hill, the lake and mountains beyond formed a panoramic view beneath the cobalt blue summer sky that was hard to put into words. Earl stopped the truck and rested his chin on the steering wheel, languishing in this moment. Neither of the boys said a word. They too seemed to be awestruck by the sheer beauty of this magnificent vista of trees and water, mountains and sky.

Earl loved this place. Secretly he knew he loved it even more than their place in Falls Church, Virginia. If he could have his way, he would pack up just what he needed to survive and move up here, but he knew Marie would never come. There was too much of the city in her. She was born and raised in Silver Spring, Maryland. She grew up with the stores, the theatres, and the hustle and bustle of big city life. He, on the other hand, came from a little town in southern Virginia with a total population of seven hundred and fifty-two where the main occupation was tobacco farming. His father owned the general store there, the only general store for nearly fifty miles.

When Earl graduated from high school, his parents sent him to the University of Maryland where he received a four-year degree in Forestry and Conservation. He graduated with honors and was offered a field position with a newly formed environmental agency that would later be known as the EPA in Washington, DC. However, as fate would have it, the job ended up behind a desk in the Washington office ninety percent of the time. The other ten percent was spent traveling between various field offices in the mid-Atlantic region. He met Marie in one of those field offices and asked her to marry him a short nine weeks later. Jason was born a year later, and the rest was history.

"Dad?"

Earl looked at the two boys and grinned. "Sorry guys. I guess my mind was wandering. You know how it is when you start getting old." He was thirty-two and they were ten. How could they possibly know what getting old meant? He knew he was still young enough to do anything he wanted to do, but sometimes he felt so very old. He was sure the desk job and all the paperwork did it. He could tell by the way that he felt when he came up here on weekends.

"You're not old, Dad," said Jason.

"My Dad is going to be forty next month," added Robert and laughed. "Now, that's old."

"What do you say we go get this truck unloaded and do some fishing?"

Earl started down the slight incline. The cabin came into view, nestled among the big trees, still and vacant but inviting.

"We want to go swimming. You said we could. Remember?"

"Oh, okay. I'll catch us some dinner, and you guys can go swimming."

The gravel driveway turned off the wider dirt road and twisted up the small hill where it made a big circle in front of the small cabin. Earl stopped the truck at the steps that went up to the porch. There were four windows in front, and they were still boarded up from the winter.

Jason and Robert got out and started toward the lake.

"Hold it." Earl called. "Where do you two think you're going?"

"Down to the lake," answered Jason.

"You said we could go swimming, Mr. Harding. Remember?"

"I know that. But I thought you'd give me a hand unloading first."

"Oh," said Jason. "Come on Robert. This won't take long."

"Sure. It's still early anyway."

The two boys started grabbing things from the back of the truck while Earl unlocked the cabin door and threw open the shutters on the front windows. He stood in the middle of the big room for a moment and allowed his eyes to feed upon the rustic beauty of the place. It wasn't a smart room by any standards and obviously decorated by a man. No interior decorator had assembled the casual collection of odd pieces. Nor would a decorator have condoned the faded chintz curtains and the clutter of books everywhere. A huge stone fireplace dominated one wall. Black, iron rods along the right side of the fireplace supported cast-iron pots. Bunk beds, obviously hand made, were against the back wall with brightly colored quilts covering them. The ceiling was open with the beams exposed.

He could be happy living out the rest of his life here. He sometimes wondered just how much of a real life he was missing sitting behind that desk in Washington.

"Where do you want this stuff, Mr. Harding?" Robert asked.

"Oh?" He turned and saw the two boys in the doorway, their arms and hands full. They'd tried to carry just about everything that was in the back of the truck in one trip. He laughed. "Any place. I'll put it away later. What do you say we check out that lake?"

"Great." Jason just let everything fall where he stood and headed outside.

"Aren't you forgetting something?"

"No." Jason answered.

"What about your bathing suits?"

"Oh, yes. Bathing suits," Robert said.

"Let's go skinny-dipping," said Jason. "It's just us guys, right? No one's going to see us."

"I don't think so, Jason. Suits. Now."

"Oh, alright." They started digging through their duffel bags until they found their suits. "Race you!" he told Robert.

"I'll unload whatever you two left in the truck. You boys stick to this side of the lake. I want to be able to hear you."

"Sure, Dad."

"Whatever you say, Mr. Harding."

Earl mussed Robert's hair. "I like this kid, Jason. Where'd you find him?"

"I don't know. He just followed me home from school one day."

"Well, I'm serious. Don't go too far, and be careful swimming. It's a little early for snakes, but you don't know what could be under the water."

"We'll be careful, Dad. Promise. Come on, Rob. Last one in is a rotten egg."

They raced past him, down the steps, and out of sight on the narrow path through the brush that separated the cabin from the lake. Earl had promised himself several times over the years that he was going to clean up all that brush so he could have an unobstructed view from the porch of the lake, but he had just never gotten around to it.

He opened the driver's door of the truck and took the carrying case that held his fly rod from behind the seat. He closed the door and started toward the cabin when Jason began screaming.

"Dad! Dad! Come here!"

He dropped the case and ran down the path, his mind picturing the worst.

"Jason!" he called. "Robert! What's wrong?"

He came out of the brush and almost ran over the two boys. They were just standing there staring down at the water.

"Look." Jason pointed.

Earl walked slowly past the boys and down to the water's edge. He couldn't believe what he was seeing. There were dead fish everywhere. They were floating in the water and washed up all along the rocky beach. There must have been hundreds of them. The boys followed him as he walked to within a few feet of the water."

"What happened, Dad? What did this?"

"I don't know, son. I don't know."

Robert squatted and started to put his hand in the water. "It smells funny."

"NO!" Earl grabbed him and yanked him away from the water.

Robert fell backward, scraping his hands on the rocks when he landed.

"What did you do that for?"

"I'm sorry, Robert, but you were going to put your hand in the water. I couldn't let you do that."

Jason had walked down the shoreline where a movement had caught his attention.

"You boys stay here and don't touch anything. I'm going to get a jar or something to put some of this water in. I want to find out what caused this."

"Sure," said Robert, and went to see what Jason was looking at.

A few minutes later, Earl returned with a glass jar. He was wearing rubber gloves. He knelt and sank the jar in the tainted water. When the jar was nearly full, he took it out and studied it. It was clear as any drinking water. He sniffed it. No odor. No. Wait. It *did* smell. He recognized that smell. What was it? He couldn't be sure. He had smelled something like it before.

He suddenly realized Jason and Robert weren't there. He stood up, screwed the cap on the jar of water, set it down, and took off the rubber gloves. That's when he saw the two boys. They were sitting on a big rock several hundred feet away and looking at something.

Earl dropped the rubber gloves next to the jar of water and went to the boys.

11

"What are you guys doing?" he called.

They didn't answer. They were staring at something on the other side of the rocks.

Earl climbed up on the rock and sat between the two boys. That was when he saw what had their attention. A great bald eagle lay between the rocks, flapping its wings and struggling to get on its feet. Once it almost succeeded, but fell again.

"Can't we help, Dad?"

Earl looked at Jason and saw there were tears in his eyes. He noticed that Robert was crying also.

"Please tell me that neither of you touched that bird."

Jason shook his head. "You told us not to touch anything, remember?"

Earl put his arm around Jason's shoulder.

"Can't we do anything, Mr. Harding?" asked Robert.

"I took a sample of the water. I can't see anything, but it has an odor I can't identify. Something has gotten into the water. I just don't know what."

"But what about him?" Jason pointed to the eagle.

"We'd be wise not to touch him until we know what caused this."

"Then we can't do anything. He's going to die, isn't he?"

Earl nodded. "I feel as bad as you, but there's nothing we can do."

Jason and Robert watched the bird. It seemed to be struggling less and less.

"Something must have gotten into Shaver's Creek. Maybe it was industrial run off, or maybe someone is dumping something in the water. Someone is always polluting our streams and lakes and rivers one way or another. I'll get in touch with our field office in the area and report this. They'll find out who or what is causing this and put a stop to it."

"Won't that be too late?" asked Robert.

"I guess, in a way, but if we stop whatever it was that did this, maybe we can prevent it from happening again."

"I wish there was a way to end pollution."

"I do too, son. But as long as there are men and machines, there's going to be pollution."

"We'll find a way to stop it." Jason looked at Robert. "Won't we, Rob?"

Robert just nodded. He wiped the tears from his eyes with the back of his hand and continued to stare at the dying bird.

"If anyone could figure out how to end pollution the whole world would praise that person. But as I said, as long as there are men and machines, there's going to be pollution. It's just a fact of life."

"Or death," added Jason. He was staring at the eagle. The bird had stopped struggling and was still.

"I think he's dead," whispered Robert.

No one said anything else. What was there to say? The bird was dead.

The wind began to pick up and dark clouds were starting to pile up along the mountainous horizon. The first drops of rain dotted the big rocks.

"We better get inside." Earl said. "Looks like a storm is coming."

# Cry for the Child

**December 4, 2001**

Bob waited, not because he wanted to, but because he had been ordered to. He knew something wasn't right. Husbands were supposed to be with their wives when they were giving birth, weren't they? From the beginning, he and Sandy had planned for this, and being away from her side wasn't part of the deal.

There were two other men in the small waiting area on the third floor of the Holy Cross Hospital. He found himself studying their faces to pass time. They both looked to be in their twenties, young and handsome. They hadn't said anything, but they seemed anxious, upset, and maybe a little angry. Apparently, they had been told to wait here also. Why? What was going on? This just wasn't done anymore. Sending husbands to a waiting area was a throwback to the Fifties.

Bob shifted uneasily in the uncomfortable, vinyl chair. He picked up the same dog-eared magazine for the fifth time and flipped through it.

This was archaic. Husbands should be with their wives at times like this, not sitting in some out-of-the-way waiting place. He was more irritated with himself than Dr. Stevens. He should have been more forceful. He had rights, didn't he?

Bob glanced at the clock above the nurses' station again. The hands hadn't moved. Maybe the damn thing was just there for appearances.

Dr. George Stevens was Sandy's gynecologist. He had been her gynecologist since she was a teenager. He was also Bob's uncle and a close friend to both families. Bob trusted him. It wasn't just because he was family; he was the best gynecologist anywhere.

Bob tossed the magazine on the table and went to the nurses' desk for the third time. There was only one nurse behind the counter. She was fiftyish, short, heavy around the middle, had hair that was completely white, and wore reading glasses that set low on a chubby nose. She looked up as he approached.

"I still haven't heard anything, Mr. Sanders," she said before he could ask.

"Can you at least go check or something?"

"Trust me. Everything is okay. She's with Dr. Stevens." The nurse smiled. "He's the best GYN on staff."

"I know that. He's also my uncle. I just want to know about my wife."

15

Sandy's pregnancy had been without incident for seven months. Everything was completely normal. Then the pains began. They had really started last night with what she had interpreted as a slight case of indigestion, and she hadn't said anything until she called his office at ten this morning. She told him she was probably just panicking. After all, she wasn't due until the end of February--nearly two months away.

Bob worked in Arlington, and even by the recently opened Metro Vacuum Rail, it still took over a half-hour to get to their Georgia Avenue apartment in Silver Spring.

When Bob opened the door Sandy was standing in the middle of the room next to a suitcase.

"I called George," she said before he had a chance to say anything.

"What did he say?"

"He said to meet him at the hospital right away."

"Hospital?"

She smiled, nodding, and then gritted her teeth when another pain hit. She held out her arms to him. "I'm scared, Bob. It's so early. What if something is wrong with the baby?"

"Nothing's wrong with our baby. I promise you." He embraced her. He could feel the baby moving. "See." He laughed and put his hand on her enormous belly. "He just wants to get out and stretch his legs."

She forced a laugh. "What makes you so sure it's a he?"

"Could be a girl, but I'm betting it's a boy."

Dr. Stevens was tall, over six feet, and still trim at sixty. His wavy, brown hair had very little gray in it, and his tanned face was only now beginning to develop wrinkles. He was wearing his ever-present, confident smile when he met them in the emergency room. He was waiting with a nurse and a wheel chair.

"Sit," he told Sandy. Bob watched while they helped her into the chair and checked her pulse and listened for the baby's heartbeat.

"What's wrong, George? Is she okay?" he asked.

"Don't worry." George placed a big hand on Sandy's. He smiled and winked. "You're just a little early, Sandy. Nothing we can't handle."

"She's two months early, George."

"I may have miscalculated. It happens." He smiled at Sandy. "You're going to be just fine, young lady. The baby too. The heartbeat is strong and regular."

Bob didn't believe him. He saw something he didn't think Sandy caught, a quick shadow that came over George's face. It may have been his imagination, or was it just concern he was seeing?

16

"Looks like this baby is ready to be born." He smiled at Sandy. "Bob? Why don't you check Sandy in and meet us on the third floor?"

"I don't want to leave Sandy, Doc. I promised." He knelt and took her hands in his. "Are you sure everything is all right?"

"I'll know more after I've had a look. It shouldn't take more than a few minutes. "Why don't you call John and Edna? Your parents too. They all must be very anxious."

"But..."

"No but. Just go. Edna will have your head if you make her miss the birth of her first grandchild." He chuckled. "Besides, I've got doctoring to do here."

Bob reluctantly let go of her hand. Sandy looked back over her shoulder as the nurse pushed her toward an open elevator door. Her lips formed the words; "I love you."

That was nearly three hours ago.

"Damn."

The other two men in the small alcove looked at him. They seemed to be aware of his presence for the first time.

"Excuse me. I just remembered. I never called our parents."

"This your first?" The young man across from him asked and added without waiting for an answer, "This is our third." There was a strange sadness in his voice. Having a baby wasn't supposed to be sad.

"Congratulations." Bob said.

"Yeah, sure. I pleaded with Joyce to get an abortion. I begged her, but she wouldn't hear it. She's Catholic, you see." He looked at his hands, studying them. "She keeps saying third time is the charm." He was a handsome young man, neatly dressed in a dark suit, but his face showed pain and stress... a lot of stress. He sat on the edge of the chair, continuously wringing his hands like a wet dishtowel. Bob thought he looked like he was about to cry.

"You really should call your parents." The other man, hardly more than a teenager, said. "They should be here. I know I would want mine here."

"This your first?" Bob asked.

"It's the first, but I'm not the father." He laughed. "I'm not even married yet. My name is Billy Sommers. My sister, Becky is having a baby. We already know it's a boy. Our parents were killed a year ago. I don't know who the father is and don't care. But if our parents were alive we'd both want them here."

"You should have made her get an abortion," said the handwringer. "I don't care what the Catholics have to say about it."

"We're not Catholic, but we don't believe in abortions," Billy said.

"Neither does Joyce, but these things *are* abortions. We can't let our wives have any more babies. They are all monsters. It has to stop."

"What's wrong with you, Mister?" Billy asked. "Babies aren't monsters, and besides, abortions are illegal now. Everybody knows that."

The handwringer forced a laugh and repeated under his breath, "Monsters."

"Mr. Sommers?"

Billy's head turned with a sudden jerk at the sound of his name. A different nurse was standing in front of the counter, trim and young. A young resident had joined her. Bob looked at the two and thought how sad they both looked. The nurse motioned him to come.

Billy grinned. "Looks like my wait is over. See you fellas later."

He joined the two, and the nurse said something to him. Billy started crying. The nurse briefly looked at the two men in the waiting area before putting her arm around Billy and leading him through the double doors.

The handwringer stared at them and whispered, "See that. They just told him. Did you see the way she looked at us? She knows. They're monsters. They are all monsters."

"What did they tell him?" Bob asked.

The handwringer looked at him, but didn't answer.

"Excuse me," Bob said and went to the pay phone. He lifted the receiver but just stared at it. Something was wrong. He could feel it. He had seen it in that nurse's eyes. What? He looked back at the man in the small alcove. He was alone, staring into space. It was what he said about abortions and monsters that nagged at him. He couldn't shake it. What was he not saying? Why did Billy start crying when the nurse talked to him?

Just seven months ago this past May, he and Sandy laid on the bank of a small creek just over the line in West Virginia. The water was clear and unpolluted there, clean and cold. They went there often to be alone, swim in the cold stream, and dry on a blanket on the grassy knoll. They often put up a tent and camped out, fishing for trout and cooking their dinner over an open fire.

They always filled their water jugs with the spring-like water. Six years earlier, they would never even have considered doing such a thing. Chemical plants upstream used to dump huge amounts of waste into the small streams and rivers until the government put a stop to it. It was about that time that things began to change. It had been all over the news. The President had even talked about it in his State of the Union address. The Environmental Protection Agency had developed some kind of formula and had chosen this particular stream as the first test site. They emptied barrels of the stuff into the water, and things seemed to change almost overnight. Now, the water was like drinking spring water, and nothing was cleaner than spring water.

That was where he proposed to Sandy. When she said yes, he was happier than he had ever been. They made love that same afternoon and were married just three weeks later. Both he and Sandy were sure the baby had been conceived that very afternoon he had proposed.

He pictured Sandy's face in his mind. She was so happy when George told her she was pregnant. He swore he would never let anything destroy that happiness.

A hand on his shoulder abruptly brought him back.

"Bob," said Dr. Stevens. "You have a son."

"Is Sandy okay?" he asked. "Is the baby okay?"

"We need to talk, Bob," he said, a noticeable sadness in his voice.

Something in the doctor's eyes told him that all was not fine. Something was wrong, dreadfully wrong.

"What's wrong, George?" He should go running to Sandy, but his legs were like rubber. "What is it? Is Sandy-?" He couldn't finish the question.

"Sandy's going to be okay, but there were some complications. It wasn't an easy birth. The baby-"

"What about the baby?" he cut him off.

"The baby was ... just before she gave birth, something happened. I'm not exactly sure what. She was so early, but everything looked normal. I was sure we were safe."

"Safe? From what?"

"Maybe we should sit."

Bob shook his head. "I asked you a question. Safe from what?"

"Something happened in the final few minutes. It's happened before, but I wasn't prepared for it this time because Sandy was so early. This is the fifth time it's happened here at Holy Cross, but there have been a dozen or more similar incidents in Hagerstown and Cumberland."

"What are you talking about? What kind of incidents?"

The doctor didn't answer. Instead, he pushed open the door and motioned for Bob to follow. After a minute, George said without looking at Bob, "This is the first time I've actually heard of anything like this happening. "Three times in the same night is against all odds."

Bob noticed George seemed visibly shaken. That wasn't like him. He was usually so cool about everything. He stopped and put his hand on the doctor's arm. "Where are we going, George? I want to see Sandy."

"We have to do this first, Bob. You have to see the baby first. Trust me on this."

There was a scream, and then the sound of people running. More screaming. Something crashed into a wall. Loud voices. George looked back over his shoulder briefly, but they were still alone in the corridor.

"What's going on?"

Doctor Stevens just shook his head, but Bob saw there were tears in his eyes. He quickly wiped them away with the back of his hand and faked a smile. "Sometimes being a doctor isn't such a wonderful thing. You're going to need to be strong, Bob. Sandy is going to need you more than ever."

He walked ahead of Bob through another set of swinging doors and down a wide hall. Bob felt like he was moving through a dream and everyone was staring at them.

They passed an open door on their right. The room was in shambles with overturned equipment. He saw Billy. He was sitting on the floor with his face in his hands. A man, he looked like a priest, was consoling him.

George closed the door and took Bob's arm.

"There's no easy way to prepare you for this."

Bob looked at George, but he didn't know what to say.

They went through a third set of doors. These had a sign on them, "Restricted, Hospital Personnel Only." At the end of a short hallway, they stopped at a glass window on their left. The curtains were pulled.

"I guess the only real way is to show you," he said.

Suddenly Bob thought he understood. The baby was deformed. Missing parts or something like that. That was okay though. Most things could be fixed these days. He could accept that. What did that have to do with the others?

"What is it, George? I want to know. What's wrong with the baby?"

George didn't answer. He put an arm around Bob's shoulders and tapped on the glass. The curtains drew back a little, and a nurse's head appeared. George nodded to her and she went away, but not before Bob saw the sadness in her dark eyes.

A minute later, the curtains opened.

Bob hadn't been prepared for what he saw. His legs suddenly became weak. George held him while he stared in disbelief. He couldn't believe what he was seeing. God wouldn't let something like this happen. He stared at the thing in the glass crib, and he recalled what the man in the waiting area had said. "They're all monsters." He was looking at a real monster. It wasn't human. This thing wasn't a baby. He felt the tears on his face and realized he was crying.

"I'm not sure if this is the right time, but a Doctor William Cromwell from the Children's Hospital in Bethesda wants to talk with you and Sandy

20

about your son," said Stevens. "He and a research scientist, Jason Harding, are with the other two babies at the moment, but they said they wanted to talk to the both of you as soon as possible."

Bob wasn't listening.

"Dr. Cromwell has assured me he can help. There are things they can do."

"That screaming I heard?"

George nodded.

"The other boy, Billy?"

Again, George nodded.

"What's happening, George?"

"These doctors are good people, Bob. They are doing some fantastic things with artificial limbs and other body parts, even synthesizing vital organs. I understand Cromwell and Harding are being considered for the Nobel Prize for their work. People say they're fanatics in their research and seem to be driven by forces no one can quite understand. I really believe they can help."

"Does Sandy know about this?"

George shook his head.

"What am I going to say to her?"

"You have to be strong, Bob. Sandy's really going to need you."

Bob looked away. He couldn't look at that thing any longer, but looking away didn't help. He could still see it. He would always see it. The thing seemed to *squirm* in the glass crib. That was the only word he could think of. It was like a slug. It belonged in a circus freak show. No. It didn't belong anywhere. It was an accident. There was nothing those doctors could ever do to change what it was.

It had holes where there should have been ears. There wasn't a nose, only skin stretched tightly across a face that looked as if it had gotten hot and partially melted. There were no arms, and the left leg ended just below the hip.

The blue eyes that had looked at him seemed to be pleading. He suddenly realized what they were saying, what had to be done.

"George." He looked at the doctor. "You said Sandy doesn't know yet?"

George shook his head.

"Then I'm going to tell Sandy our son died."

"I wish he had, Bob."

"You don't understand. That's not our baby in there. Our son was born dead."

"What about…?"

"Put it out of its misery. Show it the same mercy we'd show a dog or cat or horse." He looked back into the nursery and quickly turned away again. "For Christ's sake, George. Close the fucking curtains."

The doctor nodded to the nurse, and the curtains closed with a snap.

"If you need anything signed, tell me. I'll do anything that's needed, but I never want to see that thing again. I sure as hell don't want Sandy seeing it."

"What about the doctors? I really think you should talk to them."

He shook his head. "That's no baby in there. It's an accident. God's getting old. His hand must have slipped when he was making this one. Give that thing to those doctors if you want. Let them do whatever they want to do. As far as I'm concerned, our son was born dead. That's what I'm telling Sandy. Are you going to back me up?"

George nodded. "If that's the way you want it."

"That's just the way it has to be. That thing would make an old woman of her. We'll have more babies, won't we? Lots of healthy, normal babies."

Stevens didn't answer.

"What's wrong, George?"

"Sandy won't be able to have any more babies, Bob. Something happened during the pregnancy."

"We'll adopt, then. Yeah. We'll adopt.

"I'll tell Cromwell he can take all three babies."

Bob stared at him. "Three?" he whispered.

"Yes." George nodded. "The screams you heard a few minutes ago. It has happened three times now for one couple. The other was a young unmarried woman."

"Billy?"

"The boy in the room. Yes. Cromwell was talking to him."

"I thought he was a priest." Bob looked at the glass with the closed curtain. "My God, George! What's going on?"

22

# Chapter One

**Thursday, May 4, 1995, 11:00 p.m.**

Diane Kimball couldn't sleep. She slid from under the covers, being careful not to wake up Josh, and stood there several minutes, studying his face. He was lying on his back and sleeping soundly. Even in the darkness of the bedroom, she could easily make out his handsome features.

His brown hair curled over one closed eye. She reached out to brush it aside but stopped, her hand poised just inches above his head. Did she dare touch him? He might wake up. She was suddenly afraid. There were so many questions piling up inside her head. Did she really want to take the chance of waking him up? She might have to face answers to all those questions-answers she didn't really want to hear.

She went to the small sofa next to a window and curled up there. Light from the full moon came through the double windows and gave a false impression of twilight, even though it was midnight. Something about Josh was bugging her, and she wasn't exactly sure what it was. She watched him sleeping in the king-sized bed. He hadn't moved.

Something had happened. She wasn't sure exactly when, but it was after she had fallen asleep, after she and Josh had made love. She had to make some sense out of this. Talking to Josh wasn't going to help. It sounded crazy, now that she really thought about it, but she couldn't shake the feeling. Whoever this man was, it sure as hell wasn't Josh Hamilton. He wasn't the same man she had fallen in love with six months ago. He wasn't the same man she had fallen asleep next to a few hours ago.

Her Josh lived his life on the edge. He never accepted the safe and sure path. He took reckless chances behind the wheel of his red Corvette, driving too fast, passing on hills and in curves and even when there were cars coming at him in the other lane. Josh enjoyed skydiving and was just as reckless there, too. He liked waiting to the last second before releasing his parachute. He once told her there was something about watching the ground rushing up to meet him that he couldn't explain. Sometimes he was tempted not to pull the cord at all, just to find out what it would be like to hit the ground at that speed. He had laughed when he said it, but she had a feeling he wasn't kidding. He wasn't afraid of death-he actually flirted with it. He didn't seem to be afraid of anything. This was what intrigued her, had attracted her to him in the first place.

So, what was different about him? She wasn't sure. Maybe it was the way he had made love to her that second time. The second time? They hadn't made love twice in the same night since that first time they slept together. In the darkness, he had seemed like a totally different person. It was as if a stranger had slipped naked beneath the covers.

Josh was always able to excite her, even when she wasn't in the mood, and they made love a lot, sometimes at night, sometimes during the day. Once they had even made love on a blanket in a park in the middle of the afternoon. She would never even have considered doing that before meeting Josh. Now, she just closed her eyes and let it happen. She shut out the rest of the world and thought only about the two of them. When she had tried to do that a few hours ago, something had been different. She couldn't picture Josh. She couldn't feel him. In the dark, it was like someone else had taken his place. She didn't know this man. Even his kiss was different. The feel of him inside her was the same-yet different. His urgency slowed, and he had started to make love to her almost gently. Their lovemaking continued for the longest time. It hadn't been simply sex like it had been earlier tonight or so many other times. This time, he really made love. It was like that first time when neither of them really knew each other or what to expect. His touch was different, even the way he held her. It was like he had never made love before. That was crazy, and she knew it. What thirty-four year old man had never had sex? Maybe a priest.

What happened? What happened to Josh?

It must be her imagination. After all, she was barely awake. No, she told herself. He had touched her in places and ways she had never been touched before. She had multiple orgasms before he eventually came. And when he finally did, he embraced her tightly, kissing her face and neck and on the mouth. It was the kiss, she realized. That was different, too.

Afterwards, she told him she loved him, but he hadn't answered. She touched his face with the tips of her fingers. It was wet. Tears? Was he crying?

"What's wrong?" she asked.

He took her hand and gently kissed it and held it for the longest time. He didn't answer. Instead, he kissed her again, hesitantly, briefly, almost like he was unsure if he should.

She hadn't been able to go back to sleep. She lay there for the longest time, when something strange happened. Josh woke up suddenly and sat bolt upright. He looked around the room and at her as if he wasn't sure who she was or where he was.

"What's wrong?" she had asked.

He didn't answer, just stared at her. She could easily see his face in the

24

shadows of the moonlit room. He didn't smile or say anything. In the shadows of the bedroom his face had looked different, confused. He looked around the moonlit bedroom like he was checking it out, like he had never seen it before. Then he looked at her again, and this time he smiled. It was a sad smile, if such a thing was possible.

Josh kissed her gently and whispered, "Go back to sleep. I just had a bad dream."

Bad dream? Him too? Maybe it was something they had eaten at dinner.

He laid back and she cuddled up against him, resting her head in the hollow of his shoulder. He stroked her arm for a while, but she couldn't go back to sleep.

It wasn't just the kiss, she thought. That had been different, like a stranger's kiss. If she hadn't been certain it was Josh, she would have sworn it was somebody else. It was everything, but it was more a feeling than anything she could explain. This man just didn't feel like her Josh.

A little later, she had heard him whisper. She might have just imagined it or even have dreamed it. He probably thought she was asleep. He said, "I'm sorry."

She looked out the window at the silvery landscape and searched for answers that would not come.

\* \* \*

Susan Hensley was walking down the narrow isle of the 727 when she suddenly clutched her chest and fell. She sat up after a minute, disoriented and confused.

"Are you all right, miss?" asked one of the passengers, a handsome young man with sandy hair and blue eyes. He offered his hand. Other passengers on both sides of the isle were leaning out to see what had happened.

Susan stared at the young man's face, especially the eyes, and remembered a promise she had made. *I'll find you. I can't do this by myself. I'll find you wherever you are.* She remembered something else too. *I'll know when I find you because I'll see it in your eyes.*

She studied this handsome young man's eyes a moment longer before nodding and pulling herself up. There was no one in those eyes that she knew.

"Yes," she said and smiled. "Thank you anyway."

"The name's Dan. Dan Sanderson." He grinned. "Are you absolutely sure you're okay? You can sit here if you want. This seat next to me is empty."

She looked around. Where was she? What kind of place was this? She suddenly remembered the searing pain and clutched her chest again. She looked down at her hand, even more confused.

Dan moved to the center seat.

"Please. Take this seat," he insisted.

"Susan?"

Susan saw a young, dark-skinned woman in a uniform of some kind hurrying toward her. She had long hair that was black as coal and shiny. Her skin was like milk chocolate, and her eyes were beautiful black pearls.

"What happened? Are you okay? Let me help you to a seat." She took her arm.

Dan said, "I told her she could sit here."

"That's okay."

Susan looked at Dan again. She stared into his eyes with such intensity that he had to look away. Dan was a salesman in the purest sense of the word, and he could stare down the best of them, but there was something about the way that she looked at him. It wasn't lust or defiance. It was almost as if she was looking for something. Or someone? His curiosity had been raised. He had to know the woman behind those beautiful eyes.

Susan couldn't help noticing how handsome he was. She was tempted to reach out and touch his face. Was it real or synthetic? Real, of course.

"I'm all right. Really. I am. I must have tripped. It's embarrassing, really." Her voice sounded strange. She could hear the other passengers whispering. She looked around the cabin, at all the strange faces and sets of eyes that were looking at her, and then at her own hands. They were a stranger's hands, beautiful, with long delicate fingers. She was wearing a plain gold ring on the third finger of her right hand. Did that mean something?

She looked again at all the strangers. She had made quite an entrance, but these people weren't aware of what had really taken place. They didn't know the woman called Susan was no longer there.

This dark woman who was offering her help was wearing a nameplate that read, "Hillary Wharton, Flight Attendant." Then this was some type of aircraft. She saw that she was dressed similar to Hillary, navy blue jacket, pants, and a white blouse. Was she a flight attendant also? What was a flight attendant anyway? A waitress? That's what it sounded like. She searched her memory but drew a blank. Phil would have known. He loved history. He knew everything.

"Are you sure?"

"I'm sure. Thanks anyway, Hillary."

Hillary looked at her strangely.

"What's wrong? What did I say?"

"Since when do you call me Hillary?" she laughed.

"That's your name, isn't it? It says it right there." She punched the nameplate with one of the long delicate fingers.

"Sure, but you always call me Hill."

"Oh?" she said and added, "I'm not feeling very good, Hill."

"Why don't you go to the lavatory and put some water on your face."

"The what?"

"The lavatory, baby. You know, that room down there at the end of the plane." She pointed. "Don't worry. I can handle things here. It's another thirty minutes before we land, and June and I just finished putting everything away. You just go and sit someplace. If we need any help, we'll call Rob back from first class. Let him know what it's like to work among the peasants for a change."

"Thanks, but I'm okay now. Honest. I'll be right back."

"No, you won't. You go and sit someplace. That's an order, girl."

Susan didn't argue. It was probably best. She hadn't a clue what she was supposed to do, what a flight attendant's job was.

Dan motioned to the now-vacant aisle seat. He was still watching her with some concern showing on his face. Susan briefly wondered if it was real or faked.

"Thank you, Dan, but I think I need to take Hill's advice and go to the back."

"Any time," he smiled. "Remember. The name's Dan Sanderson." He handed her a business card. "Washington, DC. I'm staying at the Holiday Inn out on Clearwater Beach. If you need anything, anything at all, just call me."

Susan took the card and stared at it. Washington DC. Washington Post. Lincoln Memorial. Monday, May 10th. What day is this? Do I dare ask?

"What is today's date?" she asked.

Hillary laughed. "Girl, you hit your head when you fell?"

"It's Thursday, May 4th," answered Dan.

"May fourth?" she repeated. She studied the card. "Washington? Is that where we're going?"

"That's where we're from. We'll be landing in Tampa in twenty-five minutes." Hillary put her hand on her arm. "You sure you're okay, baby?"

"No, I'm not. You're right. I think I do need to go someplace and sit for a few minutes." She smiled at them and started down the isle.

"Don't forget." Dan stood and put a knee in the seat. "I'm staying at the Holiday Inn on Clearwater beach."

Susan looked back and smiled. He watched her walk to the back of the plane.

A man in the isle seat across from him, several years older than Dan, was watching her too. "Nice legs," he commented. "Strange woman though."

"Nice everything," Dan smiled to himself. "We're getting married, you know."

"Oh? You two didn't seem to know each other."

"We don't. Not yet, anyway," he grinned.

"I see."

Dan looked at the man. He had dark hair with a lot of gray in it. There were lines around his eyes and lips. He was wearing an off-the-rack gray suit and a blue tie with stains on it. Probably coffee, he thought.

"Name's Dan. Dan Sanderson." He offered his hand and a broad smile.

"James Chatfield." James accepted his hand. "You live in Florida?"

"Washington, DC. Here for a sales meeting. You?"

"Business. I make this flight about once a month. So you're going to marry that young lady, you say?"

"That's right. Momma always told me when the right woman comes along you'll know. She's the right woman, all right."

"Well. Good luck, son." He smiled and returned his attention to the magazine he had been reading.

Susan held onto the seat backs as she walked to the back of the plane. The aircraft was swaying, rising and falling. It made walking, especially on these stranger's legs, a little difficult.

The other flight attendant was returning from the front of the plane.

"Excuse me, Hillary," Dan said.

"Yes?"

"What's Susan's last name?"

"Why?"

"Let me ask you something, Hillary. Do you believe in love at first sight?"

"No." She laughed.

"No?"

"That's what *I* said."

"Those two are going to be married," said James Chatfield, without looking up from the magazine.

Hillary looked at the man. "You don't say."

"That's what he tells me."

"Well, I didn't use to either," continued Dan. "But I think I've met the woman of my dreams."

"In your dreams." Hill laughed again and started to walk away.

"Wait." He reached out and took her arm. "You didn't tell me her last name."

"I should tell you to ask her yourself. It's Susan Hensley. It says it right there on her nameplate. Can't you read?"

"I didn't notice. I was too busy looking at her face," he said. "Susan Hensley. Is she married?"

"Uh-huh. Sure. You're a real work of art. You know that?"

"You know what they say. If you don't ask… I'm a salesman." He handed her his card. "I was trained to always ask for the order at least three times."

"A salesman. I would never have guessed."

"So? Is she married?"

"No, she's not married. I don't think she's even seeing anyone."

"Thanks, Hillary. I'll make sure you're invited to our wedding."

"Sure. One thing though. Don't call me Hillary. I hate to be called Hillary."

# Chapter Two

Lauren locked the lavatory door and stared at the stranger's face in the mirror. She touched the reflected image with the tips of her fingers. The hair was shoulder length, a chestnut brown color with auburn highlights. The eyes were gray with tiny flecks of brown, and the nose was longer than hers, straight and thin. The lips were full and painted pale red. The teeth were as white as pieces of ivory, almost too perfect to be real.

"You're a beautiful woman, Susan," Lauren said to the reflection.

She unbuttoned her blouse, exposing a lacy-white bra that supported ample, youthful breasts. She had never seen a real bra before. Her small, synthetic breasts had never required that particular undergarment. She touched her chest in the valley between her breasts. There wasn't any pain. Just the wonderful feel of warm flesh and the beating of a very human heart. She had often wondered how it would feel to be totally human. Nothing she had ever imagined came close to what she was feeling now. She examined her hands, her legs, and her feet. They were all real. For the first time in her life, she was complete, a living organism held together with flesh, bone, and muscle. There were no mechanics, no computers, only that which God had designed and made to house the human soul.

"I'm not sure if you can hear me, Susan." She spoke softly and stroked the image in the mirror again. She realized she was waiting for a reply to come from this stranger's lips, but knew that was impossible. "Phil told me we would be sharing the same body. I was never completely clear what that meant. I guess I should have asked. This doesn't feel right, what we've done. If you can hear me, Susan, believe me when I say it was the only way. I didn't come back to harm you or anyone, only to set things right. My name is Lauren Jefferson, and while I am here I promise to take good care of your body."

There was a knock at the door.

"Susan? Are you all right?"

"Yes?"

"Can I get you anything? A soda maybe?"

Lauren found the slide latch and opened the door.

"Whoa there, girl," Hill laughed. "I don't think our passengers are ready for this." She started buttoning Susan's blouse.

"Oh. I guess I forgot."

31

"Sure, Baby. Are you *sure* you're all right? I'm thinking that doctor idea is sounding better and better."

She nodded, smiled, and said, "No doctor. I'll just sit for a few minutes, and then I'll be all right."

Hillary studied Susan's face. Later she would realize that what she was seeing was confusion. She wasn't exactly sure what was going on, but this was her best friend. They had known each other for more than fifteen years, through high school, college, and flight attendant school. Hillary recognized Susan's moods, knew when to shut up and leave her alone. Something was wrong. She was acting different, and it had all started so suddenly. She decided to watch her, and if she needed looking after Hill would be there for her. That's what friends were for, wasn't it? "Take your time, Hon. It's lucky for you we put in for that three day layover. I think a little R and R is just what you need."

"Three days? R and R?" Susan asked as Hillary assisted her to a seat.

"Don't sound so broken up. It was your idea. Soak up some of that Florida sun, you said. Remember? A little paid vacation. A long weekend. We deserve it, Baby."

"Oh." She sat in the isle seat in the last row. All three seats were empty. *Washington Post. Wednesday, May 10th.* She couldn't waste three days. She had to get to Washington. She only had seven days before she was supposed to meet Phil.

She saw a magazine in the seat back pocket in front of her. She took it out and studied the cover. There was a space view of the Earth and the United States. In large print at the top left was "USAir" and in smaller letters at the bottom left "Complimentary Issue."

Chimes sounded, three times altogether, and a man's voice came on the speakers.

"This is Judd Hower, your captain. We have just been cleared for landing. The current time is 4:43, and the temperature in Tampa is 75 degrees. It's currently overcast but no rain is predicted. We are on our final approach and should be on the ground in ten minutes. Please make sure your seat belts are fastened and your seats are in their upright position. Have a nice day and thank you for flying USAir."

Susan started to get up, but a hand on her shoulder pushed her back down.

"No you don't." Hillary fastened her seat belt. "I told you we can handle this."

"Flight attendants. Take your seats." A different voice said over the speakers.

She couldn't spend three days in Florida. The process only allowed them ninety days. That was two thousand one hundred and sixty hours before the process would reverse itself. She put her hand to her chest again and remembered the searing pain the artificial nerve-endings had transmitted to her brain. That pain could only mean one thing; the body she had left behind in that cave was dead. What was going to happen to her at the end of ninety days? There was nothing to go back to. Lauren Jefferson was dead.

She had seven days before she was supposed to meet Phil, she reminded herself. Three days of doing absolutely nothing might do her some good. She wasn't all that far from Washington, and she had never had the time to do absolutely nothing before. The Disciples had always kept the two of them busy. Protecting their secret had been a round-the-clock job.

There was plenty of time to get to Washington, DC, she told herself. Plenty of time to rendezvous with Phil and find Jason Harding.

She wondered where Phil might have ended up. He could be anyplace in the world. What if he couldn't get there? The answer was obvious. It would all be up to her. The mission must be completed at any cost. She reminded herself she was a soldier also. She was just as capable of carrying out the mission as Phil was. They would have eighty-three days after the rendezvous, less than three months.

The plane bounced and shuttered. She felt the vibration of the landing gears being released and locked into place. What if the plane crashed? Wouldn't that be ironic?

*Don't even go there,* she told herself.

* * *

### Tampa, Florida, Outside USAir Employee's Lounge

"What are you doing here?" Lauren asked when she opened the door and saw Dan standing there.

"I told security I was supposed to meet my fiancée'. I told them you were a flight attendant for USAir and what flight you were on. They were eager to help."

The door closed behind her.

"You still didn't tell me why you're here."

Hillary was inside the lounge confirming their hotel rooms. She reached behind her and tried the lever. The door was locked. There was a numbered pad next to the door, which probably meant there was a code, or combination she was supposed to know.

"Wait," Dan said. "Don't go yet. I've been waiting out here for forty minutes at least."

"How did you know where I would be?"

"I told you. I asked. I asked everybody that works for USAir and security finally came through for me. You know, there's a hell of a lot of people in this airport that work for USAir." He laughed.

"Okay. What did you say your name was? Oh, yes. Dan."

"I'm flattered. You remembered. It's Dan Sanderson."

"Well, Dan Sanderson. I don't have much time. What is it you want?"

"I just had to see you again."

"Well, now you've seen me."

"And ask you to join me for dinner." He pushed on. "Tonight. Any place you say."

"I thought you had some kind of sales meeting or something to be at?"

"That's not until Monday. I flew down early to soak up some rays. I earned it."

She thought for a moment. She knew she should say no. There wasn't time to get involved, but what was the harm? She was going to be here a total of four days, from Thursday until Sunday. Lauren Jefferson could use a little R and R also. Would accepting Dan's dinner invitation really affect the mission? She thought not.

"If I say yes-"

"I'll be the happiest man in Florida."

She smiled. "That's nice but don't be hurt if I say I don't really care."

"I am. I really am."

The door behind her opened and Hill came out. She looked at the two of them, frowning at Dan.

"There's a van waiting for us on the tarmac at gate 6."

Dan was standing between his suitcase and a briefcase. He grinned.

"You again?"

Dan held out his hand. Hill ignored it.

"This guy bothering you, Susan? Cause if he is I'll call airport security."

"I think Dan has already met security." She laughed; finding that funny surprised even her. "Dan has invited us to join him for dinner tonight."

"That's right," Dan agreed quickly. "I meant both of you, of course. I'm here by myself, and I hate eating alone. Don't you? I would love to have the company of two beautiful women for dinner."

"Sure. Your flattery is supposed to work on us, right?

"It usually does." He grinned.

"How the hell did you find us, anyway?"

"I asked. I asked a lot."

"Security told him," Susan said.

"So, how about it?"

"You really want to have dinner with this guy, Susan?"

"Why not? He's paying. You *are* paying, aren't you?"

"Of course. You can have anything you want."

"Okay. Not tonight though. Make it Friday at five-thirty. Susan needs to rest and relax. I think we've both been pulling too many flights."

"Five thirty is good for me. I'll meet you in the hotel lobby."

"You'll meet us? How do you know where we're staying?"

"You underestimate me. I'm a salesman. Remember? Holiday Inn Surfside in Clearwater. Right?"

"You're scary. You know that?"

"Not really. You just have to get to know me. I have a rental car. Would you like me to drive you there?"

Lauren started to say yes, but Hill put a hand on her arm and said. "No thanks. It's real late, Dan Sanderson, and we have a van waiting for us. You know. Airline rules and all. We'll see you Friday in the hotel lobby."

"Great. Five-thirty. I'll be waiting."

Lauren noticed Dan's perfect white teeth when he grinned. He had one chipped tooth. She watched how the muscles in his face moved with every expression he made. She wanted to touch his face, to feel his flesh.

Hill tugged on her arm. They started down the corridor.

"You sure you don't want a ride?"

They stopped. "Be right back, Hon." Hill left her suitcase and walked back to face him. She said softly, "Look mister."

"Dan. Remember? Dan Sanderson."

"I know. Look, mister. I have an idea what you have in mind, but let me tell you we're not those kinds of girls. I'll warn you now I carry Mace in my purse and I know Karate, and I've been known to use both."

He laughed. "Thanks for the warning. Let me assure you my intentions are honorable. See that beautiful woman over there?" He pointed at Susan and smiled. "Like I told you on the plane. She's going to be my wife."

"Have you let her in on this little revelation yet?"

"That's what dinner is for."

"Okay. This should be good. Well, Mister Dan Sanderson. We'll see you Friday at five-thirty. Don't be late 'cause we won't wait."

"That's good. You're a poet. Don't worry. I'll be there waiting."

"Bet you will too."

"Count on it."

"Uh uh."

Hill rejoined Susan.

"Come on, Hon. Our van is waiting."

"What did he say?"

"He told me his intentions are honorable. You know. I kind of like the guy. How about you?"

Lauren nodded and smiled. "He's different."

Hill laughed. "Got that right."

\* \* \*

### Josh Hamilton's Cabin, Morgan County, West Virginia, Thursday, May 4, 7:00 A.M.

Phil leaned against the deck railing and watched the wind playing through the treetops below. Out beyond the trees the valley was flat to the horizon. The horizon itself was hazy and uneven, blending into the sky with only patches of green separating the two. A wide river snaked its ways across the valley. The valley floor was a patchwork of patterns.

*Where am I?*

He listened to the birds and watched rabbits playing in the grassy yard below. He had never seen a live rabbit before, only pictures. Everything was so peaceful, so serene. He had never known anything like this. He used to dream about dying and going to Heaven. Was this heaven? Was that beautiful woman upstairs an angel? Had he really had sex with her? He knew the answer to everything except the sex was no.

Even if Heaven existed, even if there really were angels, he'd never see either. He was a soldier, a protector for the Disciples and their secrets. He was a professional killer. It was his job. There was no place in Heaven for people like he and Lauren.

Phil heard barking. What was that? A dog? Could it really be a dog? He had only seen pictures of dogs. "Man's best friend." Where he came from, dogs didn't exist. They hadn't existed for a very long time. Neither did rabbits, squirrels, or birds. They all began to disappear when the changes started. As far as he knew, most land animals had become extinct. They couldn't survive the change, and humans were too concerned with their own survival to even notice their disappearance until it was too late. The birds were the last to disappear and even that had been long before he was born. He wasn't sure how sea life had been affected by the change, or what monsters might lurk beneath the sea's calm surface.

A gorgeous yellow Labrador came out of the trees and trotted across the back yard and up the deck's steps. He was a beautiful creature. The dog came over to greet him but stopped short and sniffed him.

36

Phil knelt and held out his hand, "It's okay, boy. I won't hurt you."

The dog backed away and made a low rumbling growl. The dog knew. How?

"I see Harley's back!"

Phil looked up and saw a gorgeous woman standing in the doorway. She wasn't much over five feet tall, thin and delicate. Her strawberry blonde hair was shoulder length and a mass of curls. She was wearing a man's shirt (His?) and holding a cup of coffee. Harley went to her, and she raked her fingers through his thick fur.

"I see he likes you."

"Harley understands me, accepts me. I guess I have a way with animals." She smiled and winked. "I hope you don't mind, Josh. I made a pot of coffee." She hesitated, then asked, "Would you like some?"

"Sounds great. Sure."

She tilted her head and looked at him curiously, almost questionably.

*I said something wrong. What? Something about the coffee.*

She came over to him, stood on her tiptoes, and kissed him. He started to put his arms around her, but she backed away and studied his face curiously.

"Take mine," she said and faked a smile. "I'll pour another cup."

"You sure?"

She nodded, and he took the mug, sipping the hot liquid. It was good. He had never tasted anything like it. Phil set the cup on the deck railing. She stared at it.

"You're up early," he said.

"What?" She looked at him. "Oh. No. You're the one who's up early."

He laughed but thought, *this isn't going to work. I haven't a clue where I am, or who this woman is.*

She smiled again. If he had ever seen a real smile before he would have known instantly, this one was a fake also. He noticed she had a dimple in her cheek. Dimples were once considered to be deformities. Her blue eyes even smiled, her whole face did. Machines could never replace what he was seeing. They had thought themselves so perfect, better than the real thing, but when it came down to it they were just machines. Machines could never replace the real thing. He didn't realize the smile, the expression, the words, were all faked.

Diane suddenly put her arms around his neck and kissed him.

"What was that for?"

"I just needed to know something."

"Well?"

"I think I got my answer."

"What answer would that be?"

"You're not Josh Hamilton, are you?"

*She knows. She knows I'm not Josh. The dog knows it too. How?*

He studied her face. She wasn't smiling and now looked determined.

Did it matter who he was? The transference had worked. He looked away, out across the tranquil valley below. He was here, and he had ninety days to make things right. That was all that really mattered. He didn't have time to play a game of pretending he was someone whom he wasn't. But he needed to be this Hamilton person, he reminded himself. For the next ninety days, if the mission took that long, he had to be Josh Hamilton, and everyone had to believe that. He didn't need any unwanted questions.

Diane backed away and waited for his answer.

Phil turned and just looked at her. He wasn't sure what to say, but he knew he had to say something.

"Who the hell are you?"

"I'm Josh. Who else would I be?"

"That's what I would like to know. You're lying. I don't know how you did it, but somehow you did something to Josh. Where is he? What have you done with him?"

Phil picked up the mug and drank the coffee. It was hot and sweet. He leaned against the rail and looked out across the valley. "This is really good," he said without looking at her.

Diane slapped the cup out of his hand. He watched it fall in the grass below.

"The Josh Hamilton I know hates coffee."

"Oh."

"He can't stand the smell of it. Who the fuck are you?"

Diane waited, unsmiling, determined.

"What makes you so sure I'm not Josh? How do you know I'm not just acting different this morning?"

"It's not just the coffee. It's the way you made love to me. It's your kiss. It's the way Harley just growled at you."

"Your dog doesn't like me very much. That's all."

"*My* dog? Sure. I guess you would think that. Harley belongs to Josh. The two are inseparable."

"Oh."

"That's right. Harley doesn't know you either. Animals always seem to sense when things aren't right. And something is definitely not right here."

Phil looked away again. He was a soldier, he reminded himself. He was on a mission. This was a job. It was just a job. It didn't matter what this woman thought. He had a mission to complete. Nothing was more important than the mission. Besides, when this was all over she would get her precious Josh back.

"Last night. You raped me. And don't you dare try to tell me you didn't know what you were doing."

"I'm sorry. It just happened."

"Yeah, that's what they all say. Last night you said you were sorry. Right after you did it. Was that supposed to make it all right?"

"No. I didn't know you heard me. I thought you were asleep."

"Sorry for what? For raping me?"

He didn't answer.

"Who are you? Why are you here, and where is Josh? What have you done with him?"

He looked away again. He couldn't handle this. He was feeling things he hadn't felt before. Where were these feelings coming from? He was a trained soldier, dammit. He wasn't supposed to have these feelings. His eyes had become wet. What was that about?

"I'm sorry."

"Look at me."

Phil turned around. There were tears in his eyes. She had never seen Josh cry, not ever. She was looking at the face of a stranger. She looked into those familiar blue eyes, but Josh wasn't there.

He reached out to touch her, but she stayed beyond his reach.

"Do you even know my name?"

"Why?"

"I just want to know. Do you know who I am? If you're going to replace Josh then you must know my name."

He didn't answer.

"Just say it."

"But--"

"Say it," she insisted, demanded. Tears came to her eyes and rolled down her cheeks. "I want to hear it."

"I can't."

"Why not?"

"Because I don't know your name."

He turned away and went down the steps and out across the back yard. The grass was cool and damp from the morning dew. She watched him from the deck. Harley came up beside her and started to whine. She patted the top of his head. He licked her hand and watched this man whom neither of them knew.

Phil stopped where the yard sloped away. A little ways down the hill the trees began, a barrier between the cabin and the valley below. He stood there with his head down. He looked defeated, confused. What was happening? Who was this man? Where was Josh? This man looked exactly like him. He was able to replace him, but he didn't know a little thing like her name. This whole thing was just impossible.

Phil turned around and looked up at her. He was at least fifty feet away, but she could still see the sadness in his eyes.

"I'm sorry," he said.

She barely heard him.

"Sorry for what?" she said.

"You're right. I don't know your name because I'm not really Josh Hamilton. My real name is Philip Rollins, and I'm from the future."

# Chapter Three

Jason rolled over onto his left side and reached out to touch Patricia, but he discovered her empty pillow instead. The room was dark but danced with shadows from the streetlights. It was just light enough to see she was not there. He pushed himself up and looked around the dark room. He saw she was standing at the window. She was wearing his white shirt and nothing else; her slim form outlined beneath was back-lighted by the streetlights.

"What's wrong?" he asked.

She jumped at the sound of his voice.

"Can't sleep. I didn't want to wake you."

He patted the place next to him.

"Well, no chance of that now. Come back to bed. We'll work on the problem."

She just smiled slightly and turned back to the window.

"Something is bugging you, isn't it? What's up?"

"I was just wondering if it was still there."

"And what would that be?"

"The car."

"What car? Never mind. Is it?"

She nodded. "It's been there every night this week. The same car."

Jason got out of bed and went to her. He put his arms around her from behind and kissed her neck. Patricia pushed back the curtain so he could see.

"It's probably just a coincidence," he said against her ear. "This is a small community, and there's not much parking."

"I don't think it's a coincidence. There are two men in the car, and they just sit there. Don't laugh, but I think they are watching the house." She squeezed his hands against her belly.

"I doubt that," he laughed softly against her ear.

"I told you not to laugh."

"Sorry."

"I'm being serious, Jason. They've been there all week. I just haven't said anything."

"Would it make you feel better if I went down there and asked them what they are doing?"

"Don't you dare."

"You know I will if you want me to."

"I know."

"Anyway. They probably work for the Agency."

"The Agency?"

"You know? The EPA. The place where I work? Remember? I don't know if they are, but if it will make you feel better, I'll ask Albert first thing tomorrow."

"Who's Albert?"

"Albert Fenwick, the guy who signs my paycheck. You met him back in February, at that party we went to up by the National Cathedral."

"I met a lot of people that night."

"You said he looked like a penguin. Remember?"

She laughed. "Oh, him. Now, I remember. That was before I knew he was your boss."

You were right though. He does look a little like a penguin. So, how about it? Do you want me to call him?"

"Would you?"

"Of course. Now come on back to bed." He took her hand.

"Why do you think they are watching us?"

"Maybe they aren't," he said. "But if they are, maybe it's like the Secret Service or something like that."

"You mean they may be protecting you like they do the President?" She pulled her hand from his and put her arms around his neck.

"Maybe. I don't know. Come on." Without waiting for an answer, he picked her up and carried her back to the bed.

"What do you think the big shots down at Hecht's would say if they could see their general manager right now?"

Patricia rolled onto her back and Jason sat across her legs. He slowly unbuttoned the white shirt and peeled it back. His hands glided across her stomach, breasts, and arms. When their hands touched, they locked fingers. Their faces were only inches apart. They smiled at each other. He kissed her lightly on the lips, the chin, the neck, and then kissed each of her breasts, his tongue circling each of the hard pink tips. His lips and tongue softly massaged each breast before he moved on. He kissed the valley between her breasts where a tiny stream of sweat had formed, then his lips brushed across her stomach as lightly as a feather. She inhaled audibly when his lips brushed her pubic hair. He felt her body trembling and knew that for the moment she had forgotten about the two men in the car.

"I'd tell them we're having an early breakfast."

"What do you say we skip breakfast and go for a nice big helping of dessert?"

"I love a man who likes dessert," she laughed. She held his head in her hands, running her fingers through his thick hair.

Outside, in the car, the two men waited patiently while they listened to the sounds of lovemaking coming through the small speaker sitting on the dash.

### May 4, Thursday, 8 A.M.

"If you're not Josh, then who the hell are you, and what have you done with him?"

Diane was trembling. Harley seemed to sense something wasn't right and began to whine. He licked her leg as if trying to assure her that everything was going to be okay, but everything wasn't okay.

This stranger in Josh's backyard just stood there as if this place belonged to him, and he had every right to be there. He didn't answer. He just stood there and looked at her.

"Where is Josh?" She repeated, "What have you done with him?"

"He's here," he said barely above a whisper, pointing to his head.

"What? I didn't hear you."

"I said your Josh is here," he said louder this time.

"Where?"

"Inside my head." He started toward the deck.

"Don't. Stay where you are."

Harley barked and started growling again.

"Good boy." Diane petted Harley.

"I need to talk to you. I can explain everything."

"You can explain from where you are."

"No. Not from down here. Let me come up."

"First you tell me what you did to Josh."

"I already told you, he's still here. I didn't hurt him. He's inside my head... Josh's head," he corrected himself.

"That's impossible. Let me talk to him."

"I can't."

"You mean you won't. You're lying."

"No. As long as I am here, Josh can't be. It's really as simple as that."

Diane shook her head. "Bullshit. This is some kind of hoax. Things like this just don't happen."

He reached the bottom of the steps and started to come up.

"Stop! I warn you. You take another step, and I'll tell Harley to take your leg off."

Harley ran to the top of the steps and started barking. The hair on his back was standing up.

"I believe you."

43

"Who are you? I want the truth this time."

"Philip Rollins," he answered. "I didn't know it was going to be this way. We didn't think."

"You didn't think? What do you mean? What did you do to Josh?"

"I told you. Josh is still here. It's just that I have to be Josh for a while."

"I don't understand."

"Of course you don't. How could you?" He put a hand on the handrail.

Harley's growl rumbled deep inside his throat.

"Don't worry. I'm not coming any farther." He looked at Diane. "Listen to me. As crazy as it may sound Josh and I are one and the same. You'll have your Josh back when this is over. I promise."

"No." She was shaking her head. "You're still lying. You're making all this up. Something like this just can't happen."

"We thought it would be so simple. Really. I would be transferred. My mind, my thoughts, my spiritual being. The mind of the host, your Josh, would be compressed and forced into an area of the brain that's like an empty room and sealed off. No one would ever know that I had taken over his body. It was so simple. It was the only way we had to do this."

"You're saying you just took over Josh's body?"

"I'm sorry. You have to believe me. There was no other way. We're not like them. We have feelings. We still care. But what I have to do is too important. If it ever comes down to it, even Josh is expendable-because I'm expendable."

"Expendable? Expendable? Who are you to say who is expendable?"

"I understand."

"No you don't. How could you? I love Josh, and I want him back."

"You'll get him back. I'll do everything in my power to protect him. When this is over I'll be gone, and everything will be back the way it was before."

"I want him back now."

"That's not possible."

He started up the steps again.

Harley went into a barking frenzy.

Diane sat down on the deck and started to cry.

Phil stopped halfway up. He looked at her and waited.

"My name is Diane Kimble," she said without looking at him.

"Diane. That's a pretty name." He smiled. "I wish we could have met under more pleasant circumstances."

She glared at him. Phil had never seen so much hate in another person's eyes.

"I told you my name, because if and when I find a way to destroy you and get Josh back, I want you to know the name of the woman who did it."

\* \* \*

Jason lay on his back. He was asleep, but Patricia was wide-awake. She snuggled up against him, her head on his arm. Her fingers played in his chest hair, and she watched his chest rise and fall with even, shallow breathing.

Early morning sun came through the windows, its warm rays forcing back the shadows and some of the fears she had experienced earlier. She could hear the sounds of Georgetown awakening. Patricia listened and tried to identify all the familiar sounds. It had become a part of her waking-up process each morning. A private game. The sounds seldom changed, and all of them had become familiar. Now and then new ones sneaked in but never stayed like the regular sounds. She identified the garbage truck and heard the banging of the trash cans being emptied. A jet plane roared overhead. That would be USAir's 8:00 A.M. commuter flight from National to New York. A horn sounded twice. That never changed either. The same cab showed up every morning to pick up Jason's neighbor. She heard familiar music approach and slowly fade. That would be the person who likes Rod Stewart. It was the same song every morning at the same time, "My heart can't tell you no." She liked Rod Stewart too, but this person was either a real fanatic or only owned the one tape.

She remembered the car outside and wondered if it was still there. What exactly did Jason do for the EPA anyway? The EPA stood for the Environmental Protection Agency. What kind of job could he have there that was so dangerous? Why would he need watching or protecting? She didn't know anything about what he did, and when she asked, he would tell her it was just a boring job that she wouldn't find very interesting. She *was* interested. She was interested in everything about this man she had fallen head over heals in love with.

\* \* \*

Sounds penetrated the dreamlike fog. Delicious smells. Coffee brewing, bacon frying, eggs. She never cooked for herself. That was Jason's thing. She would just as soon go to the IHOP across the river in Arlington or the Little Tavern around the corner. The International House of Pancakes was conveniently located just a few blocks from the Hecht's department store at Ballston Commons. They knew her well there and greeted her by her first name. A bagel with cream cheese and a diet Coke were delivered to her table within seconds after she was seated. They knew her all too well.

Patricia listened to the sounds outside. They were different now. Day sounds. That meant she was going to be late for work again. This man downstairs was a bad influence. She looked at the clock radio and saw it was almost 9:30. Already late. What the hell.

She turned over and squeezed Jason's pillow against her face. It smelled like him. She always liked the way he smelled. The man never smelled bad. Not to her anyway.

"You going to sleep all day?"

Patricia put the pillow down. Jason was standing between the window and her, the sun making him a silhouette. Dust danced in the sunlight that surrounded him, giving him an aura. Something about that image suddenly caused chills to run up and down her spine. She tried to push the thoughts aside as she had the men in the car outside. It didn't work this time either.

Jason was holding a bed tray with a complete breakfast, including orange juice and a bud vase with a single, fresh-cut red rose. IHOP knew her better, but he was trying. She gave him credit for that.

"Well?" he asked.

"You're making me late for work again. You know that, don't you?"

He set the tray on the bed and kissed her. He touched her cheek lightly with the back of his fingers and smiled.

"I love you anyway," she laughed. "But I really should be getting ready for work."

"And let all this go to waste?" He kissed her again. "You're serious, aren't you?"

"Of course I'm serious. I'm the boss. Remember?"

"That's right. How could I forget? You have all the keys."

"And I'm late."

"Well, this is also your day off, boss lady with all the keys," he chuckled. "You told me last night not to set the clock. Don't you remember? You're off until Monday."

"Is this Thursday already?"

He nodded.

"I'm becoming senile. I don't remember yesterday."

"Could it be when you're with me you lose track of time?"

"Don't flatter yourself. Aren't you eating?"

"Already did. Ate while I cooked."

He sat on the edge of the bed and watched her.

Patricia picked up the fork and pushed the eggs and bacon around on the plate before taking a small bite of the eggs. They were scrambled and cooked well, but she just wasn't an egg person-or a bacon person either, for that matter.

"I wasn't sure what you liked, so I cooked everything I had in the house that seemed like breakfast." He watched her. "You don't like it, do you?"

She picked up the buttered toast and took a small bite.

"It's not that. I think it's wonderful you made breakfast for me."

"I hear a but coming."

"No one has ever served me breakfast in bed before."

"I hope not," he laughed. "But?"

"I usually just have a bagel with a little cream cheese."

"That's it." He got up. "I knew I was missing something. No bagels in the house. I'll go get some. It won't take a minute."

"Hold it right there, buster." Patricia reached out for his hand and pulled him back to the bed. "I don't want a bagel. I think what you did is just wonderful. Really thoughtful. I-"

"Want to hear a joke?" He grinned and kissed her on the cheek. She could smell the bacon in his hair. "I thought of it while I was cooking."

"You sure beat the hell out of 'Good Morning America.' Sure. Let's hear it."

"What goes ugh, ugh, ah, oh, oh, ouch?"

"I have no idea."

"Guess."

"I don't know?" She giggled.

"Me naked in the kitchen frying bacon. Ouch."

They both laughed.

She lifted the apron he was wearing and looked under it.

"I hope our friend didn't get burned."

"If he had?"

She smiled. "I would have to kiss him and make him all better."

"Well," he said. "He did get burned just a little. Right here." He pointed.

"Sure." She laughed again and took a bite of toast. "So what are we doing on my day off, or did I forget that also?"

"Anything you like."

"Why aren't you working?"

"If you can take the day off, I can too."

"Have you called Mr. Fenwick?"

"Albert?" Jason nodded. "He doesn't know anything. He said maybe they're with the FBI or Secret Service. He told me he'd check it out and call me."

"I don't like it, Jason. I don't like this feeling it gives me."

Don't be silly. I'm sure there's a logical explanation. Stop worrying. It's going to be a beautiful day, and neither one of us has to work."

### Thursday, May 4, 11:30 a.m.

Cottony clouds drifted across the blue summer sky. A warm breeze flirted with the leaves high up in the old oaks that bordered the dirt path on this side of the reflection pool. The morning was brisk and cool, luring out joggers and bicyclists.

Pigeons flew between the trees and played tag with squirrels in the thick, green grass. Children in their summer shorts and pullovers and sneakers chased the pigeons, tempting them with generous handfuls of peanuts and other goodies. Their laughter was like music in the clean morning air coming in off the tidal basin and the Potomac.

Jason leaned against a tree and Patricia sat between his legs, the back of her head against his chest. They had been sitting in silence for the last several minutes, watching the children playing and the ducks floating gracefully in the reflection pool. Patricia's brown hair cascaded over his hands as be began to massage her neck and shoulders. She felt the tension melting away beneath his touch.

She was wearing white jogging shorts, a striped pullover, and Nike running sneakers. Jason was wearing blue NBA shorts, though he had never played basketball in his life, and a white T-shirt that had the words "Mother Earth. She's All We Got," printed in big green letters across the front.

Every time they had a chance, they jogged a five-mile path that paralleled the Rock Creek Parkway, the Georgetown Canal, and circled the Reflecting Pool. A month of unusually warm spring weather in April had given them both handsome tans.

"Jason?"

"Yes."

"See those two men over there?" She pointed across the pool.

"Sure. What about them? Don't tell me. You think they're the men from that car that's been parked out front of the townhouse."

"They've been following us."

"What makes you think that?"

She turned and looked into his dark, almost black eyes. His face was brown and strong, his smile warm and loving. His black hair glistened with perspiration.

"I've just had this feeling all morning."

"You know what I think?"

48

"Probably." She laughed.

"I think you're paranoid."

"I don't care. I have this feeling about them, and it scares me."

"I told you they're probably Secret Service or FBI."

"Sure, and I'm old Mother Hubbard," she laughed.

"Seriously.'

"You're just trying to shut me up. Well, for your information, it's not working."

He leaned over and kissed her. "What do you say we get an ice cream?"

"Isn't that a contradiction?"

"What?"

"We've just run five miles to shed a few calories and then we-"

"No arguments."

He stood, pulled her up and they walked across the freshly mowed grass toward Constitution where several vendors were parked.

Patricia looked back over her shoulder.

"What are you doing?" He laughed.

"I was just checking."

"Look, honey. Scouts honor." He held up his right hand in the traditional Scout greeting. "The work I'm involved in right now is very important. They probably *are* FBI."

Patricia opened her mouth to argue.

"No. Not another word. I tell you what. You can keep watch. I'm going to have an ice cream."

"You sure you don't want to invite your friends?"

"I personally don't give a shit about them, but if they want ice cream they'll have to buy their own," he laughed.

Patricia started to look back again, and Jason tugged on her hand. "Stop that."

"Okay," she pretended to pout. "But I'm not eating."

"Your loss."

"Exactly," she laughed.

The two men came around the end of the Reflection Pool and stopped near the Vietnam Memorial. Patricia watched them while Jason ordered his ice cream. They were so obvious, their plain dark suits stood out in the colorful crowd of tourist that had invaded Washington now that the national vacation time was approaching.

The shorter of the two men turned to his partner and said something. His partner shrugged and nodded, but he never took his eyes off them.

* * *

"So?"

"So what?"

"Aren't you going to tell me about this job of yours?"

They were sitting on a park bench and Jason was eating his ice cream.

"Let's walk." He got up and took her hand.

"You need it after that." She took the cone from him. "Are you going to tell me?"

"You either eat that or give it back."

"You haven't answered me yet," she persisted.

"You just don't give up, do you?"

"You know that."

"Here. Have some ice cream." He took her hand and forced the cone to her mouth, smearing it across her face.

"Oh, now you're going to get it."

"You've got to catch me first." He started to run.

Patricia dropped the cone and chased him. Later she thought how easy he had been to catch. They both fell on the grassy mound behind the Vietnam War Memorial. She straddled him and kissed him, smearing the ice cream that was still on her face across his. They were both laughing when he put his arms around her and pulled her against him. They kissed hard, unaware they were not only being watched by the two men but also by a dozen snickering children who were just leaving the Wall and heading toward the Lincoln Memorial.

"So tell me."

She was sitting on him and holding his arms back above his head.

"Kiss me again."

"Tell me."

"Kiss me. Then I'll tell you. Scout's honor."

"You weren't ever a Boy Scout."

"How do you know?"

"Julie told me. Don't you know? She tells me everything."

"I've got to have a talk with that sister of mine. What else did she tell you?"

"That won't work, and you know it?"

"What?"

"You're trying to change the subject. I asked you a question. I want an honest answer."

"Okay, okay. Let me up first."

"I don't know. Can I trust you?"

"Yes. Let's go sit on the steps and keep Lincoln company. Then I'll tell you all about it."

"Really?"

"Don't you believe me?"

"Seems too easy."

He held up two fingers.

"Stop it with that Boy Scout bullshit. Do you really mean it?"

"Sure," he laughed. "It's no big deal anyway."

They sat halfway up the steps facing the Reflecting Pool and the Washington Memorial beyond.

"God! I love this city." Jason said suddenly.

"What brought that on?"

"Shut up. I'm answering your question."

"This better be good."

"We've lived here all our lives. Well, at least I have. I don't know how long you've lived here. You don't have a sister that will tell me everything about you."

"For your information, mister smart ass, I was born over there across the river." She pointed behind her, indicating across the Potomac. "Arlington Hospital. I grew up in Falls Church. My parents had this little brick house on a street with big trees. They don't live there anymore, but I still remember that house. I'll take you there sometime."

"I'll hold you to that." He smiled.

"So?"

"Okay. You love this city every bit as much as I do, don't you?"

"I don't know. Sometimes. Sometimes I think it's just a dirty, crime-infested place that lives up to its name as the murder capital of the United States."

"True, but it's still a beautiful city."

She looked at him and saw the seriousness in his dark eyes.

"I used to go hiking when I was a kid. I'd hike the tow path along the C & O canal up around Hancock and Berkeley Springs and sometimes even farther north near Cumberland."

"What has any of this got to do with those two men? Look." She pointed. There they are. By that tourist bus."

"Stop pointing. I see them," he said. "They've been following us for almost three weeks."

"You knew and you didn't tell me?"

"Will you forget about them for a minute? I'm trying to tell you

51

something here."

"Okay, okay. I'm listening."

"I always carried drinking water with me. There aren't many springs near the river, and I never trusted boiling the river water. It's actually better, closer to Georgetown, but it's really bad up near Harpers Ferry and Shepardstown. It looks so clean until you put it under a microscope. They say it's getting better, but I think it's even worse now. Anyway, there's a little creek up there called Cacapon that's so bad you can smell it before you can even see it."

"That name sounds familiar."

"You're probably thinking of the Cacapon resort. Anyway, this Cacapon creek smells like shit, literally. Once I got so sick from the smell there, I actually threw up. The banks are coated with scum. The trees are dead. The water is black and greasy. It looks like something you'd see in a cheap horror movie." He laughed. "You keep expecting to see the Creature from the Black Lagoon rise up out of that water."

"What happened? What caused it to be that way?"

"Lot of things. Chemical plants and coal mines and years of just plain not giving a shit. Did you know five quarts of motor oil can ruin 300 gallons of water? I bet you didn't know that, did you?"

She shook her head.

"It's true. The pollution isn't just happening here either. It's everywhere. Lake Erie has been biologically dead for years. The Tennessee River has so much mercury in it in places that commercial fishing has been banned. Oil spills, garbage dumps, chemical run-off, and toxic-waste dumps. You name it. We've all had a hand in it. We all share the blame. Virtually every river in the country has been affected to some extent."

"I didn't realize it was that bad."

"I was just a kid when Dad took me and Rob up to this cabin we used to have in West Virginia. It was a beautiful place on this huge lake. I should remember all the good times I had there, but all I can remember about it are the dead fish and the bald eagle that I watched die."

Patricia squeezed his hand. Jason was looking out at the Reflecting Pool, but she was sure he was seeing something else entirely.

"You've probably seen those big tanks laying around at the older service stations."

She nodded. "I always wondered about them. They seem to be digging up all the stations around here."

"Underground gas storage tanks used to be made of metal. The new ones are made of fiberglass. Those old metal tanks are beginning to leak. Think about what five quarts of oil can do and then picture about five thousand gallons of gas leaking into the ground. That's potentially a million and five hundred thousand gallons of water ruined. Now, multiply that by just the gas stations that are ten years and older. It's staggering. Everyone is so concerned about air pollution. They don't even think about what's right under their feet."

"That's terrible. Can't anything be done about it?"

"That's why they've started to replace those aging fuel tanks, but it's too little too late."

"Isn't there some way to neutralize the gas and oil? Can't we do something?"

Jason laughed. "Not really. Not yet anyway. That's where I come into the picture. As Paul Harvey would say, 'Now for the rest of the story.'"

# Chapter Four

**July, 2217, Nashville, UCA (United Cities of America)**

A laser shattered the glass above Phil's head. Broken shards of glass showered the street around him. A blinding white light reflected off the glass of the building across the street seconds before the sheets of polished glass dissolved into fragments and rained down on the pavement.

Phil skidded to a stop, his back pressed against the wall. He examined his left arm. The hand was gone, neatly sliced off at the wrist. The synthetic flesh was still hot and smoking circuits dancing and hissing like so many tiny snakes. The pain monitors had been short-circuited and hadn't registered the wound, or if they had, he hadn't noticed.

"Come on, Lauren." He searched the dark sky between the glass towers. "This is no time to be late."

Phil stepped away from the wall, firmly planted his feet, and lifted the gun with his good right hand. Micro-motors and gears beneath the skin moved his arm and hand into position and held it steady. He waited.

An agent came around the corner full speed. He never expected Phil to be waiting for him. His surprise lasted for only an instant. Phil squeezed the trigger. The gun vibrated slightly as a blue beam of light passed through the assassin's mid-section. His clothes smoldered, his flesh cauterized instantly. He automatically lifted his own weapon but couldn't pull the trigger. Phil had evidently hit some vital mechanism that controlled his hand. The fingers wouldn't close. The would-be assassin stared at the hole through his mid-section and the burned, synthetic flesh.

He suddenly removed the gun from the disabled appendage and raised it with his right hand. Before he could get off a shot, Phil fired again, this time aiming at the man's head. The shot hit him between the eyes.

Phil smiled, taking satisfaction in the kill. It wasn't often these days that he got such satisfaction. A shot to the head was always terminal. He really enjoyed this part of his job. He should feel guilty about the way he was feeling, but too many of their own had fallen to the guns of these UCCIA agents.

Shattered and abandoned buildings closed in on all the deserted streets. Gutted vehicles, wrecked, burned, and abandoned, littered the streets and sidewalks. Smoke came from some of the buildings where fires never seemed to completely burn themselves out. The fire and police departments had given up on this part of the city years ago, condemned it, and surrounded it with an electric barrier. The only way in or out was by air, and the government, the UCCIA, strictly controlled the airspace. But when one knew the routine, they could easily slip in between patrols. He, Lauren, and Sandy did it all the time. All those other times no one had even suspected.

He should have been suspicious when Sandy insisted they meet here, but she had convinced him it was the safest place, and it was urgent that she see him immediately. She was right about it being the safest place. No one should have suspected, and hadn't they met here hundreds of times? What was there to be suspicious of? The UCCIA didn't come to this part of the city that often. Sandy was a soldier of the Disciples, just like he and Lauren. She was a trusted member of the group. Why would anyone, especially her own brother, have reason to doubt her loyalty?

A dark blue craft came down between the buildings and hovered in a clear area about fifty feet away.

"It's about time." Phil holstered his weapon and ran for the now open door. He leaped through the opening just as laser fire hit the pavement where he had been standing moments before. A water main ruptured and a fountain shot up nearly a hundred feet. Another laser beam narrowly missed the van as it began its ascent. The beam of light struck the building off to the right, and the building exploded in a shower of plastic and metal and glass.

"Where have you been?" he screamed above the wind noise.

"Car trouble," Lauren called back.

"Very funny. Keep the door open!" he yelled.

"I have to close it!" Lauren called back. "I can't get up to speed with it hanging open like that. The wind will rip it off."

Phil ignored her, steadying the gun between his knees with his good right hand. He aimed, pulled the trigger, and held it. A laser beam swept the street below. Even as the door was closing, he saw three UCCIA men were caught in the beam and engulfed by the burning light. They were dead before they knew what had hit them.

The door thumped closed, and the locking mechanism whirred and thudded into place.

Phil crawled between the seats and slid into the passenger seat.

"What kind of car trouble?"

"You know." She saw the destroyed flesh and missing hand. "You've been hit."

"It's nothing. I still got my other hand."

"We'll have to get Daren to repair it. He must have a spare hand around someplace."

"I don't think we'll have time for that."

"What do you mean?"

"Just get us out of here. Oh, and I'm glad you had car trouble."

"Why?"

"I'll explain later."

She turned the aircraft around one hundred and eighty degrees and accelerated, gaining altitude quickly. They ascended above the electric barriers, above the shattered towers of the abandoned suburb, into the open space several thousand feet above the ground. Just to the north, the hub of Nashville proper glowed brightly like a sun in the center of a dying solar system.

"There will be others, won't there?" she asked.

"You better believe it. They can't be far behind."

"How did they know? We've done this so many times and no one has ever suspected."

"One guess."

They were headed north, leaving behind them the third largest of the twelve United Cities of North America. The suburb of Bowling Green began to glow along the horizon. The stars mixed with the city lights.

Lauren checked the scope for chasers as she set their course.

Nashville itself was a congested city of mile-high buildings and a maze of transporter tubes and shuttleways. Most of the airspace in the city center was restricted to official use only. Official these days meant UCCIA traffic. Civilian aircraft was permitted by special permit and strictly monitored, forbidden altogether in the abandoned zones.

For the moment, they were alone in the sky.

The main hub of the city radiated outward for more than a hundred and fifty miles in all directions, taller buildings gradually giving way to retail centers, industrial parks, private residences, and government-controlled farming lots. Then there were the suburbs. Chattanooga and Huntsville to the South. Gatlinburg, Asheville, and Knoxville to the East. Memphis and Muscle Shoals to the West. Bowling Green and Louisville to the North.

"What about Sandy?" Lauren asked a few minutes later.

"Sandy won't be joining us," he said.

"But she's part of the team. The three of us-"

"I'll explain later. Okay?"

"What does this do to our schedule?"

"Screws it all to hell," he laughed. "We can't wait. It has to be tonight."

"Tonight? But-"

"Tonight," he repeated. "They know about us. We don't have a choice."

"What about the others?"

He didn't say anything, but she thought she knew the answer.

"Daren says we still need to divert more power to synchronize the transfer process. We can't do this without him and the others. We're just soldiers, Phil. We don't know enough about the process."

"We're not *just* soldiers, and you know that. We can do it. The Disciples taught us everything we need to know."

She was shaking her head.

"No. I think we should wait. We can call the others from the cave."

Now it was Phil's turn to shake his head.

"Don't you understand, Lauren? There are no others. It's just you and me. We're it. We're the last hope."

The aircraft dropped suddenly as her hands slipped from the controls. She recovered quickly and pulled back on the wheel. The craft started to climb again.

"What happened back there? What were all those agents doing there?"

Phil didn't answer immediately. He looked out the side window and watched the city of Nashville sliding past beneath them. Nashville was dying-like all the other great cities. People were killing each other off. The sperm and egg banks were nearly depleted, so those people who were killed weren't being replaced. The government had become quite selective in fertilizing eggs lately.

"They're all dead."

"How?"

"Why do you think the UCCIA showed up? They never go into that part of the city. Sandy sold us out. She sold us all out."

"Why? What on earth did she have to gain?"

"Maybe she didn't want things to change. Maybe she liked the way things are. They could have promised her a new body. She always was vain, and she never liked the one she had. You know that."

"No." Lauren shook her head. "Sandy wasn't that shallow. She wouldn't turn us in."

"Shallow? No." He laughed. "I wouldn't say that. Christ was betrayed for a lot less. Looks like the Disciples had their own Judas."

"Maybe we should just hide and wait this thing out."

"Where? They know who we are. And you can bet your ass they know about the cave."

"Maybe the others got away too."

Phil shook his head.

"How do you know? How can you be so sure?"

"Sandy told me. She always did like to gloat. I think she actually enjoyed what she did."

"You believed her?"

He nodded. "Why would she lie?"

"Can we really do this without the others?"

"We have to give it a try. What other choice do we have?"

"I don't know enough about the process."

"You know as much as I do."

"No."

"Daren explained it to us both. It sounds pretty simple. We can do it, Lauren. Our faith is what got us this far in the first place."

"I'm not so sure."

"I, for one, believe in God. But God only helps those who help themselves."

"Well, I believe in this." She put her hand on the gun at her side. She looked at him and smiled. "And I believe in you."

He suddenly realized Lauren really didn't know much about the process. Daren had explained it to both of them, but as he recalled she hadn't seemed very interested. She really didn't understand how the process worked, but she knew enough to make it work.

Daren had once drawn him aside and told him they would be in those other bodies for only a short time. If they were successful, they would probably cease to exist. He had asked Daren not to tell Sandy or Lauren. He was afraid it might affect their performance, jeopardize the mission. The truth was, he wasn't sure how they would take it.

"Shit."

Phil asked, "What's wrong?"

A light flashed behind them. Phil looked back and saw three black aircraft coming toward them at high speed.

"Oh. Guess we've got company."

Lauren checked the radar. "Six hundred meters and closing. They're coming at us at twice our speed. We'll never be able to outrun them."

"Those are UCCIA pursuit vehicles. They go fast but don't do so well in tight places. We can lose them."

"We can't go to the cave."

"We have to. They probably know about it anyway," he said. "Swing around behind that hill up ahead and dive for the trees."

"Won't they just follow us?"

"Probably. It's going to take them a while to get turned around though, and I'm hoping the trees will give us cover."

A blue laser beam screamed against the side of the craft. The aircraft rocked back and forth and veered off course slightly before Lauren regained control.

"That was close."

"Probably just a warning. You better get us out of the sky."

Lauren cut their speed. The craft dropped below the treetops. The three black pursuit aircraft flew past, laser fire hitting several trees.

"That worked."

"They'll be back," she said. "I give them five minutes."

"That's all we need."

"What do you have in mind?"

"Just get us on the ground. Over there." He pointed to a small clearing at the foot of a low hill. "There's an old abandoned entrance to the cave not far from here. It's not on any of the newer maps."

"How do you know?"

"I found it a couple of weeks ago when I was checking out some of the tunnels. I haven't seen it from this side before, but I think I can find it."

"You *think* you can find it."

"I'm *sure* I can find it. Okay?"

They climbed out of the craft as it settled in the small clearing. Phil checked his gun. It had only a half charge remaining.

"How's your gun?"

"Full charge."

"Good. Mine is only half. That should be enough though." He just needed enough to blast that door open and then seal it closed once they were inside.

They started climbing.

"What happened to Sandy?" Lauren asked.

"Sandy's dead," he said and kept walking.

"I'm sorry. What happened?"

"You don't have to be sorry. I'm not. I killed her."

Lauren was startled. Not so much about Sandy being dead but at the way Phil said it. Sandy was Phil's biological sister. Sister? She was his sister only because the eggs from which they came from were harvested from the same woman more than a century ago. They weren't even close. They had never been close. And she had betrayed them all.

"I just can't believe Sandy turned us in. She always seemed so loyal. She was such a good soldier," Lauren said as they were climbing the hill.

"Every army has its share of traitors."

"How did you get away?"

"Pure luck." He laughed. "I opened the door, and she was standing there with a gun aimed right at my head. Her big mistake was waiting. She should have killed me right then, but I guess she wanted to gloat about what she had done. She started telling me how she had been promised all these things. She said that I should understand. She had to turn us in. There was no other way. She said she had already told the UCCIA about the others. You and I were supposed to be the last. She told me she had bargained with the UCCIA to be the one who killed us. After all, I was her brother, and you were like a sister to her.

"Anyway, a street person saved my life. The woman opened the door across the hall and screamed when she saw Sandy holding the gun on me. Sandy jerked the gun around and killed her. That split second was all the time I needed. I jumped aside, pulled my own gun, and shot her between the eyes."

"I'm sorry."

"Why? She turned us in. She had our friends killed. She betrayed us.

"You know, she stood there for the longest time, just staring at me with those lifeless eyes. I know she was already dead. She had to be. I shot her between the goddamned eyes. And this is where you're going to think I'm crazy. She smiled. I swear it. Right before she fell. She smiled. It wasn't a robot smile either. It was real. It was human. I don't know how or why, but I think she was happy it was finally over."

Lauren didn't say anything. She wasn't sure what to say.

After a moment Phil said, "Come on. We better hurry if we're going to make this work."

"How? I don't even know who I'll be. Who you'll be. I don't even know where you will be."

"We'll find each other, Lauren. I promise. It doesn't matter where in the world you are, I'll find you. You and me. I'll find you."

"How?"

"I'll know. I'll look into the eyes of every woman I see. I'll know when I find you, and you'll know it's me. Trust me."

"We have to find that door first," she laughed. "If they find us first, neither of us will have to worry about finding anyone."

"Right."

The ground had become steep and rocky. There were a few pines and a lot of weeds.

"It's just up ahead. I think it should be about halfway to the top of this hill."

Phil stopped. Lauren started to say something. He put a finger to his lips and pointed to two circles of light moving back and forth across the barren hillside. They could hear voices.

"We better find some place to hide before they find us," she whispered.

"What good would that do?" he said softly. "We don't have to anyway. There's the door."

It looked like an ordinary wooden door in a not so ordinary place. Trees and brush had grown up around it making it nearly invisible. It was locked. For some strange reason that was funny to Phil and he chuckled.

"What's funny?"

"Nothing."

He fired at the padlock, and it dissolved. Phil forced the heavy door open. The hinges screamed in protest. When they crossed the threshold, ancient sensors registered their movement or body warmth and lights began to glow.

"Do you believe this?"

Lauren was still standing in the doorway. Phil laughed and pulled her on inside just as one of the lights found the doorway, and an amplified voice ordered, "Stop or be shot!"

"Not tonight, Jack." Phil answered. "You go ahead. I'll slow them down a little." He shoved the door closed and noticed Lauren was still standing there.

"That's not going to stop them."

Phil looked down the long tunnel. The countless steps created an illusion of going all the way to the bowels of the earth.

"This will." He blasted the stone and supports around the doorway. The ancient supports splintered and rocks started to fall. "Now, will you go?" he asked.

She didn't move.

"I'll be right behind you."

"You better be or-"

"Or what?" He grinned.

"Or I'll come back and drag you down by your hair." She grabbed a handful of his thick hair.

"I bet you would."

"You better believe it."

"Don't worry. We've got more important things to do than stay here and play with our new friends."

The steps had been carved into the stone in some ancient time when the cave had been a tourist attraction. She imagined the sounds of laughter and of children going down the steps. That other time was something she had only read and dreamed of. It seemed like fiction. Was there ever a time like that? When children actually laughed?

Phil stopped after they had descended forty or fifty of the steps. He turned and took aim at the pile of rubble in front of the doorway and fired again. More rocks came down, and dust billowed out from the collapsing ceiling. A few of the rocks tumbled down the steps and past them.

Phil holstered the gun and took her hand.

"What?"

"Come on. Let's find out where this tunnel goes."

It took them twenty minutes to reach the end of the stone stairway.

There was another door, but this one wasn't locked. Phil turned the knob and pushed it open. They went through the opening. On the other side was a huge cavern with concealed lighting that began to glow from dozens of places.

"Not heat sensors," Phil commented. "Probably motion detectors."

He turned and looked up the seemingly endless tunnel. He unholstered his gun, took aim, and pulled the trigger. He held the trigger until the beam of light faded and died, the charge finally gone. Distant rumblings told him the tunnel was starting to collapse. Rocks were clattering down the stone steps.

Phil threw the gun down and shoved the door closed. He grabbed Lauren's hand, and they started to run, just as the ancient door splintered and dust billowed through the opening.

* * *

Phil watched Diane. Her expression hadn't changed since he began telling her his story. Did she still hate him? Did she still want him dead? Of course she did. But it wasn't like Josh was dead. He was just away. His thoughts, everything that was Josh Hamilton was still here, just locked away for the time being.

They were sitting out on the deck. He looked out across the peaceful valley and tried to imagine what the world must be like. Everything was still real and full of life. There were real birds and rabbits and deer... and people. Nothing had changed... yet.

When exactly did things start changing? Officially, Jason Harding dumped the first batch of the bacteria in the Cacapon creek on July Fourth, 1995. Was that when it really started, or could it have been before then? Maybe there had been an earlier test that hadn't been recorded? An accident, maybe. This month? Next week? Maybe it had already happened. Maybe everything they were doing was all for nothing.

How much time did he really have? A week? A month? Days? Hours? He couldn't know for sure until he found Jason Harding and talked to him.

# Chapter Five

## July, 2217, Nashville, UCA

When Jerrell Hardman and the men from the pursuit craft arrived a few minutes later, they discovered several men standing around a splintered doorway with a pile of rocks spilling from it. Hardman examined what remained of the door and the opening that was now choked with boulders.

"It was an abandoned remote entrance to the cave, sir," Collins volunteered.

The dust still hadn't completely settled. It hung in the still night air like a fog.

"Why wasn't I told about this?"

Collins didn't answer as quickly as he should have. Hardman immediately picked up on his hesitation.

"I asked you a question. I'm waiting for an answer."

Collins had been the only person with direct contact to Sandra Rollins. He had earned her trust over several months, made her promises, and paid her handsomely. She told him about the others, the handful of rebel leaders, what they were up to, and the purpose of the underground. Apparently, there were many involved in this underground movement but only fifteen that actually knew of this facility a few miles east of the village Cave City. Twelve of those fifteen were now dead.

The names of the final three were included on her original list. Daren Kosman's location hadn't yet been determined, but finding him was just a matter of time. Phil Rollins and Lauren Jefferson hadn't been killed, because Sandra had asked to be the one to do it. He supposed it was a family thing. They were supposedly brother and sister, fertilized eggs from the same donor. Collins had agreed to her request without consulting with Jerrell Hardman. She told him that when they were all dead, she would tell him everything else. He believed her. He trusted her, but she never told him where the Disciples were meeting or exactly what they were trying to accomplish. She had only hinted that it was going to change everything.

"Well?"

"She never told me, sir."

"She never told you? What have you been doing for the past four months?"

He shook his head. "She was going to tell me everything. Right after she killed Jefferson and Rollins."

"You believed her?"

"Why shouldn't I? Everything else she told us was true, wasn't it? We eliminated all the others, didn't we?"

"Not quite. There is one other, but that's another matter. You told me you knew everything about the project. You said we didn't need any of them."

"Sandra wouldn't do it any other way. She said they all had to be dead first. Then she would tell me everything."

"And you believed her." This time it was a statement, not a question.

Collins nodded. He walked over to the splintered pieces of the door and the pile of debris. Without looking at Jerrell, he said, "I guess I made a mistake."

"Yes, you did, but don't worry. You won't be making any more."

"No. It will never happen again." Collins turned and saw Jerrell was pointing a small black object at him. He recognized the deadly weapon immediately.

"Don't do this, sir. We can still catch them. It's not too late."

Jerrell squeezed the black object. Collins' head exploded.

"That was messy," said Hardman. "Very messy."

He aimed at the piles of debris and squeezed the small weapon again. He blasted the pile of rocks again and again. More of the hillside came down to replace what was blasted away.

"Is there another way into this place?"

He turned and looked at the others. They didn't answer. They were staring at the headless corpse.

"There's a main entrance." Richard Levi pointed across a shallow ravine that separated them from another series of low hills. "There's an abandoned cluster of buildings and a parking lot not far from here."

"Let's go, then. We've wasted enough time at this place."

"What about Collins?" One of the men from the original group asked. Collins had been in charge of this group.

Jerrell looked at the corpse. "He's dead," he said, but he fired another shot at the crumpled pile of synthetic flesh and metal anyway. The body melted in the heat of the blue laser light. Jerrell smiled, but it gave him little satisfaction for the man's incompetence.

"Levi?" he looked around.

"Yes, sir," a voice answered out of the dark several yards away.

"How far is that other entrance?"

"I think about two miles," Levi said. "It's been closed for more than a hundred years though. I'm not sure if we can get in there."

"Collins didn't leave us any other options. If those two get away with this, they'll screw up everything. Do any of you have any idea what that means?"

He looked at the others. They were shaking their heads. Of course they didn't. They were just ignorant fools, bred and trained by the UCCIA. Their only purpose was to serve the Company. He and Collins and Levi were the last of a special breed. He was the oldest of the three by more than fifty years. The three had worked for the original CIA before it became the UCCIA, right after the formation of the twelve United Cities. They had formed this special task force right after they found out about the Disciples and what they were up to.

"I'll tell you what it means," he said. "Everything we know is about to be destroyed. All of you. Every one of us will cease to exist. We will not let that happen. I won't let it happen."

* * *

Phil looked at Diane again. He looked into her eyes, desperately searching for Lauren. Of course, she wasn't there. He had no idea where in the world she might be.

"What are you looking at?"

He shook his head. "Nothing. I was just thinking how beautiful you are. How much you remind me of Lauren."

Diane laughed. "And you were thinking about her last night too, weren't you? While you were fucking me, you were thinking about her."

"It wasn't like that."

"Sure. It doesn't matter who you are or where and when you come from, you're still basically a man, and men only think with one thing, their dicks."

"That's not true. That was the first time I've ever done anything like that."

"Sure, and I believe in Santa Claus." She laughed.

"It's true. People from my time don't have intercourse. They can't."

"What are they, machines?"

He didn't answer, and she thought she might have come close to the truth.

"Go on. I want to hear the rest of the story. I want to know what happened to Lauren."

"I don't know what happened to her. I hope she's out there someplace. I pray we'll find each other in time."

"I suppose you would like me to help you find her?"

"I can't ask you to do that."

"Why not? You took over Josh's body. You already fucked me once, why not again?"

Phil didn't answer. He turned away from her and looked out across the

67

peaceful valley again, collecting his thoughts. Lauren would find him if she could. There wasn't time to go looking for her. First, he had to find Jason and stop him.

* * *

Lauren's hand was poised above a glowing light on the large console. She was waiting for Phil's signal.

They were in what was once referred to as the Snowball Room. She wasn't exactly sure why it had been called the Snowball Room, but it may have had something to do with it always being a good ten degrees colder than the rest of the cavern. There was a constant breeze through the cavernous room that was caused by the elevator shafts leading to the surface. This may have been the reason it got its name back when Mammoth Cave was a major tourist attraction in the old state of Kentucky.

Phil gave her a thumb's up and she pressed the button. There were muffled explosions from charges that had been set years earlier in anticipation of what was happening now. Dust billowed out from the closed elevator doors. More distant explosions followed. They could hear the mountain above them exploding and collapsing and both realized that they had just sealed themselves in. There was no turning back now. There was only one way out of here.

The lights flickered, went out, and came back on again as the outside power failed and the auxiliary generators came on-line.

Walking across the huge cavern, Phil suddenly realized just how alone they were. They were two of a kind, and they were the last. He took her hand and held it for the first time since they had known each other.

This place had once been used as a cafeteria for the hundreds of tourists that went through here daily. This huge room had once echoed with the sounds of children's laughter back when children still laughed. That had been more than a hundred years ago.

For the last fifty years, the Disciples had used the caverns as a lab to perfect the time-transference device. There were fifteen beds for the three soldiers and the twelve Disciples. The Disciples were the leaders of the movement, and all fifteen of them were supposed to make the journey. Phil was more than a little sad that only he and Lauren had survived to see if it really worked, if all that they had sacrificed was worth it.

The transference device was Daren's creation, and he had seen it through all the stages of its development. He worked longer hours than anyone did, and he dreamed of the day he would make the journey. He and Lauren and

Sandy were the soldiers who were supposed to protect the secret. Now Daren was dead. Sandy was dead. All the Disciples were probably dead also. Only their ghosts could ever return here. But even as Phil was thinking this, he knew he was wrong. They were all still here. Their hearts and souls were in these machines they had built. Their thoughts, their voices, their very lives were here. Each and every one of them would accompany him and Lauren on this journey. The two of them were Earth's last hope. Into their hands had been thrust the fate of the entire human race, the future of all humanity.

In 2036, Earth had reached for the stars in an effort to escape the plague, the change. They completed the space station Freedom and from it, they launched several spacecraft bound for Mars and beyond. They took with them the frozen seed of mankind in hopes of creating test tube babies free of the bacteria that had infected Earth. But instead of escaping, they took with them Earth's plague. The bacterium was in the food, the water, and their bodies, even the air. Earth's destiny became its legacy for all the worlds it would touch.

A livable surface for Mars was terra-formed over the next hundred years. Satellites circling the planet reflected and magnified the sun's rays, melting the polar caps, releasing water that had been trapped as permafrost, and giving life to long dormant plant seeds. Mars slowly became a thriving, vibrant world.

No answers were found. Children continued to be born with severe deformities, and artificial bodies continued to be used. Babies were raised in plastic cocoons. Wires were attached to their brains, and from these connections they were taught everything they needed to know.

The computers gave them knowledge, but could not give them love or compassion. The babies became adults, were placed in artificial bodies, and went about performing their pre-programmed destinies.

The only emotion that seemed to flourish was hate. Civil wars and rebellion spread across the globe and out into space. People were killing each other faster than they could be replaced. The sperm and egg banks were being depleted. By the year 2217, the people of all the countries of Earth and its colonies in space were on the verge of extinction.

\* \* \*

"Any regrets?" Phil asked as they entered the Transference Chamber.

Lauren didn't answer. She was staring at one of the fifteen beds along the far wall. Someone was laying on the fourth bed from the end. This was the bed that had been programmed for Daren. Could it be? Daren was always working late. Maybe he never went home yesterday.

"Look." Lauren pointed. "Daren's here. They didn't kill him. He looks like he's sleeping."

"He can't be asleep. Not after all those explosions."

"Daren!" Lauren called, running to the bed. "Wake up!"

He didn't move.

Daren was lying on his back, his hands at his sides. His head was suspended inside a large ring. The ring was eleven inches wide, made from spun strands of gold and copper. Inside the ring were hundreds of tiny needles connected to the ring and pointing toward his head. These were probes that collected the thoughts and memories, sending them to the computer where they were compressed and packaged for processing.

Lauren shook him, but he didn't wake up.

Phil came up behind her and put his hand on her shoulder.

"He's gone, Lauren."

"What?"

"I mean, he's already made the journey. He must have found out what was happening. that's the only reason I can think of that he wouldn't wait."

"He looks so peaceful. Just like he's asleep."

"In a way he is. His brain is still functioning. His mechanical heart is still pumping vital fluids. His body is still alive, but Daren's gone."

"I don't understand. I thought we were going back in time."

Phil took her hand and went to one of the consoles. They were running out of time, but she needed to know this. He showed her one of the monitors. There were two red lines across the screen, one was a series of curves, the other flat.

"This represents Daren's body." He pointed to the curved line that undulated across the screen in regular patterns. "This line," he pointed to the other line, "represents Daren's thoughts and memories. It should be virtually identical, but now it's flat."

"You're saying he's dead."

Phil chuckled, shaking his head. "No. Transferred."

He went on to explain the process in greater detail. He told her that the transference began after the processing was completed. Daren's thoughts, all his memories-his soul-were compressed to the size of a single electronic impulse and then accelerated in a reversed circular motion within the circular mechanism at the speed of light.

"Are you sure? He really looks like he's dead."

Phil grinned. He shook his head again. "Look." He switched screens. "This is Daren's body. The temperature is 96.4 degrees, just below normal for both the mechanical and human bodies. His artificial heart is still beating at seventy-two beats per minute. His mechanical lungs are still processing air."

"That doesn't prove anything. His body is a machine."

"You're right, but our brains make all this machinery work. That part of the brain is still here, over there in that bed. The thoughts and memories and everything that was Daren is gone. The activity in the brain consists of electrical pulses. It's like a fantastic computer. To put it simply, everything in this room has been designed to code those impulses, code and compress them, then do a little cutting and pasting. They're cut here and pasted there."

"I guess I was thinking our bodies were going back."

"No. That's why Daren told us to place the ad in the newspaper when we got there. Remember?"

She shook her head.

"I guess none of this was ever really explained to you, was it?"

She shook her head. "Or I wasn't listening."

"Well, Daren told us to place an add in the Washington Post Classifieds under the Announcements section."

"Like what?"

"Each ad is to be identical. 'Fellow Traveler. Just arrived from Mammoth. Meet me at the Lincoln Memorial Wednesday, 6:00 p.m., May 10, 1995.' The ad is to be signed with the first and last initial of the person placing the ad."

"Why didn't someone simply transfer into Jason Harding's brain?"

"Couldn't," he said. "We can't choose our hosts. The genetic code was matched by sex and age, but that was as close as they could get. They couldn't even control what country we'll be transferred to. That single electric impulse is like a sliver of iron being attracted to a magnet, but not just any magnet will work. The recipients, both male and female, will be between thirty and forty years old. Daren thought that age would probably be the easiest to work with. Besides, Jason Harding is thirty-four."

"Then we won't know who we'll be or even where we'll be?"

"You got it. That's why the ad. That electric impulse is sexually coded. We will be transferred by sex and age, but we have no way of knowing who we'll be. That's why we have to place that ad in the Classifieds of the Washington Post as soon after our arrival as we can. We'll be on our own when we get to wherever it is we end up. It has to be up to each one of us individually, you, Daren, and me. Seven days should be enough time to make the rendezvous."

"Don't worry about me. I'll find you. I know I can't do this by myself.

I'll find you wherever you are."

He laughed. "There won't be any time to waste looking for each other. Watch for mine and Daren's ad in the Classifieds, and be there at the Lincoln Memorial at six p.m. on May Tenth-but if we don't show us, don't wait for us. Jason Harding has to be stopped even if it means killing him."

Lauren took his face in her hands and stared into his eyes.

Phil laughed. "What are you doing?"

"Looking at your eyes. I'll know when I find you because I'll recognize your eyes."

"They won't be *my* eyes," he said.

"I'll still know if it's really you."

"We better get started. We've already wasted too much time."

They started walking.

Lauren said, "Just think. You're going to meet your father."

Phil laughed. "You mean Jason? He's not really my father."

"Wasn't it his sperm?"

"Sure, but he was just a college student who happened to need extra money so he donated his sperm to the sperm bank. He probably did it more than once."

"That still makes him your father."

"I suppose. I just never really thought about it that way."

She stopped and looked at him.

"Could you really kill him?"

"If I have to. Whatever it takes. Too much has already been sacrificed."

"Your own father?"

"Biological father, remember? Yes. I will if it comes to that."

# Chapter Six

Diane watched him intensely. Her expression hadn't changed since he began. She hadn't said a word, hadn't interrupted him once-and she hadn't taken her eyes off him for a second.

"I have to ask you something," she said.

There was no emotion whatsoever. A simple question. She didn't blink or look away. He found himself admiring the way she boldly confronted him, pressed for all the details.

"Sure. Anything."

"You told me Josh, I mean the real Josh, is still here."

Phil nodded.

"Does he know what's going on? Can he hear us?"

"I doubt it. I mean I don't think so. Of course, there's always that possibility. The way it was explained to me, it's like he's asleep. When I leave, he should simply wake up. He'll never know any of this ever happened."

"What happens if you never leave?"

"I *will* leave, Diane. It's inevitable."

"What makes you so damn certain?"

"I have ninety days to accomplish the mission. We didn't plan it that way. It was an unknown factor that entered into the process. We couldn't get around it. I suppose it's just as well. We might have been tempted by this life and given up on the mission."

"So what happens at the end of ninety days?"

"The process reverses itself. We return to our real bodies-if there are bodies left to return to."

"And I'll get Josh back?"

He nodded again.

"I can't kill you. I can't even hurt you because that would be like doing it to Josh. Right?"

Phil didn't answer, just nodded.

"Well, go on with your story. I want to hear what happened next."

"Okay, but there's not much more that I can tell you."

"I want to hear it anyway. Right up to the minute you were fucking me."

Phil opened his mouth to protest. Diane held up a hand. "Just tell me what happened."

73

\* \* \*

The caverns began to vibrate. Rocks were shaken loose and started to fall. From someplace far away came muffled sounds of explosions.

"What was that?" Lauren asked.

Phil went to one of the monitors. Long ago cameras had been placed at all access areas. This particular monitor was located just above the elevator doors in the main lobby. "Looks like they're trying to blast their way in."

"I'm picking up tremors. I think they may have disturbed some ancient subterranean fault. Its epicenter seems to be several miles from here. It's measuring 7.6." She looked at him from across the room. "The shock waves are going to cross through these chambers in less than a minute."

"We better get moving then. If we lose the auxiliary power the computers will be useless."

"I'm ready whenever you are."

Phil came across the room, took Lauren's hand, and walked with her to her bed and helped her up onto the soft surface of the bed.

"When you lie down, this headpiece will slide forward, and your head will be suspended by a low energy force field. It will feel like a cushion of air. Don't worry about all the needles. They won't actually touch your head. These are the controls." He pointed to three buttons on the right side of the table. "The top button activates the transference computers, the middle button is the standby, and this button is the abort. Got that?"

"Got it. Don't worry about me. Just get in your own bed. We have less than a minute."

Lauren laid back and the headpiece moved forward.

"You sure?" He placed her hand over the three buttons.

"Go."

"Remember the ad. Washington Post Classifieds. May 10."

"I know. Now, go."

"Wait for my signal."

She stared at him.

"Okay. I'm going."

Phil quickly checked the computers and then went to the first bed. He stretched out on the soft mattress, and the headpiece moved forward. He felt the tingling sensation from the force field that had automatically been activated.

There was a loud explosion. Dust billowed into the room. Rocks started to fall.

Phil reached across with his right hand and felt for the buttons. He looked at Lauren. She was watching him, waiting for his signal just like he had asked her to. Past her, he saw three men enter the chamber.

"Now, Lauren!" he called and pressed the top button.

He saw laser beams darting across the chamber and exploding. He tried to turn his head but couldn't move. He attempted to call out to Lauren, to warn her, but no sound came out of his mouth.

There was a sudden flash of light, an explosion, searing heat... then nothing.

\* \* \*

That's it," Phil said. "For a minute there I thought we were both dead. Then an instant later, I was having sex with you. Imagine how I felt. I know this is hard to believe, but I have never had sex before. Where I come from, we can't. It's impossible."

"Impossible, yes. Impossible to believe."

"It's the truth," he said. "It's just something we can't do. I had never experienced anything like it before. Maybe it was just primal instinct, but I couldn't stop. I didn't want to stop."

"Well, I hope you enjoyed it because it won't be happening again. What happened to your Lauren?"

"I don't know. I'm pretty sure she made it too. The transference was fast. I didn't even feel the earthquake. If she pressed that button when I told her to, she's okay, and all I have to do is find her. I have to place that ad in the Washington Post as soon as possible. She'll be looking for it."

"So what happens now?"

"I have to find Jason Harding before it's too late."

### July, 2217, Nashville, UCA

Hardman examined each of the three bodies in turn, starting with the one on the first of the fifteen beds. All of them appeared to be sleeping, but appearances could be deceiving. He knew this by experience, having learned the hard way.

"What's going on here, Levi?" Hardman's voice was a deep baritone and his question was easily heard across the large chamber. "You got any ideas, I'd like to hear them."

Levi was on the other side of the large room examining the monitors there. He was very impressed with what he was seeing.

"I can only guess at this point," he answered. "This technology is new to me. I haven't found out how to get into their system yet, so I'm not exactly sure what's happening."

"How long will it take?"

"An hour. Maybe longer."

"You have ten minutes, and that may be too long. Can you at least tell me what they are trying to do here?"

"I'd say they have already done it."

"Done what?"

"Gone back."

Hardman looked up. Levi could see the penetrating, cold look in his dark eyes. It was as powerful as any laser beam and just as deadly.

"What does that mean?"

"I'm still guessing, but we know they were working on some method of time travel. Give me some time, and I'll know more about what they were doing."

"We don't have time. Ten minutes, and that may be too long. I want answers."

"Yes, sir."

"What about this one?" He waved the gun over Lauren, probed the chest wound with the barrel. Her chest had ruptured from a direct hit. There was no blood, because everything inside had been instantly cauterized, the mechanical heart melted instantly, the artificial arteries and veins sealed.

"One of these monitors is showing two flat lines. No brain activity. The power chip was melted by a direct hit. She dead."

Jerrell waved the gun toward Daren. "What about that one?"

"Brain activity at the subconscious level. Regular heartbeat. The power chip is still active. He's still alive, sir."

"Did he go back with the other two?"

"I don't know."

"I suggest you find out."

Hardman aimed his gun at Daren's head and squeezed the trigger. The short burst of light made a neat hole between his closed eyes.

"What do you see now?"

"Brain activity has ceased. Chip is still functioning, but for all intents and purposes, he's dead."

"Good." He went over to Phil's bed and blasted his head. "And now?"

"Same thing. I believe they're all very much dead now."

"Which means we stopped them, right?"

"I'm not so certain. They probably went back before we got here."

"How can we find out?"

"First I have to get into these computers. They must have notes around here. We have to find out how the process works, exactly what and how they did whatever it was they did. There are twelve vacant beds. Those were probably for the others we terminated. That could mean we have twelve possibilities of going after them."

"Then get to it. I need volunteers." Hardman looked around the room. No one said anything. "Well?"

"I don't think that would be wise, sir. We still don't know how the process works. Give me some time."

"We don't have time."

"But we do. Once we know exactly how they did it, we simply go back to an earlier date. We'll be there waiting for them."

"Brilliant. Perhaps we can even find Jason Harding first. Help him out a little. Move up the schedule."

"I don't understand."

"If we can get the formula into the water supply before they get to him, they won't be able to change anything."

"Very good, sir. I never considered that."

"Get on it then. Learn everything you can about this setup. I'll authorize all expenses and people you need. I want to know exactly how this time traveling works. Call me only when you have the answer."

"Yes, sir."

# Chapter Seven

**Thursday, May 4, 1995, 3:45 p.m.**

Jason and Patricia held hands and strolled along the canal near Minnesota Avenue. Tourist season hadn't gotten into full swing yet, so there weren't a lot of crowds. Next month, school would be out for the summer and vacationing tourists would flood the city, spending their money freely, and pumping much needed dollars into the ailing District economy. The District's economy was always ailing, Jason thought. Wealthiest country in the world and its capital was close to bankruptcy.

It was a time the locals would prefer to be somewhere else, unless, of course, they were business owners or depended on those dollars for income.

Jason looked back over his shoulder. Two men. The same two men who had been following them all day. When they were eating, he had entertained the idea of inviting the two men to join them. He wondered how they would have handled that.

He wondered why Albert hadn't called back. Maybe no news was good news.

Jason wasn't naïve. He knew how important his research and the experiments were, but most of what he did had been kept from the media. The EPA didn't want a lot of advance hype, and they controlled all news releases.

What did they want anyway? The formula? Maybe, but anyone, even Bill, would have a difficult time reproducing it without his cooperation. He told himself he had been reading too many spy books. He was trying to make this into something more than it was. There was probably a good and simple explanation-Secret Service, FBI, or even the EPA. Maybe he should call Albert again. No, he told himself. Albert would call when he found out anything.

They found a vacant bench along the brick towpath and sat. Georgetown Mall was directly across the canal, and they could see through the glassed entrance.

Jason liked to people-watch. It was one of his favorite pastimes. It was six-thirty on a Friday night, the evening was warm, and there were still a lot of people strolling the towpaths or just window-shopping.

Patricia was quiet. She seemed to be watching the ducks swimming in the canal and the children playing in the small park in front of the mall, but Jason knew better than that. He instinctively recognized her mood and was pretty sure her thoughts were someplace else. She was already arranging and organizing her day, going over her appointments, and reviewing mental notes for meetings. She had been away from Hecht's one whole day. She hadn't made one phone call to the store. He had deliberately hidden her beeper and turned her cell phone off. He had put his own work aside for the day so they could have this time together. He was being pressed to show some substantial progress, but the two of them needed this time.

Patricia had belonged to him all day, but he lost her at dinner. Her thoughts had slipped away without him realizing it. For once, he hoped she was thinking about Hecht's and not the two men.

Jason started digging in his pockets for change but came up empty.

"What are you doing?" Patricia asked.

"I was going to give you a penny for your thoughts, but I seem to be all out of pennies." He laughed, took out his wallet and handed her a bill. "How about five instead?"

"They aren't even worth the penny." She started to take the five he was waving in front of her, but he jerked it away.

"First your thoughts. Be honest. You're thinking about work again, aren't you?"

"Not really."

That should have surprised him, but it didn't. Those two men were spoiling everything.

"I recognize that mood you're in. You're thinking about everything you've got to do tomorrow and how these two days off have totally screwed up your schedule, and you're probably wondering where the hell I hid your beeper and cell phone."

She laughed, shaking her head. "You're so totally wrong. I know exactly where my beeper and phone are."

"You do?"

She nodded, smiling.

"How? Never mind. I said be honest. Remember?"

"Actually I was wondering if this stuff you're working on really works, does that mean even this dirty old canal water would be drinkable?"

He laughed, relieved. "You were thinking about my work? When did this start?"

She pretended to pout. "I always think about your work. It's just before today I wasn't really sure what that work was. Well?'

"Well, what?"

"The water. Could we drink it?"

"Eventually," he answered. "Of course there's the algae and fish poop.

Can't do much about that stuff. Would you believe even the District's water will be drinkable again?"

"That would take a miracle."

They were both referring to the trouble the District was having with its water system. The Mayor repeatedly assured the city's residents they had no cause for alarm. The water was constantly being monitored, and chlorine was being added as necessary. The only possible threat might be to people with immune system problems, such as AIDS patients, and the elderly. The news media was really playing it up, though. There must not be a whole lot going on in the rest of the world if this was their big story. Sometimes he felt sorry for the Mayor and people in government in general. The media always seemed to be attacking someone in their group like a pack of starving wolves.

"Didn't you know? Your Jason deals in miracles. That's my work."

"Well, I think what you are doing is just wonderful."

"You do?"

"Well, don't sound so surprised. I wish I were as smart as you. I'd love to be able to help. I've never really had a cause, like you do."

"You're plenty smart," he squeezed her hand. "Smarter than me. There's just different kinds of smarts, that's all."

"I love you," she said suddenly.

He was caught off guard. He wasn't sure what to say. When someone told you they loved you, you were supposed to say, "I love you, too," weren't you? Wasn't that how it was supposed to go? Then why was he hesitating? Jason found himself staring into her dark eyes. Before he could reply, his cell phone rang.

"You brought your phone."

"How else was Albert going to reach me?" He flipped open the phone and said, "Hello."

Jason smiled at her and winked as he listened to the caller on the other end. "Thanks. If you find out anything else call me." He closed the phone and put it in his pocket.

"Well?"

"Albert."

"I guessed that. What did he say?"

It's not the Agency or the FBI. He's pretty sure it's not the Secret Service either. He said not to worry. He's going to do some more checking and question-asking. He'll call me when he knows something."

"I'm frightened, Jason. What do they want?"

"There's only one thing I have that's worth having. That's the formula. Don't worry. If that's what they're after, we're safe. They can't take a chance hurting either of us."

"What makes you so sure?"

He didn't answer.

She put her arms around his neck and kissed him.

"Don't worry," he whispered against her neck. "I'll never let anything happen to you."

* * *

Chadwick Bowerman leaned against the railing of the Minnesota Avenue Bridge that crossed over the canal. His partner, Evan Lockner, had gone off to get a soft drink. That left him alone to watch the couple sitting on the bench a half block away.

Lockner was a good man, a professional, and a trusted partner for fifteen years. They went to college together, attended the FBI academy in Lorton together. They had been partners, field agents, in Washington until their retirement two years ago this July. A stroke of luck had brought them together again.

Bowerman was the one who got the offer. He brought Lockner in because he knew he couldn't do it by himself. He needed someone he could depend on, someone to watch his back. And Lockner needed the money. He had a big mortgage, two kids in college, and a history of bad investments. His financial situation was in a shitty state, and wasn't going to get any better. This was an opportunity of a lifetime. Pull this off and they both would be set for life.

Bowerman considered it a reward for all the years of faithful service they had given the FBI. All he needed was patience . . . time and patience. The testing wasn't scheduled to take place until July Fourth. Plenty of time. He just had to wait for the right opportunity to present itself.

* * *

If Hill hadn't awakened her, she'd probably still be asleep. Lauren wasn't tired, but Susan's body must have been exhausted.

"Wake up, girl," Hill said. "It's time to put your bod in that little two piece you bought in Washington and soak up some of that famous Florida sunshine."

"I just want to sleep." She covered her head with the pillow. "You go on."

"No way."

"What time is it anyway?"

"Almost four. Girl, you're too young to sleep like this. Come on, now.

Get out of that bed." She jerked the covers off her. "I'm not going anywhere without you."

"Speak for yourself. I need the sleep."

"Okay. I'm going. But if you're not down there in fifteen minutes, I'm coming to get you. You hear?"

"Yes, ma'am," Lauren laughed.

After Hill had gone, Lauren got out of bed and thoroughly searched the overnight bag. She found a smaller bag in it that contained a toothbrush, toothpaste, shampoo, perfume, lipstick, comb and brush, and other essentials. There was a wallet with photos, a driver's license, two plastic cards, money, and other pieces of paper she didn't recognize. The cards had her name and raised numbers and were printed with CitiBank Visa and First National Bank MasterCard. The photos were of a young boy, a middle-aged man and woman, and a cat. She studied them for a long time. All these things were important. She must memorize everything.

Thirty minutes later, she was sipping a frozen drink and watching the sunset. She had never been to the ocean, had never seen so much water in one place. She loved closing her eyes and listening to the sound of the crashing waves. It was a wonderful sound, so relaxing.

It was hard to feel the urgency of her mission in such a calm and relaxing atmosphere. She knew she should feel guilty. She should be on her way to Washington. She should have already placed that ad. "Tomorrow," she promised herself. "Tomorrow."

\* \* \*

"I have a proposition for you, if you're interested," Jason called from the kitchen.

Patricia had slipped out of her shorts and taken off her blouse. She had thrown them in the hamper, and was in the process of unfastening her bra.

"What? I didn't hear you," she called back.

Jason came up the stairs with a bowl of vanilla ice cream. He stopped and watched her from the back as she removed her bra and tossed it in the hamper. She was wearing white cotton panties, the kind that were cut low and hugged the hips. Nothing else. He admired her well-tanned, lean body. She had long, muscular legs, and the muscles in her back were well-defined. Her waist was small and accented her hips and gorgeous ass. He admired her reflection in the mirror, her perfect breasts, her long neck, her lips, and especially her eyes. God, he loved this woman. Then why couldn't he tell her? Didn't he owe her that much?

She saw him in the mirror and smiled.

"I said I have a proposition for you."

"What kind of proposition?" She turned and stood in the bathroom doorway, smiling mischievously.

"I-" He looked at the ice cream. "You think-"

She came over and took the spoon from him. She scooped up a rounded spoonful and put it in her mouth. Then she put her arms around his neck and kissed him. Her mouth and tongue were cold as she shared the ice cream with him. He was becoming aroused. He could feel his whole body responding to her erotic kiss. Her breasts flattened against his chest as she pressed him against the doorframe. Her hand moved to his zipper, opening it.

"Or maybe you had something else in mind?" She smiled, scooping up more ice cream this time with two fingers.

This wasn't exactly the proposition he had in mind. He was going to ask her if she would like to visit the test site near Berkeley Springs with him and Bill. At the moment, this seemed like a much better idea.

Later, they were lying on the bedroom floor naked. Patricia's head was on his chest and he was raking his fingers through her thick hair.

"I never answered you earlier," he said.

"Answered me?"

"When you told me you loved me."

"It wasn't a question. I wasn't looking for an answer. I just felt like saying it. That's all. Just because someone says they love you, it doesn't mean you have to say it too."

"Well, I do love you. I may not say it, but you must know that by now."

"I do. I did. But it's always nice to hear it anyway."

Patricia smiled and kissed him. He turned her around and embraced her tightly, their naked bodies pressing together, remains of the ice cream sticky on both their bodies.

The phone rang. Jason started to get up. Patricia pulled him to her.

"Let the machine get it."

\* \* \*

"Makes me want to go home and screw the old lady," said Lockner.

"Shut up," Bowerman barked.

"What are we going to hear? They're fucking. That's all. That's all they ever do. I don't know why we're out here anyway. Why don't we just go in and get the formula?"

"We're here because we don't know where the damn formula is.

Sometimes people say things when they're screwing they'd never say at any other time."

"By the way, dear, I hid the formula in my sock drawer. Sure. That's just what you're going to say when you're fucking a beautiful bitch like her."

"Maybe. Maybe he talks in his sleep. That formula is going to make us rich."

"Or put us in jail for the rest of our lives."

"Possibly. I don't know about you, but I'm willing to take the chance for a million bucks. You can still get out if you want. It's not too late. I can always find someone else. I just thought you needed the money."

"You know I do. I'm still in. Don't worry. Besides, I'd probably still be charged as your accomplice if you got caught."

"I'd never say anything."

"I need the money, OK? Maybe I can give Marge the life she always wanted."

"The phone is ringing," said Bowerman.

Two weeks ago, they had carefully searched the entire townhouse. They hadn't found anything, but they had time to tap all the phones and place bugs in all the rooms.

"Pick up the fucking phone," said Lockner. "I hate it when people don't answer their goddammed phones."

It rang four times before the answering machine picked up. There was a click and then a dial tone. The caller didn't leave a message.

# Chapter Eight

"Harding. Harding." Phil ran down the list in the phone book. "There certainly are a lot of Hardings."

"What did you expect?" Diane asked. "Do you know where he lives?"

Phil shook his head. "Someplace in Washington. That's all we know for sure."

Diane ran her finger down the first column and then the second. There was almost a full page of Hardings listed. "There are three J. Hardings, one J.R. Harding, and two Jason Hardings."

"He must be here, then. He works on Wisconsin Avenue, and he walks to work. I know that much."

"You know all that, and you don't know where he lives?"

"It wasn't part of the public record. And much of the information about this time period was destroyed by a virus that got into the computer network in 2002."

"Well. Let's see. Where on Wisconsin Avenue did he work?"

"1101," he answered.

Diane got up from the table.

"Where you going?"

"I have a street map of Washington, DC. We'll see what's close to 1101 Wisconsin Avenue." When she came back, she opened a large map book and laid it on the table.

"This is Wisconsin. 1101 would be at an intersection. It should be around here, near L street. Let me see the phone book again." She looked down the two columns. "Here you go. Three Hardings in the Georgetown area. One is Jason, one is J and one is J.R. What was his middle name?"

"Robert. That's got to be him."

"Who?"

"J.R."

"What about the other two?"

"You're right. It could be either one of them."

"Well. That's only three out of two hundred to check out. That shouldn't take you long. Why don't you call the J.R. first?"

Phil didn't hesitate. He took the phone and dialed the number. It rang four times and an answering machine picked up. Phil listened to the man's voice on the other end; "We can't come to the phone right now, so, at the tone leave a message."

He hung up.

"No answer?"

"An answering device."

"Why didn't you leave a message?"

"I didn't know what to say."

Phil put his hand over Diane's. She closed her eyes and pretended for a moment it was really Josh's hand and not this other man that had taken over his body. She opened her eyes and looked at him. There was something about the eyes. They were different. Someone once said the eyes are windows to the soul. They were Josh's eyes, but Josh wasn't there. Where was he? Did he know what was happening? Would she ever get him back again? She removed her hand from beneath his.

"I really appreciate your help," he said.

"Anything it takes to get Josh back."

"Look, Diane. I'm going to take care of this body. I promise you. I'll do my best to get through this thing in one piece. You'll get your Josh back. I mean it."

"You damn well better."

\* \* \*

### Friday, May 5, 1995, 8:20 a.m.

"Remember that proposition I started to make last night?"

Patricia peeled the covers away from her face and looked at Jason. He was standing in the doorway, fully dressed in jeans and a blue plaid shirt and hiking shoes. Hiking shoes?

"I thought we settled that. What are you doing up so early?" She pushed herself up, stretched and yawned.

Jason sat on the edge of the bed and kissed her lightly on the lips.

Patricia covered her mouth. "Um. Bad breath."

"Me?"

"No. Me. I have a bad taste in my mouth. It's got to smell awful."

"I didn't notice. Well? How about it? Up for a little drive?"

"You're dressed for more than driving."

"There may be a little walking involved too. How about it?"

"I really should go to work. We started those damn 'red dot' sales today and half the things didn't get keyed in. It's going to be a zoo."

"I don't want to hear it. You're on vacation, remember? What are department managers for, anyway? Isn't that why they call them managers?

88

This is the first time you've taken off in a year."

"Okay. Bring me a diet Coke while I shower and dress."

He kissed her again. "I have coffee brewing. Want some?"

"You know I don't drink that stuff. It's bad for you."

"So are sodas."

"Do I get breakfast before we go for this drive?"

"I went to that bakery on the corner this morning."

"How long have you been up?"

"Couple of hours. They had just put out fresh blueberry bagels. I got you a half dozen. Please tell me you like blueberry"

"You really don't know me very well, do you?"

"I'm trying. You have to give me credit for that."

"I do. How are we going to go on this drive? You don't own a car."

"Bill's driving."

"I see. It's not just the two of us then?"

"It was going to be, but Albert called again. He called Bill, too. He wants us to inspect the test area."

"Why? I thought that was just a park."

"There's a small field lab there. It will be used to continue monitoring the water afterwards. He just wants to make sure everything is secure."

"Why doesn't he send someone else? Did he say anything about those two men?"

"I volunteered. I thought you might enjoy a day in the mountains. And, no, he doesn't know anything yet. He's still checking."

"He's not doing anything, then?"

"I didn't say that. He's asked the FBI to get involved. You'll probably see some of their agents following us soon."

"Great. Let's all play follow the leader."

\* \* \*

"What the hell is going on?" Bowerman asked as he handed Lockner a Styrofoam cup through the open car window. He opened the door and slid into the driver's seat.

"Albert Fenwick called Harding right after you left to get the coffee. Apparently sometime Thursday, Harding called him and told him he was being followed. I guess he spotted us. What do we do now?"

"What did Fenwick have to say?"

"He called the FBI. I don't like this, Bowerman. What if they find out who we are?"

"Don't worry. No one is going to find out. No one else knows about us."

"What about your friend?"

"Don't worry about him."

"What if they find the bugs?"

"There's no way they can trace them. Things like that disappear all the time. Besides, I took all that stuff over a year ago from a surveillance stakeout that went bad. There's no trail that can lead them to us."

"They'll know they are FBI bugs. They will know what job they came from. You know as well as I do they will figure it out. It's just a matter of time."

"Just means we have to do something soon. Maybe today. Didn't I hear them say something about going to Berkeley Springs?"

Lockner nodded. "Just the three of them. Alone in the mountains. We've already searched the fucking house. The formula isn't there. So, what do you have in mind?"

"We follow them. This may be the best opportunity we get."

"To do what?"

"What ever it takes. I say we get the fucking formula today."

\* \* \*

"The Washington Post. How may I direct your call?"

"I would like to place an ad," Phil told the female voice on the other end of the phone connection."

"Please hold." There were several clicks.

"Classifieds. May I help you?" A man's voice.

"I want to place an ad in the Announcements section." Phil answered.

"How do you wish it to read?"

"Fellow Traveler. Just arrived from Mammoth. Meet me at the Lincoln Memorial at 6:00 p.m., Wednesday May 10, 1995. P.R."

"That it?"

"Yes."

"How long do you want it to run?"

"Ten days. Through the Tenth."

"I can put that on four lines for thirty-seven dollars or five for fifty."

"Make it five for fifty and make Fellow Traveler bolder and bigger so it will stand out."

"That's going to take more space."

"I want it to stand out."

"How about one column by four inches with a border."

"Sure."

"That will be one hundred and fifty dollars. How do you wish to pay?"

Phil hadn't thought about that. He looked at Diane.

"What?" She stood on the other side of the kitchen counter sipping a hot cup of coffee.

"They're asking me how do I want to pay for it."

Diane laughed. "That's no problem. Josh is filthy rich." She set the cup on the counter and left the room. When she came back, she handed him a wallet and a gold colored plastic card. "Use this. American Express gold. No limit."

"Sir?" The voice on the other end of the phone sounded irritated. "How do you wish to pay for the ad?"

"Plastic." Phil answered. "American Express."

"I need the number, your name as it appears on the card, and the expiration date."

Phil read it to him, and the man repeated it back. "Is that correct?"

"That's right."

"Your ad will start tomorrow in the Saturday edition. Will there be anything else?"

"No. Wait. Have there been any other ads similar to this one placed recently?"

There was a brief pause. "That's strange."

"What's strange?" Phil asked.

"Another ad identical to yours."

"Are you sure? How is it signed?"

"D.K. But the rest of it is just like your ad. Word for word."

"That's great. Thanks." Phil almost burst out laughing. He wasn't alone. Daren hadn't been killed, and he was here!

"Will there be anything else, sir?"

"No. Thanks."

"Thank you for calling the Washington Post."

Phil hung up the phone.

"What was that about?"

"Daren Kosman. A friend of mine. He's here also." He began inspecting the wallet.

Diane took it out of his hands. "What are you doing? This is Josh's wallet."

"I know." He took it back from her and started looking through it again. "I'm Josh. Remember?" He laughed. "I think it's time I get to know him."

"You bastard. This is like a game to you. Isn't it?"

91

Phil laid the wallet on the counter and looked at her. "This is no game," he said. "This was never a game. I lost someone I love too. Remember?"

"You don't know that."

"No. But then, neither do you. For all you know, Josh is listening to us right now."

"You're lying. You're just saying that to make me feel better."

"Maybe. But how can either of us be sure?" He picked the wallet up again and started to search through it. "There's a lot of money in here. You said Josh is filthy rich. Just how rich is he?"

"I don't know. He inherited a big chunk of change when his parents were killed. A lot of it went into a trust and is paid out to him in a monthly allowance. I think he has a hundred thousand in his checking and savings accounts. He owns a Corvette, a Jeep Cherokee, and a small plane. He has this house and a condo on New Hampshire Avenue in Washington."

"You seem to know a lot about him."

"Josh and I are going to be married. Were," she corrected herself.

"Are," he said. "You still are. When this is over-"

"If it's ever over."

"It will be. I promise."

Phil picked up the phone again and dialed the number where he had reached the answering machine last night. The phone rang four times and the same message was repeated. He hung up without leaving a message again.

"Machine again?"

He nodded.

"Why didn't you say anything?"

"What was I supposed to say? Hello, you don't know me, but I'm your son and I've come here to kill you. We don't even know if he's the one I'm looking for."

"I don't care. I just want this to be over."

# Chapter Nine

Lauren stretched and tilted her head back, languishing in the wonderful heat of the Florida sun. She and Hill had spread two beach towels near the pier early this morning before the wide beach became crowded with sun worshipers.

She reminded herself she should call the Washington Post. What was she waiting for? Did she think all this was just going to go away? She wasn't being fair to the others. They had given their lives for this mission. Daren and Phil were out there someplace. They would be looking for her message in the Washington Post. Waiting. She should feel guilty. No. She had never experienced anything like this before. She had never known a real body. She had never taken the time to just lay back and enjoy life. She deserved every second of this.

"Good morning."

Lauren opened her eyes. She saw Dan's handsome, grinning face, looking down at her. He was holding two drinks.

"I hope you don't mind. When I went out on the balcony this morning I saw the two of you on the beach. I said to myself those two look like they could use a drink. How about it? Strawberry daiquiris okay?"

He offered the drinks again. They took them and sipped the sweet frozen concoction.

"So, what are you ladies up to today?"

"Exactly what you see," Hill said. She set the drink in the sand next to her, laid back and closed her eyes.

"You feel up to a little volleyball? That group over there needs a couple more players." He pointed back toward the hotel.

"I don't know how to play." Lauren said.

"I'll teach you."

"I don't know."

Dan stood and offered his hand. "Come on. Give it a try. You might actually enjoy it."

"Why not." She gave in and accepted Dan's hand.

He pulled her up. "That's what I like. Someone who's not afraid to try something new."

"You haven't seen her play yet," Hill said.

"Hill's right. You haven't seen me play yet."

93

"Who cares? It's just a game anyway. Life is just a game."

"Sometimes I wish it were," she said.

* * *

Jason was in the kitchen when he heard the horn. His townhouse was three blocks west of Minnesota and four blocks north of M Street. He didn't see a lot of traffic here. The clusters of townhouses were gathered along several narrow, tree-lined, dead-end streets. The big and ancient trees seemed to absorb most of the sounds from the business area of Georgetown. A car horn here was not a welcome Saturday morning sound.

The kitchen was in the front, just to the left of the entrance foyer, and the two short windows above the sink faced a small courtyard and the tree-shaded street. He looked out the kitchen window and saw Bill's red convertible double-parked in front of his townhouse. Bill hit the horn again.

"Bill's here." Jason called upstairs. "You just about ready?"

Patricia came down the stairs without answering. They nearly collided as she came around the corner.

"Oh. Guess you are. Don't you look good? You should dress like this more often. I like this natural look."

She was wearing faded jean shorts, a white pullover sweater, a green and white checked shirt, unbuttoned, and carrying a canvas duffel bag. He noticed she was wearing the brown hiking boots he had talked her into a few weeks ago. He knew she didn't like them and hadn't wanted them, but he had talked her into them anyway. This was the first time she had actually worn them. She had pulled her hair back into a ponytail. He liked this new look.

"Natural? Are you saying I don't normally look natural?"

"That's one of those questions a man can't answer, isn't it?"

"Is this how the West Virginia women dress?"

"Trust me. You look better than any of the women I've met up there."

"I have your approval then?"

"Definitely. I especially like the boots."

"I know you do. I thought I may as well give them a try. They cost you a fortune."

He laughed again. "Sure did. Julie let me use your discount, and they still cost me two weeks of lunch money."

She loved the sound of Jason's laughter and the way his eyes reflected his feelings. She could always tell when he was truly happy. The opposite was also true. When he was sad or angry it was just as obvious. His eyes gave him away every time.

94

He was wearing a forest-green checked shirt, faded jeans, and hiking boots. Jason should have lived in the wilderness, because that was where he was the happiest. He didn't like suits and only wore them when he was forced to attend meetings to justify his work for continued funding. Even when working in his lab, he dressed casual.

"What's in the bag?"

"Nothing."

"Let me see." He snatched the bag and opened it. "Your Nikes?"

"Just in case."

The horn blasted again.

"Your neighbors are going to hate you. Why don't you ask him in?"

"They're going to hate Bill, not me."

Patricia went to the front door and opened it. Bill waved. He got out and stood beside the car.

"Come on in, Bill," she called. "We're just about ready."

"Can't. I might get towed. You know how Jason's neighbors are."

"I can't imagine why. Can I get you anything, coffee or a soda?

"No thanks. You two about ready?"

"Almost," she answered.

"Hurry up, will you? Before a cop shows up."

She laughed. "I advise you to lay off the horn." She went back to the kitchen and opened the refrigerator. She selected a diet Coke and opened it. "Where's that bagel you promised me?"

"I was just putting cream cheese on it. I'll wrap it in a paper towel and you can take it with you."

"You know this is why I love you, don't you?"

"What do you mean?"

"I mean my spending the day with you and Bill."

"Listen. We'll check things out, get Bill set up, and then we'll be on our own. I promise. You'll have a great time."

They heard a different horn and then yelling.

"Sounds like Bill's about to meet some of your neighbors."

"Trust me. He's met them before." Jason laughed. He put his arms around her and kissed her. "Come on. Let's go before he gets himself arrested."

Outside, Jason started to lock the door, but remembered the disk.

"Be right back," he said. "Forgot something."

"Hurry, or we're going to have a fight to break up."

"Bill can take care of himself. Trust me."

The formula was on two floppy disks. Jason kept one of the disks with him at all times, and the other was in a locker at the Trailways bus terminal in Silver Spring, Maryland. The formula was actually quite simple, but only Jason knew the specific combinations that would create his particular strain of bacteria. These vital combinations were missing from both disks, and only Jason could enter the correct sequence that made the formula work. Since the questionable accident that had taken Rob's life, Jason didn't trust anyone with the complete formula. He was the only person who knew a second disk even existed, and, just to be safe, he probably should update that other disk.

Even if Bill had known about the second disk, both were still useless without the information that only Jason could supply, and that information was inside his head. Jason never allowed the formula to be saved in the computers. Any changes that were made were copied to the disk that he always kept in his possession.

* * *

Bill parked near the main building. It was a single-level log structure with a porch on three sides and cedar shingles. The building was still under construction. The windows hadn't been installed yet and the double doors were missing. In the back, extending out over the murky water of the small creek, was the lab. It looked like the rest of the building, except it was completely finished and furnished with all the necessary equipment and computers. The parking lot, a quarter mile off the main highway, had just been paved. Paving equipment was still parked at one corner of the large lot, probably waiting to put on a second coat, since the surface was rough and had an unfinished look to it. All this land along the east side of the creek was owned by the EPA and would be donated to the state for use as a park during the upcoming ceremonies.

"I'll open it up," Bill said and went inside.

"I'll be along in a minute," Jason replied.

"Doesn't Bill need your help?" asked Patricia.

"Naw. He can handle this part," he laughed.

Jason had such a wonderful laugh, she thought. Maybe today would be a good time to tell him the good news. No, she thought. She really should wait until she was absolutely sure.

Jason pointed to a large structure under construction at the distant end of the big parking lot. "They call that the theater," he said. "On that stage Fenwick and the President and yours truly will be speaking. After July Fourth, this place will be listed on maps as a special place to visit. It's going to be famous."

"Why did Bill want to come up today?"

"He keeps trying to convince me that something is wrong with the formula. Ever since Albert made him my assistant, he thinks he knows more about it than me."

"What does he think is wrong with it?"

"He thinks something is wrong with the bacteria. He wants to change the formula."

"Change it? How?"

"I don't know. Doesn't matter."

"Aren't you a little curious?"

"No, besides, everything is set to go. I've checked everything about that formula more times than I can remember. It's safe and it works."

"Then why is he here?"

"I have to humor Bill. He would probably call Fenwick if I tried to shut him out. That way, I let him think he's doing something constructive. When he gets through, I save what he's done to the disk and make sure everything is removed from the computer. That's why I suggested he come along today. Besides, we needed a ride."

"There was always my car."

"Don't you like Bill's convertible?"

"Sure."

"Then what's the problem?"

"I thought it was just going to be you and me, that's all."

"Sorry. I guess I wasn't thinking again, was I?"

"What's new?" she smiled.

"Thanks a lot. It's just that I still don't know much about Bill. He kind of just appeared after Rob was killed. He's likable and really knows his stuff, but he doesn't believe in the formula like I do. He's always wanting to do testing and more testing. I've tried to tell him we're ready, but he doesn't agree. When I ask him why, he just gives me vague answers. He still hasn't told me exactly what he thinks is wrong with the formula. Do you want to come in while I load the disk?"

"Sure."

Patricia watched the two men go about turning on computers and setting up the testing equipment. She quickly got bored.

"I'm going outside."

"I'm almost through here," Jason said.

"That's okay. Take your time. I think I'll climb that hill on the other side of the parking lot. It looks like a good place to soak up some sun."

Jason followed her to the door. He took her hands and whispered against her ear, "Be careful."

She looked at him strangely. "Why?"

"Our friends. The two men who have been following us. Remember? Just be careful."

"I promise." She smiled and kissed him. "I won't cross the road and I won't talk to any strangers."

"Seriously. I'll be out in a few minutes."

"What are you two talking about?" Bill asked. "What friends?"

"Someone has been following us." Jason said. "No big deal."

"No big deal? Why didn't you tell me?"

"I was going to. Albert asked me to come up and check on things."

"And I thought you were doing it for me." He laughed.

"Albert said he'd let me know if anything turned up or he found out anything. He has the FBI checking it out. Nothing yet."

"That's just great. That's another reason we should postpone this whole thing."

"No way. You've been trying to persuade me to postpone this for the past month. We're ready to proceed with the next phase. We've been ready."

"I don't like it. I didn't think anyone was supposed to know about this."

"There's probably a very reasonable explanation, Bill."

"Well, I still don't like it."

Jason squeezed Patricia's hand. "I'll be right out."

Patricia made up her mind. "Well, hurry. I have a surprise to tell you."

"A surprise?" What is it?"

"I'll tell you when you get through here."

He turned to Bill. "Can you handle things from here, Bill?"

"Sure, just give me the disk."

"No, I'll load it for you. You'll need the combination anyway."

"Why don't you just give me the code? That way you two can go off and do whatever you want."

Jason turned to Patricia and said, "I'll be right out."

Patricia climbed the grassy hill that overlooked the parking lot. At the crest of the hill she had a panoramic view of the highway, the creek, and the park that was still under construction. The West Virginia mountains were hazy blue in the distance. The wind was gusty up here, and she was glad she had put her hair in a ponytail.

She sat in the grass and watched, looking for any unexpected movement below. Nothing was out of place. She didn't see the black Chevrolet Impala parked nearly a mile away on a dirt farm access road just off Highway 522, nor did she see the two men hidden in the trees less than fifty yards from the unfinished park building and lab.

* * *

Patricia had barely gotten to know Rob Williams before he was killed in that awful accident. He and Jason had been close friends, and she knew Jason really missed him. The accident had happened just two months ago. The two of them had grown up together, went to the same college, even shared the same dorm room. They had accidentally discovered this new bacteria strain similar to the spirilla type while they were in college. The bacteria strain had actually been discovered in a beaker of water taken from the Shenadoah River. At first inspection, it looked like any other spiral bacteria, but as they experimented with it, they discovered it behaved differently from other bacteria strains they had studied. When the bacterium was subjected to small doses of radiation, its structure changed. It actually mutated into an entirely different form. By controlling the amount and duration of radiation exposure, they learned how to control the mutations and to work with the different strains they were able to create. They were excited about their discovery, but had no idea exactly what they were creating.

Like so many great discoveries, theirs was a complete accident. They were washing test tubes and beakers one evening after cleaning the lab when the dirty, soapy water suddenly started to change. The suds began to rapidly disappear and the oil on the surface began to separate and shrink. In less than a minute, the water in the sink and even the test tubes and beakers were sparkling clean. They just stared at the phenomenon. It was impossible, but it had happened. The water in the sink appeared to be as clean as drinking water. They tested it and discovered it was nearly 100 percent pure. There were no contaminants or visible bacteria of any kind to be found.

They tried to recreate what had happened, but couldn't. They eventually determined it had been some combination of substances from the different test tubes and beakers. They bottled and sealed the sink water and continued to experiment with it. During their senior year, they co-authored several papers concerning the bacteria strain and its possible impact on the environment. After they graduated, they were offered positions with the EPA and were given their own lab. They worked together for twelve years but only made small advances in their primary research while managing to solve some minor problems concerning land and air contamination. They were never able to recreate the incident the accident had caused that evening in the college lab.

But last year, Jason discovered the elusive combination and recorded the exact formula and procedures he had used to recreate it. Then Rob was killed in a freak accident on I-395 at King Street in Alexandria in March.

Two weeks after Rob's death, Bill Dodds appeared. He was a black man who had graduated from Mississippi State about the same time Jason and Rob received their degrees from the University of Maryland. He had been studying the effects of different types of pollution on the environment and the ozone and had apparently made quite a name for himself. The agency was impressed with his credentials and appointed him as Rob's replacement. He was good. Jason was impressed. He knew his stuff. Sometimes he even seemed clairvoyant, like he could see into the future. He was able to predict dates and times and effects as accurately as if they had already happened.

He didn't believe in the formula like Jason did, and Jason still hadn't been able to convince him they were ready for the actual field-testing and release.

\* \* \*

"What are they doing?" Lockner asked.

Bowerman was looking through binoculars. "I can't tell. There's only one window on this side of the building. I can see the black man, but I don't see Harding or the girl."

"That's Bill Dodds. Forget him. Harding has what we want."

"I don't see him or the girl." Bowerman scanned the building and the big parking lot.

Lockner tapped him on the shoulder and pointed, "There she is. Up there on the hill."

Bowerman swung the binoculars around. "I don't see Harding. He must still be inside."

Lockner pulled his gun and started to get up.

"Wait." Chad ordered. "We need them together."

"I say we get the girl. We got her and we get anything we want. He'd be a fool to let anything happen to that sweet little piece of ass."

"There he is now."

Lockner took the binoculars from Bowerman and looked. Jason had just come out of the building. He stopped and looked around, saw Patricia up on the hill, and started toward her.

\* \* \*

He had only gone a few yards through the tall grass when he stopped and turned. He looked around and then at the park building. Up on the hill, Patricia watched. What was he doing? She looked everywhere, but didn't see anything.

100

"Jason," she called.

Before he could answer, the log building suddenly exploded and erupted in flames. A fiery black cloud mushroomed above the trees. Burning projectiles flew in all directions.

"Oh, my God! Jason!" she screamed and started running down the hill. She stumbled, fell, got up and kept running.

"Get down!" Jason suddenly loomed up in front of her and fell, taking her with him. He held her down, covering her with his own body as pieces of the building showered down all around them. They heard trees cracking and falling. Another explosion. The car. Smoldering pieces of metal peppered the ground and ignited the brush and trees. He looked back and saw that the lab had become a mass of smoke and shapeless burning things.

Jason could only think of one thing: what the hell happened? What had Bill done?

"Are you okay, honey?"

"I think so. What happened, Jason?"

"I don't know. There shouldn't have been anything in the building that could do that. You sure you're okay?"

"I think so. What about Bill?"

"He was still in the lab."

"Go. I'm okay."

He got up and searing pain suddenly shot up through his left leg. Everything started spinning, and he knew he was going to pass out if he didn't sit back down.

"Jason!" Patricia screamed. "Your leg!"

There was something sticking out of his left leg just below his knee. When had that happened? He hadn't felt a thing. There wasn't any blood, but the pain was getting worse. His jeans had been burned around the metal object and were still smoking. He felt sick. The sour taste of bile filled his mouth, and he knew he was about to vomit.

Patricia took her shirt off and wrapped it around the hot, jagged piece of metal, and started pulling it out. At another time Jason would have been proud of her quick thinking, but right then he was in agony. He clamped his teeth and clawed hands full of grass and dirt as it tore through the flesh. She threw the thing down and examined the wound.

"God! It hurts like hell."

"Good news."

He attempted a weak laugh.

"That I still have a leg?"

"That too. No. I think the heat must have cauterized the flesh. The wound isn't bleeding and that thing was so hot I don't think you have to worry about any infection."

"Great. Do you see Bill?"

She shook her head. "I don't think he got out in time."

"He had to. I've got to look for him."

"You can't, Jason. You can't even walk."

"Sure I can. Just help me up."

"At least let me wrap something around the wound."

"Okay. Here." He handed her a knife from his pocket. He called it his McGyver knife. McGyver had always been his hero. He might be a fictional character, but he was someone who really cared about the environment. Jason had seen every episode ever filmed, some more than once.

She opened the knife and cut the material away. The wound looked worse than she had thought. The skin around the wound really looked nasty. "We have to get you to a doctor."

"First we have to see about Bill. Besides, the fire department will probably be showing up pretty soon."

"We're more than thirty miles from Berkeley Springs. That could take a long time, even if there were anyone around to report it."

She ripped pieces of her shirt that wasn't burned, wrapped them around his leg, and tied them securely in place.

"There. That should at least keep the dirt out."

"Help me up."

He leaned on her, and she did her best to support him as they slowly made their way to the burning wreckage. Jason was hoping against hope that somehow Bill had escaped in time.

"There's no way he could have gotten out of that alive."

"You're wrong." Patricia laughed and cried at the same time. "Look." She pointed.

There was a body laying face down at the edge of the stream. It was Bill. His clothes were smoking, and he wasn't moving.

Jason hopped mostly on one foot the twenty or thirty feet to the stream and fell next to Bill. Patricia knelt next to them and turned Bill over. She placed her fingers against his neck and felt for a pulse. He was alive. She did a cursory examination and didn't find any injuries other than a goose egg bump and cut on his forehead.

"He must have hit his head when he fell. Lucky it didn't kill him."

"Bill." Jason shook him. "Speak to me, buddy."

Bill opened his eyes, "Who are you? Where am I?"

# Chapter Ten

**Friday, May 5, 4:45 p.m.**

Bowerman and Lockner watched, speechless, as the building exploded and huge chunks skyrocketed in all directions. A black, fiery cloud mushroomed and blotted out the evening sun. There was a second explosion a moment later. That would be the car.

"What the hell happened?" Lockner asked.

"How the fuck should I know?" Bowerman looked through the binoculars. "Where's Harding and the girl? Do you see them?"

Lockner shook his head and started to laugh. "It's over. Harding is dead and a million bucks goes up in smoke."

"Harding is alive," said Bowerman. "Looks like he got hit with something, but he's alive. His girlfriend is with him."

"What about the other one? Dodds?"

"He's not important." Bowerman looked for him anyway. "There he is. Near the water."

"What the shit happened? You don't suppose the disk was ruined, do you?"

"Naw. Harding will still have the disk on him. He hasn't trusted anyone with that formula yet. Robert Williams didn't even have a copy and he was in on the discovery."

"You had to bring his name up, didn't you?"

"We came close to fucking up everything, old buddy. It won't happen again."

* * *

Diane heard the explosion and thought it was thunder. She went out on the deck and saw a dark cloud mushrooming up from the valley floor near state highway 522. Fires had already begun spreading through the surrounding grass and trees.

She went back inside and dialed the Berkeley Springs fire department.

Phil was in the kitchen pouring a cup of coffee. "That sounded like an explosion. What happened?"

"It was. Something blew up down in the valley. It looks like it happened where they're building that new park. I just called the fire department."

"How long will it take them to get there?"

"Twenty or thirty minutes. Why?"

"How long would it take us?"

"Probably five minutes."

"Then let's go."

"Okay." She knew she sounded surprised but couldn't hide it. Was this man actually wanting to help someone?

"I'll get some blankets and a first aide kit," she said. The blankets were in the hall closet. The first aide kit was kept in the utility room. She handed Phil the blankets and grabbed the keys to the Jeep Cherokee from the wall hook in the kitchen. "I'll drive."

"No problem."

\* \* \*

"That was a nasty hit you took, buddy."

Jason and Patricia had helped Bill to a large oak nearly a hundred yards away from the fires and burning wreckage. He was leaning against the tree, while they examined the lump on his forehead.

"This cut should be cleaned, but I don't think we should use the creek water."

"I definitely agree," said Jason.

"What's wrong with the water?" Bill asked. "Who are you? What happened?"

"I thought maybe you could tell me." Jason said. "What caused that explosion, Bill? What the hell were you doing in there?"

Bill looked confused. He honestly didn't know this man or what he was talking about. He shook his head. "I don't understand." He touched the bump on his forehead and then looked at his fingers. Blood? *Always go for the head,* he heard a voice say. He knew that voice. It belonged to his close friend, his only friend, Philip Rollins.

Bill closed his eyes and remembered a darkened room with familiar machines. He remembered lying on the transference bed. There was a sudden flash of brilliant light, and then he was standing on a crowded street corner at a busy intersection. There were buildings and people everywhere. Antique machines of all descriptions, sizes, shapes, and colors flew past. He looked up at the tall buildings and then out across the wide river.

There on the other side of the slow moving river was a familiar skyline that no longer existed. He recognized that famous skyline from pictures and old videos he had seen. There was a building close to the water that looked like an ancient temple. Just beyond, a white marble obelisk stood tall and straight, its sharp point aimed at the heavens. In the background, the white dome of the capitol building was easily visible.

He was looking at the resurrection of Washington, DC. He hadn't thought much about actually seeing this famous city, or even what it would be like. It had been destroyed nearly fifty years before he had been born. The capital of the United States had been moved to a large southern city, a city that had also been destroyed by civil war but had risen out of the flames like the phoenix, a fabulous bird of ancient legend. Legend had it when the phoenix reached 500 years of age it burned itself on a pyre from whose ashes another phoenix arose. The phoenix was always a symbol of death and resurrection. Out of the flames of a civil war Atlanta was reborn and eventually became the jewel of the south, the new capital of the United States.

Had Washington, DC shared this same destiny? No, he told himself. The future was an unpainted canvas. It was a story yet to be written, and he and the other eleven Disciples were its authors. With the assistance of Phil and Lauren and Sandy, they would set the course that would dictate how the story would unfold. The civil war that destroyed Washington had not happened yet. It would not. He hadn't told the others, but he had chosen this place and time to start his work. The others would be along in four to six weeks.

Daren Kosman. The name suddenly came into his head, and he remembered who he was and what he had come here to do. Had the mission been accomplished, or was he in the middle of something else?

Daren looked at the man and woman. He felt that he should know them. They were obviously very concerned about his condition. How long had he been here? Where were the others? Were they here also? Were these people Disciples? Should he ask?

"Stay here, Bill. Stay with him, Patricia. I'll go and find help."

"You can't go anyplace with that leg," she said.

"There's a farm house less than a mile from here."

"You can hardly stand up. How are you going to walk a mile? Besides. If it's that close someone should be showing up to see what happened."

"What if no one was home? I have to get to a phone. Besides, it's not that bad. Honest."

"Sure. Mr. Macho. You stay here with Bill," she said. "I'll go."

"I'm all right." Daren started to get up. "Why don't we all go?"

"No, you don't." Patricia put her hand on his leg. Daren looked at it strangely and then at his own hand. His hand was black, both hands were black. Had he been burned? They didn't hurt. Wouldn't there be pain? He rotated his hands and studied them. Then he touched his face, his nose, and his lips. Was he a black man? An Afro-American?

105

"Both of you stay here." Jason ordered. "That's a nasty hit you took, Bill. You might even have a concussion. Patricia will stay with you while I go get help. No more arguments."

"I will not." Patricia stated. "You're staying with Bill, and I'm going. So just sit yourself down and accept it."

They called him Bill? The man called the woman Patricia? Then they weren't anyone he knew. Or maybe they were, and they just didn't know who he was. Should he tell them? Who was Bill? What was Bill's last name? How did he fit into all this? The explosion? Had he made it happen? Was it part of the plan? Had the mission been accomplished? No. He told himself. He was still here. If he was still here the mission had not been accomplished, at least not successfully.

"Where are we?" he asked, but no one answered him.

Patricia made sure they both were okay and then she started across the parking lot.

"I said, where are we?" he repeated.

"Stay here, Bill." Jason patted his leg. "Patricia!" he called.

She stopped and turned to look at him. She saw the agony on his face as he struggled to get to her. Was it agony or just plain stubbornness? She met him halfway.

"Please stay here, Jason. I know how you like to be in charge, but let me do this. Okay?"

She called him Jason? Jason Harding? Could it be? No, Bill told himself. He could never be so lucky. Of all the places in the world, it was a million to one odds that he'd show up with the man he had come here to find.

"I guess you're right. I'm not sure if I could even reach the highway."

"Then stay with Bill. He can use your help."

A red Jeep Cherokee turned off highway 522 onto the paved road and slowly came to a stop in front of them. A man and a woman got out and approached.

"Didn't I tell you someone would hear the explosion and come?" Patricia said.

Daren watched them while a thousand questions raced through his mind. What if he just blurted out his name? Nothing else. He'd hit his head. He might say anything. If none of them recognized the name it wouldn't matter.

"Daren Kosman!" he called out and waited to see their reactions.

Phil jerked around and stared at the black man leaning against the big tree.

*Daren?*

\* \* \*

### May 5, Friday, 5:10 p.m.

Dan Sanderson was waiting for them in the second floor lobby. When they came out of the elevator he stood and grinned at them.

"I reserved us a table at a little place a few blocks from here. It's right on the beach. I think you'll like it. They have great grouper sandwiches and the best crab soup outside of Maryland."

"Anything besides seafood?" Hill asked. "I could really go for a steak."

"You're in Clearwater, Hill. When you're at the beach, you order fish. When you're in Texas, you order steak." He laughed. "Trust me. You have to try the grouper. You've never had grouper until you've had it here. It's just a few blocks from here. I hope you don't mind walking."

"Walking's okay." Lauren said. She trembled. What made her do that? It was such a strange sensation, like nothing she had ever felt before. It was like electricity was flowing from Dan's hand to hers. Was this normal? She didn't know, because this body she was in was like nothing she had ever felt before.

Dan felt her tremble and said, "Wait a sec. I have a jacket in my room. It won't take but a minute to run and get it."

"Really. I'm okay." Lauren assured him.

Hill interrupted. "You must be starving, girl. I haven't seen you eat anything since that tiny salad at the airport in Washington last night."

She wasn't starving. She wasn't sure what she was feeling, but for some reason it felt wrong. It was almost like she was betraying the others. Phil was out there someplace waiting for her, waiting for her message to appear in the Washington Post, and this handsome stranger she had met on the plane was here romancing her. It was wrong. She knew that. There wasn't time for this foolishness when the fate of the human race depended on what they did here in this time. She needed to place that ad. She should be on a plane back to Washington. Phil would be waiting for her at the Lincoln Memorial.

Later, she told herself. There's still plenty of time.

\* \* \*

### Friday, May 5, 5:15 p.m.

Phil stared at the black man in the distance. He was standing now but leaning against the big tree. He hadn't taken his eyes off them.

The smoke swirled around them and the flames were spreading from tree to tree.

"That's Bill." Jason said. "He has a big knot and a cut on his forehead, but

I don't believe it's life threatening."

"Daren?" he asked.

Patricia was supporting Jason where they stood between Bill Dodds and Phil. Diane came up behind him, but he didn't notice. He was staring at the black man with the nasty cut on his forehead. *Daren Kosman? Can it really be you?* Phil walked past Patricia and Jason and knelt next to Daren.

"Do you know Bill?" Jason asked.

"What?" Phil asked without looking. To Daren he said too softly for the others to hear, "Daren? Is it really you?"

Daren nodded. He didn't recognize this man, but how would he? Who are you, he wanted to ask. Cole? Newton? Babcock? One of the others? No. They were all dead. Betrayed and executed. He remembered now. There were only four of them left; He, Sandy, Philip, and Lauren.

"Phil?" he asked.

Phil nodded slightly and Daren smiled.

"You made it," he whispered and squeezed Phil's hand. "Thank God."

Jason sat down next to them with Patricia's support.

"Bill took a nasty hit on the head." Jason said. "Doesn't remember who or where he is."

"I heard him call you Phil?" Patricia said. "Do you know each other?"

Phil looked up at her and smiled. "We've met before." *Who are you supposed to be Daren? Who are these people?*

"I'm Diane Kimball. This is Josh Hamilton." Diane said. "We saw the explosion from Josh's house up on the mountain." She pointed in the general direction of the cabin, but there was no way to see the house from here.

"I'm Patricia Everest."

"Jason Harding." Jason offered his hand.

Phil accepted it and returned a firm handshake. *"The* Jason Harding?"

"You know me?"

"Everyone in the world knows you."

He laughed. "I don't think so. You must be thinking about someone else."

Daren watched them without saying anything. Jason Harding and Patricia Everest? Philip Rollins? Lauren? Sandy? Did he dare ask?

How long had he been here? What had happened? Did he cause that explosion? Had the formula been destroyed? There were too many questions and not enough answers. The only certainty was that the mission had not been accomplished. If it had been, he and Phil wouldn't still be here staring at each other.

The fires had spread to the other side of the narrow creek. The sky was black with smoke. In the distance the sound of sirens grew steadily louder.

\* \* \*

"Ain't this just a fucking mess," Bowerman angrily stuffed the binoculars in their case.

"We better get out of here. We can't do anything now."

"Why not? We're the only ones with the guns."

"There's too many people, Bowerman. What are you going to do, kill them all?"

"It wouldn't be the first time."

"I won't do it, Chad." Lockner shook his head. "I won't. I've been thinking."

"That's your problem. If we don't do it now we may never get another chance. You can bet your ass the police are going to be investigating this little incident. I guarantee you Fenwick and his boys and the FBI are going to be in on it too. What a fucking mess this is turning out to be." Bowerman took his gun out and checked it.

"Wait." Lockner put his hand on Bowerman's arm. "Look."

Jason had just taken something out of his shirt pocket. Bowerman took out the binoculars again and zoomed in for a closer look. Jason examined the broken piece of plastic, shook his head, and tossed it in the creek.

"He just threw the disk in the creek." Bowerman said. "It was ruined."

They heard the sound of sirens in the distance.

# Chapter Eleven

**July 16, 2217, Mammoth Cave (Five days after the transfer)**
"Jerrell Hardman," Levi said into the plastic cardphone.

"Who's calling?"

Levi heard background noise that indicated Hardman was already in transit. These cardphones were wonderful gadgets. Even two hundred feet of solid rock didn't interfere with their reception. He knew the background noise came from the injection turbos of Hardman's personal DS-2 pursuit vehicle, and the voice that answered was undoubtedly Hardman's driver.

"Let me speak to Mr. Hardman." Levi demanded. He didn't have time for silly games with the phone. Who else could possibly be calling on this secured narrow-band frequency? How many people actually had access to cardphones?

"What is it, Levi?" Hardman was obviously irritated. "Because of Collins' fuck- up I have to stand before the council in Atlanta, and I'm already late."

"You told me to call you when I made any progress."

There was a brief moment of silence. Levi could picture Hardman nodding, half-listening. He knew from past experience when Hardman spoke again he would have already made a decision and it would be useless to argue in favor or against that decision.

"Continue."

"We know how they did it, sir." He was having a difficult time keeping the excitement out of his voice. "How far away are you right now?"

He heard him inquire to the driver. He said, "Fifty miles. Why?"

"How soon can you be here?"

"Fifteen minutes if I choose, but as I said I have been ordered to stand before the council. I'm already late. What is it that can't wait?"

"You may want to call and postpone that meeting."

"I would have to have a very good reason."

"We're preparing an experiment. I'm sure you will want to be present."

"This experiment. If it is successful, what does it mean?"

"That we will be ready to go after them."

"That's what I want to hear. That's what the council wants to hear. I'll request my leave and be there at once."

Levi heard the disconnect sound and the line went dead. He put the cardphone in his jacket pocket and smiled. This was going to mean a promotion, a big promotion, maybe even a bonus to go along with it. Collins had been a good agent, even a close friend, but he had screwed up royally. Levi smiled. He regretted Collins' death, but he was delighted with the ultimate outcome. Yes, indeed. He was going places in the UCCIA.

"Okay people. Listen to me," he said as he moved across the large room. "Mr. Boss will be here in fifteen minutes. Kershaw?"

A stocky, older man looked up from one of the consoles. He didn't look any older, but Levi knew Kershaw was at least sixty years his senior. Everyone looked about the same age. These days the only visible thing left that was real were the eyes.

"Sir?"

"Is the subject ready?"

"Yes, sir."

Levi stood in the center of the room and studied the dozen or so faces that were turned toward him. He had persuaded Hardman to gather the best minds available, and he had pushed all of them non-stop around the clock for the last three days. They were all showing signs of exhaustion, but their efforts had paid off quickly. They now knew exactly what these Disciples had done and how they did it. They still weren't sure exactly how the transfer process worked or what made it work, but that wasn't important. What was important was that they were able to improve on the process itself and utilize what was here. On the surface, it all seemed so simple, and he found himself wondering why no one had ever thought of it before, but he wasn't so naive to believe it was as simple as it appeared. Given time they would probably figure out all the whats and hows and whys, but at the moment that wasn't necessary. All they needed to know was how to make the transfer. When the situation was resolved he and his group would have all the time in the world to unravel the mysteries held within these machines.

\* \* \*

"Who is she?" Hardman went over to the fourth table on the far side of the chamber and studied the face of the young woman strapped to the table. Her eyes were closed, and she appeared to be asleep.

"She's nobody. Just a woman from one of the local farms."

"Kidnapping is still a federal offense, Levi."

Hardman looked at him and grinned. Levi wasn't sure if he was serious. Since when did Hardman have any qualms about kidnapping? Here was a man who killed at the drop of a hat without giving it a second thought. He decided Hardman must be making one of his rare jokes, and forced a guarded laugh.

"She volunteered, sir."

"What did you promise her? Does she know what is going to happen?"

"She thinks she does." Levi grinned. "She also thinks she's going to be very rich when this is over."

Hardman smiled. "You are beginning to think like me, Levi. I like that. How will you know if this experiment is successful?"

"I'll take that as a compliment, sir. We think we have discovered a way to monitor the transfer, but we won't know for sure until we actually make the transfer. We're pretty sure we can pinpoint the exact time of arrival. We can't choose the place or the person. I don't believe the Disciples could either, but we can follow the transfer. We think we can actually watch it happen."

"What do you mean watch it happen?"

"The transfer seems to leave a trail. It lasts about a minute before it breaks apart and dissolves. We should be able to see through her eyes exactly what she sees. We think we'll even be able to hear what she hears."

"How do you know all this? I thought you hadn't made a transfer yet."

"We haven't. We have been studying the data from those other three transfers, and discovered a very interesting phenomenon. I'm not sure if any of the Disciples were even aware of it."

"I don't understand any of this," admitted Hardman. "I still believe actions are better than words, so just show me."

Hardman stroked the woman's synthetic arm and studied her sleeping features. The doctors responsible for her body did an excellent job. Her head seemed to be suspended inside a large golden ring that encircled her head. The ring consisted of spun strains of gold and copper. On the inside surface of the ring hundreds of tiny needles pointed toward her head but didn't actually touch her.

The woman appeared to be sleeping. It was impossible to tell how old she was. Everyone appeared to be about the same age. Hardman guessed she was young, though. An older person would never have been so easily convinced. She was either heavily sedated or hypnotized.

"Shouldn't she be awake and aware of what is happening?"

"We thought it would be better this way, less traumatic."

"How do you plan to monitor the transfer?"

"It's difficult to explain. It will be easier to watch."

"What are you waiting for? We're wasting time here. Proceed."

"Yes, sir. The transfer is being set up now."

Hardman stroked the young woman's arm again before turning away and walking around the room. He briefly studied the assortment of machines and computers. Now and then someone would attempt to explain how a particular device worked, but Levi, who followed discreetly a few paces behind, would shake his head slightly and the attempted explanation would be quickly aborted. Hardman made a complete circuit of the room and ended back at the side of the still-unconscious woman.

"Wake her up."

"Do you really think that is a good idea?"

"I want to see how she reacts. If one of us is going to do this I want to know what to expect." He stroked her arm, and then touched her cheek with the back of his fingers.

"She doesn't have to be awake. She's wired. The machines will tell us everything she experiences."

"I want to see her eyes. I want to see how she reacts when she gets to wherever it is she's going."

Levi knew better than to argue with this man. He remembered how easily Hardman had blown away Collins back at the cave entrance. That had been five days ago, but the memory of it would be etched into his brain for a very long time.

"Do you have a problem with that?" Hardman looked at him with cold, dark eyes and Levi shivered.

"No, sir. We can give her a shot. She'll be awake in less than a minute."

"Good." Then he did something that would seem completely normal for anyone else, but for Hardman was strange, very strange. He smiled for the second time.

As the needle was being removed from the young woman's neck her eyes opened. Hardman was delighted with the immediate results. Whatever the drug was, it certainly did work fast.

"Is the experiment over?" The woman asked. "Can I get my money and go home now?"

"Be still," Hardman ordered. "We're not through yet."

The woman looked into Hardman's dark, sinister eyes, and shivered. She was suddenly afraid. No. More than afraid. She was horrified. She had never seen this man before and wasn't aware of his reputation. If she had she would have been even more than horrified. She would have been scared shitless. The eyes were the only things that were real for any of them, and the eyes could not hide the truth. She was afraid and scared at the same time because what she saw in this man's eyes wasn't human; it was as black as the clothing he wore.

In that instant she realized she had been lied to. It had all been a trick. There wasn't going to be any money. She wasn't going to be rich. She had been a fool. They were going to kill her. She had to make them stop before it was too late. She had to get away.

"I've changed my mind. I don't want to do this!" she said, fighting hard to control her voice. "You can keep your money. I just want to go home."

"I am afraid you can't do that," Hardman said.

"Find someone else. I said I changed my mind. Let me go." She fought against the restraints. They wouldn't budge. She tried to turn her head. Something was holding it in place. "Please let me go," she begged.

Hardman found it interesting to see a stream of tears erupt from her eyes and flow down her artificial cheeks. He had never seen a synthetic person cry before.

"I asked you to be still." Hardman looked at Levi. "Can you give her something?"

"I thought you wanted her awake."

"I do. I mean something to prevent her from moving."

Richard motioned to one of the nearby technicians and a small vial was quickly placed in his hand.

"This will block the brains impulses that control the body machinery."

"I want her to be completely coherent."

"It won't have any effect on her mind. They use this stuff to control patients in psychiatric hospitals. It's fantastic."

"No!" The woman screamed. "Let me go! Please!"

Hardman bent close until his face was only inches from hers. He put a finger gently against her lips and said, "Hush, young lady. You made a deal with us. Remember?"

"I don't want to do this. I just want to go." She began to cry.

Her body had suddenly gone limp. She couldn't make her arms or hands or legs move. She couldn't feel anything. It was like someone had removed everything that was below her neck.

"What's happening? What have you done to me?"

"It's working," said Levi.

"Hush now." Hardman put two fingers to the woman's lips. "This isn't going to hurt. In a few minutes it will all be over."

"I don't believe you."

Hardman ignored her. "Get on with it."

"You heard the man." He turned to the others. "Begin the sequence."

Hardman didn't take his eyes off the woman's eyes. The drug had now paralyzed her voice box along with that area of her brain that controlled the operation of all the mechanical parts of her body. Her brain was now held captive. But her eyes still revealed the terror she was feeling.

"We're filming her reactions in case we miss anything," someone said.

"Has it started?" Hardman asked.

"When that ring around her head begins to glow brightly it will indicate the transfer has begun."

Hardman studied her eyes and face intently as the ring began to glow. It lasted less than thirty seconds. At its peak of brightness Hardman thought he saw a glint of light leap from the paralyzed woman's eyes and dance briefly above her body before disappearing. It could have been a reflection or just his imagination.

"Did any of you see that?" He looked away from the woman for the first time. He studied all the nearby faces. It was obvious they had seen nothing. He looked back at the woman, at her eyes. There was no life left in them.

The glowing ring lessened in brightness, then died altogether.

"We have a flat line," someone on the distant side of the room said.

"She's gone," said Levi.

"Dead?"

"No. Gone."

"Just where did you send her?"

"Take a look." Richard smiled. "We can't control where. Just when. She went to November 23, 1969. But we can see exactly where she ended up. We'll be able to monitor her movements for about a minute. Let me show you." He went to one of the monitors. Hardman followed.

The monitor was displaying a blue sky, a sandy strip of sand and a small mountain jutting out into the blue ocean. There were dozens of nearly naked sunbathers playing, walking, and laying on the beach. The view changed suddenly, and they were looking at high-rise buildings jammed against each other, each competing for a piece of the white, sandy beach. The transmission began to fade and a moment later it was gone altogether replaced by five lines of text.

Transfer Completed.
Arrival: November 23, 1969
Time: 0400 Hours
Location: Hawaii
Specifically: Honolulu

"In a manner of speaking she's been born again. I think she will enjoy this new life we've given her much more than the money she was promised. Once the initial shock wears off she'll probably be very thankful if not downright grateful."

116

"Is there a danger of her changing anything?"

"It's always possible. She has taken over another person's life. She will now control that person's actions because she has now become that person. Anything she does will be different from what that person was going to do just as the three that transferred out of here five days ago are affecting our past. The past will be changed from this moment on. There's no preventing that from happening. But it's very doubtful this poor creature is going to make any dramatic or even insignificant changes in the past. If she does we'll never know it."

"Why is that?"

"Because her future will become our past. From the instant Philip Rollins, Lauren Jefferson, and Daren Kosman appeared in 1995 our history began to be rewritten. Their future is our past and as long as they stay alive our past will continue to change. That's why someone has to go back. We have to stop them before they really screw up everything."

"We can't take any more chances. Bring her back."

"We can't."

"What do you mean?"

"I thought you knew. As far as we can tell, the transfer is one way. Once that residual trail dispersed any connections we had to her disappeared also."

"No, I didn't. No more experiments until one of us is ready to go. You understand?"

"Yes, sir."

"Now, we have possibly four subjects to take out."

"Even if we kill all four of them their futures will still have been altered. We have no idea who or where they are. The people they replaced may have been nobodies. On the other hand any one or all of them may have played a key role in our past. We have no way of knowing now, because whatever any of them may have done wasn't."

"We're still here, and we haven't changed. That's all that matters."

"How do we know? How can we be sure?"

"Bullshit. I don't even want to think about it."

Hardman took out his laser pistol and fired a point blank charge between the woman's open eyes.

"She's already gone," said Levi.

"Then this is useless luggage."

He holstered the pistol and crossed the large room. Before exiting he stopped and turned. His eyes swept the circumference of the chamber and eventually stopped on Levi.

"I'm going to Atlanta. I'll be back in three days. Have everything ready."

"Who do you plan to send?"

"The only person I completely trust. Myself." He turned and left.

* * *

The recording was set to automatically repeat itself until he turned the machine off. He had watched the one-minute clip more than fifty times now. He had studied the scene frame by frame. Hawaii. Honolulu. Waikiki beach. It was a time when people were real. He studied the people on the beach, their bronze bodies maybe not as perfect, but much more beautiful than anything they had ever created.

It was late, and Levi was alone in his apartment. He couldn't remember a time when he wasn't alone. He had accepted this way of life more years ago than he cared to remember. He was one of the rare and fortunate few. He hadn't been born completely deformed. He had a face, a real face; a perfect face. Unfortunately, the remainder of his body was deformed beyond recognition. The scientists experimented with him, took samples, studied him. He lived in that body for almost ten years before the operations began.

He recalled how he had hated it at the time. Now, he remembered how wonderful it had felt. Regardless how awful that body had been, it had all been real. He studied his synthetic hands, turned them over so the palms faced up. He remembered the long hours, even days, after the operations, when he sat alone and studied the wonderful body and appendages they had given him. This body was perfect. God couldn't have created a more perfect specimen.

What exactly were they trying to accomplish? Sure, they were alive. The human race, the minds that *were* the people, continued to exist. But weren't they all trapped? Their brains were imprisoned in plastic shells. They couldn't reproduce. They could only replace the parts when they wore out or were broken. Their destiny had been written. The human race could not continue like this. They were all robots, just like the ones portrayed in ancient science fiction movies. They thought themselves better, more perfect, than God's own creation, but something was missing. He thought he knew what it was. Compassion. Was there anyone left that still had any? He wondered.

The real heroes just may have been these twelve who called themselves the Disciples. Wasn't it possible they could be the saviors of the human race? Let them correct the great wrong. Would it be so awful?

Levi looked at his hands again and wondered what it would be like to actually see birds in the sky, hear a dog bark, see a horse galloping along the beach. These weren't memories. They were only fantasies, visions from ancient movies of another time. None of that existed anymore, but wouldn't it be wonderful if it could exist again?

He looked up at the screen. The clip was repeating itself again. There was no sound, but he could almost hear the laughter.

# Chapter Twelve

"Every year I come to Clearwater for one of these sales meetings," said Dan. "Do you know what I enjoy most about these trips?"

Lauren shook her head but didn't say anything. She wasn't sure what she might say. She inhaled the wonderful salty air, languishing in the wonderful feel of the ocean spray against her skin. The Gulf was calm and the waves rolled into shore with a gentle, rhythmic sound that was both soothing and comforting.

"The walks on the beach at night." Dan looked at her and smiled. "Look out there." He pointed toward a small cluster of bobbing yellow lights. "That's probably someone's yacht. It's going to disappear over the horizon in a few minutes. Sometimes I wish it were me out there. No cares. No sales quotas. No meetings. Just a world of water and unspoiled islands waiting for me."

"That does sound inviting."

Dan slipped his hand in hers, squeezed it gently, and then let go. She walked ahead, and he stood there for a moment and watched her from the back. The moon was full and its silvery light danced on the water and gave the wide beach a strange luminance. He loved this woman more with every passing minute. He was telling everyone that this was the woman he was going to marry-everyone but Susan, that is. He wasn't sure if anyone had taken him seriously.

"Susan!" he called and tried to run in the loose sand. "Wait up!"

She stopped, turned, and smiled. Her long, brown hair was blowing in the night breeze.

He caught up to her and took her hands. "Where have you been all my life, anyway, Susan Hensley?"

Lauren looked at Dan's hands. They were big, strong, yet gentle and soft. He was making it so difficult to remember the importance of the mission. Dan smiled, staring intensely into her eyes. A delightful, hot rush swept through her body, causing her to tremble like she had earlier. She had never felt anything quite like it before. She started to remove her hands from his, but hesitated. Lauren realized what was happening, but she also knew there was no time for involvement.

Dan leaned close, his lips missing their target and brushing her cheek as she suddenly turned aside.

"What's wrong?"

"Nothing," she said. "Nothing you've done. I've had a really wonderful time tonight, Dan."

"You're making it sound like the night's over."

"I really should go back and check on Hill."

"I'm sure Hill can take care of herself." Dan walked up behind her and put his arms around her. She laid her head back against his chest and closed her eyes. "She looked like she was having a great time when we left. She probably doesn't even know we're gone."

"She was drunk."

"Yes, that she was." He laughed lightly. "I think she's having a really great time though. I picture Hill as a woman who really knows how to have a good time."

Dan turned her around and said, "You know what really feels fantastic?"

"I'm afraid to ask."

He suddenly flopped to the sand and started taking off his shoes.

"What are you doing?"

He grinned up at her. "Taking my shoes off. Care to join me?"

"Why?"

He stood, laughed. "She says why, and I say why not. You should never wear shoes on the beach. It's just not right. You've got to feel the sand between your toes."

"I really should check on Hill," Lauren stalled.

"You're making excuses. Ditch the shoes and walk with me. I dare you." He dropped the shoes and took her hands and looked intensely into her eyes.

"How about it? Walk with me," Dan asked again. "Trust me. There's nothing like walking barefoot on the beach at night."

"I don't know. I really should go."

"Why don't I decide for you?" He pointed his finger toward the beach and then back toward Hill. "Beach. Hill. Beach. Hill. Beach. Beach wins three to two. Now, take off those shoes and let your feet feel the sand."

Lauren laughed in spite of herself. She really did like this man. They were just going to walk for a while, nothing else. There wasn't anything wrong with that.

"Okay," she relented. She bent over, unbuckled her sandals, and stepped out of them. Dan picked them up and stuffed one inside each of his much larger deck shoes.

Dan was right. The sand was warm and wet and felt wonderful.

She caught him staring at her.

"I'm sorry. I'm staring and that's very rude, but you are just so beautiful,

I can't help it," he laughed. "That sounds like a pick-up line, doesn't it? Pretty corny, huh?"

Lauren didn't say anything.

"Honestly, I don't say stuff like that often. You are, you know. Beautiful, I mean."

She couldn't think of anything to say.

He laughed again, seeming to understand. "You don't have to say anything." He took her hand again and added. "Come on. Let's go for that walk. You may find it so much fun you'll just never want to stop."

# Chapter Thirteen

Patricia recognized Albert Fenwick immediately, though she had only met him once at that Massachusetts Avenue party. He came through the emergency room doors with two other men. He was the shortest of the three, stocky, and really did resemble a penguin. He was an older man, in his early sixties, with thinning gray hair and a neatly trimmed mustache. He was wearing a black suit, white shirt, and dark tie.

The trio stopped and quickly surveyed the nearly empty waiting room.

There was a woman with two small girls watching the television. They had arrived only a few minutes ago with a man who was rushed inside with a bleeding head wound. Patricia, Diane, and Phil were sitting together on the opposite side of the room, near the nurses' station. Bill and Jason were still with the doctors. Other than the nine of them and one nurse, the room was empty.

Fenwick, without any hesitation, came across the room and took Patricia's hands in his. She studied his fat, soft hands and couldn't resist wondering if they had ever done any physical work. She stood and gently pulled her hands free.

"I came as soon as I heard. Are you all right, my dear? You weren't hurt were you?"

"I'm okay."

"How are Jason and Bill? I'm told they were injured in the explosion."

"You were told?"

"Of course."

"Bill may have a concussion. Jason is still with the doctors."

"Douglas?" Fenwick said to the taller of the two men. The tall and thin quiet man was like a shadow in the background.

"Yes, sir." Douglas answered and went to the Nurses' station.

Phil studied the two men and thought how much they looked like military types. Maybe they were soldiers out of uniform, he wondered. In another time they could have been UCCIA agents. He knew the type well. They both had close-cropped hair, square tanned faces, muscular bodies, and were wearing nondescript dark suits. More perfect specimens could not have been fabricated. He reminded himself this was not his future. The human race was not yet capable of manufacturing artificial bodies. Hopefully they would never have to.

"Chambers? Call the police in Berkeley Springs. Ask them if they have any clues about who or what caused that explosion."

"Yes, sir."

"Change that. Tell them I'll be there in an hour, and I'll be expecting a full and comprehensive report."

Patricia said, "Jason told me there wasn't anything in that building that could cause such an explosion."

Albert smiled. He took her hands again and said, "Of course there wasn't. That's why I'm going to get to the bottom of this."

Patricia's shorts and pullover shirt were dirty and torn. Her face was smudged with oily grease marks and dirt, but right now she didn't care about how she looked.

"Why don't we sit? You can fill me in."

"I thought you already knew?"

"Only that there was an explosion and that my boys were hurt." He smiled.

They sat in the brown plastic chairs. Fenwick pulled one around in front of her. He seemed to notice Phil and Diane for the first time.

"I'm being extremely impolite, as usual," he told Patricia, and held out his hand first to Diane then Phil. "I'm Albert Fenwick with the Environmental Protection Agency." He had a much firmer handshake than one might expect from someone his size and age.

Phil shook his hand and said, "Josh Hamilton."

"Jason says Albert *is* the Environmental Protection Agency." Patricia forced a laugh.

"Compliments like that is how he gets everything he wants." Fenwick chuckled. His expression suddenly took on a very serious posture. "Without Jason there wouldn't be an agency. Jason is the real center of attention right now."

Douglas returned.

"What did you find out, Jim?"

"Mr. Harding has a serious leg wound, sir. They are taking x-rays of it now. Mr. Dodds has a slight concussion and seems to have a loss of memory. The nurse said she would let us know when she found out anything more."

"I'm Diane Kimball." Diane introduced herself. "Josh and I saw the explosion from Josh's cabin."

"Jim? Call Sayers. He should be informed of this."

"Sir? Do you realize what time it is?"

"Yes. The President will have to know also. We'll let Sayers do that for

126

us." He smiled. "He's good at that sort of thing."

"Who is Sayers?" Patricia asked.

"Head of the FBI. I've already been in touch with him concerning those men Jason called me about. The FBI has two of their best agents working on it."

"Do you think those men may have caused the explosion?" she asked.

"That's a possibility. It certainly warrants a few questions, I should think."

"Josh and Diane got there right after the explosion," said Patricia. "I owe them a world of thanks."

"The Agency thanks you also. I thank you," Fenwick said and then asked, "Just how did you manage to get there so quickly?"

"Josh's cabin is up on the mountain." Diane answered. "It's less than a mile away."

"Diane called the fire department in Berkeley Springs." Patricia added. "That's the only reason they arrived so fast."

Chambers returned from the pay phone in the corridor.

"Well?" Fenwick asked.

"Fire has been contained. The building was completely destroyed. Mr. Dodds' car was gutted, and some of the construction equipment was heavily damaged. A detective, his name was Jarveson, said the good news was the fire department arrived in time to prevent a major forest fire. A Diane Kimball called and reported the explosion. Thanks to her the fire was quickly contained. He said they will start investigating when it gets light. There wasn't anything more that he could tell me. He did say he thought it would be a waste of your time to come up tonight. He would know more tomorrow and would call us. Should I check this Kimball woman out?"

"Don't bother," Fenwick said.

"I'm Diane Kimball," Diane said.

"I'm curious, Ms. Kimball. Why did you go there after you made the phone call? Why not just let the fire department take care of things?"

"I thought if anyone was hurt we could get there faster," Diane answered. "The closest house is a farm on highway 522. It belongs to Ellen and Sam Parsons. I knew they were away visiting Ellen's sister in Jackson, Mississippi."

"I see. Very good."

"Is there some reason you're questioning us?" Phil asked.

"No. Of course not. I just ask a lot of questions. So you live up on the mountain? That right?"

"Diane just told you that."

"The FBI will probably want to ask you a few questions. Do you mind?"

"Why should we?" answered Diane. "We don't know anything more than what we've already told you."

"It's just routine," he assured her with a warm, friendly smile.

The hallway doors opened and a young doctor appeared. He went to the nurse, and she pointed to the group. He came over, and they all stood.

"I'm Doctor Blake Jenson," he introduced himself.

"How is Jason?" Patricia asked. "May I see him now?"

"Jason is going to be fine," he assured her. "He was lucky. No bones were broken and no permanent damage. Somebody did a good job bandaging the wound. We redressed it, gave him a tetanus shot and some antibiotics. He needs to stay off his feet for at least two weeks though."

"Then I'll be good as new. Right, Doc?" Jason appeared in a wheel chair, pushed by a hospital volunteer. He saw Fenwick and his two assistants. "Albert. What are you doing here?"

Patricia went to him and knelt next to his wheelchair.

"The fire department notified the Agency when they discovered the site belonged to EPA. I was called immediately, and I tracked you down from there."

"Good work, Albert," laughed Jason. "You'd make a good detective. Remind me never to try hiding from you."

"Why would you ever want to?" he smiled.

"Mr. Harding is going to be okay," said Doctor Jenson. He turned to Jason and said, "Just stay off that leg like I told you. Crutches okay after a week. No weight on it for at least five days."

"How is Bill?" asked Phil.

"Bill's okay." Jason answered for the doctor. "I was just talking to him. He's acting a little strange and has a real goose egg on his head. I guess we were all pretty lucky."

"We'd like to keep Mr. Dodds for a few days." Doctor Jenson said. "For observation. It's possible he may have a concussion."

"I don't think so," said Phil.

Everyone looked at him.

"How's that?" asked Fenwick.

Phil immediately realized what he had said. "I'm sorry. I was just thinking how much I hate hospitals. Of course he should stay."

"Well, I for one think Bill would be happier at his own place," said Patricia.

"He can stay with us." Jason added. "We have a spare bedroom and we're just minutes away from George Washington Hospital Center."

"We'd be happy to drive you home," offered Phil.

"What Josh means," Diane quickly added, "we were going to Washington this evening anyway. Josh has a condo on New Hampshire Avenue." She looked at Phil, her eyes telling him not to say anything else. "The Jeep has more leg room than a car, which means Mr. Harding would probably be more comfortable."

"That's asking too much," said Patricia. "You have already done enough."

"It's out of the question," said Fenwick. "We have two cars outside. I'll send Chambers and Douglas to Berkeley Springs to assist with the investigation, but they say there's no reason for me to go. You may as well let me drive you home."

"Don't be offended, Albert. I really would prefer the Jeep. I've ridden with you in that Chevy of yours."

"You have something against my car? Or is it my driving?" He chuckled.

"Both," laughed Jason.

"I've written a prescription for pain killers. I suggest you get it filled right away," Doctor Jenson said. "Come morning, you're going to start feeling some pain."

"Oh, yes." Fenwick said. "If you see two men at your place, they're on our side. Their names are Johnson and Bricker. FBI agents."

"It's too bad they weren't around today," said Patricia.

"I know." Fenwick agreed. "Don't worry though. From now on they will be just like your shadows."

\* \* \*

"I need to get home. Marge is going to have my hide." Lockner set the empty glass on the bar. He wiped his mouth with the back of his hand and started to get up.

Bowerman put his hand on Lockner's arm. "Sit down."

It was just past one in the morning. Bowerman and Lockner had been sitting at the bar in this small pub in Georgetown for nearly an hour. The place was never crowded, and Bowerman often wondered how the place stayed in business. There was no entertainment other than a single television suspended from the ceiling at one end of the long bar. Sometimes the place was frequented by "ladies of the night." Not often, though. Bowerman suspected the business wasn't very good for them, either. At this hour the place was even less crowded than usual. There was one waitress, a good-looking woman alone at the other end of the bar, an older couple at a table in a dark corner, the bartender, and the two of them.

"I really need to go. You know how Marge gets. We can talk about this tomorrow."

"Fuck Marge."

The woman at the end of the bar looked up.

"What did you say?"

"You heard me." He lowered his voice. "In case you haven't noticed, we've got a big problem here. The disk was destroyed, and they know we're following them. I'm sure the EPA has called in the FBI by now. We've got to end this thing and do it quickly. I don't want our investors thinking we're getting cold feet."

"What are they going to do? Fire us?"

"Worse. They can pull out. They can always find somebody else to do the job."

"You'll figure something out, Chad. What I need is a good night's sleep."

"We don't have time to sleep. We have to get to Harding. It's time for a little persuasion."

"What are you saying?"

"What the fuck do you think I'm saying?" he whispered. "I'm not planning to invite them for dinner. We convince Harding it's in his best interest to cooperate and give us the formula. I want that formula, Evan. I want to collect the money and get out of the country."

"I'm worried, Chad. I don't think we can get away with it now. After that explosion, there's going to be cops and FBI agents and who knows who else."

"We'll find a way. Everything is in place. Once we have that disk we'll disappear in less than an hour. They'll never find us. I guarantee it."

"What about Marge?"

"I already told you. You can get word to Marge after we've relocated."

"Just how do you plan to get the formula?"

"We ask him for it, ask very politely. On second thought, maybe we ask his girlfriend for it," he said, still keeping his voice just above a whisper.

"That's crazy. She wouldn't have the formula."

Bowerman patted his chest, and Lockner understood. The suit jacket completely concealed the holstered .45 beneath. "It may take a little persuasion, but I think both of them can be convinced."

# Chapter Fourteen

**Sunday, May 7, 3:00 a.m.**

"There's a Denny's in Frederick." Jason said from the back seat. "I don't know about you guys, but I sure could do with something to eat."

"I think we should get you two home and in bed," Patricia said. "The doctor said you should stay off that leg. Besides, look at me. I'm a mess."

"You're beautiful."

"And you're blind."

"There's nothing to eat at the house anyway. I cooked up everything for you Thursday morning."

"Look at us, Jason. We look like refugees."

Jason was wearing loose green scrubs the hospital had given him after they mutilated his jeans. Bill's shirt was torn and bloodstained.

"We can always order in," she added.

"Three o'clock Saturday morning? I doubt it. Besides, it's Denny's and it's in Frederick. No one will even notice us."

"We don't mind stopping. Really." Phil looked back at them and smiled.

Diane was driving. She just shook her head. She hadn't said more than a dozen words since they left the hospital.

"Are you sure you don't mind?" Patricia asked.

"How long have you been here, Phil?"

Daren's question came out of the blue and everyone looked at him. Diane even looked at him in the rearview mirror.

Phil glanced at Diane. He looked back at Daren but didn't answer.

Daren quickly realized what he had said and attempted to correct it. "Where did that come from? It's Josh, isn't it? I meant to say Josh, of course."

Patricia sat between the two men in the back seat of the Jeep Cherokee. She put her hand on Bill's forehead. It was cool. He didn't have a fever, but he was acting strange.

"Who's Phil?" Jason asked.

"I don't know. The name just popped into my head."

"Forget it. That was quite a hit you took. We've both been through the mill today. Guess you might say anything."

"You're right. Things are still pretty confusing," agreed Daren.

He had to talk to Phil. He had to know what had been happening since he arrived. He felt he might have caused that explosion, but he was only

131

remembering bits and pieces. He still had no idea what he had been doing since his arrival. He wasn't sure how he had hooked up with Jason and apparently became his assistant.

Diane turned off I-70 on a long and straight downhill exit that merged with US 40. A couple of miles east on the four lane road, just past the Frederick Towne Mall, she made a left turn and pulled into the Denny's parking lot on the right. Jason had telescoping aluminum crutches from the hospital. He opened the back door of the Jeep, extended the crutches and locked them in position. Phil helped Daren from the Jeep and Patricia joined Jason.

Jason had been wrong about people not noticing. Denny's was surprisingly crowded for three in the morning, and several heads turned their way and blatantly stared at the man in the surgical scrubs being helped into a booth near the front of the restaurant. They slid into the booth and a waitress appeared with glasses of water and silverware wrapped in paper napkins.

"The rest rooms are up front," she volunteered.

"Thank you." Patricia replied. To Jason she said, "No one will notice, uh?"

"Well, you *are* a little dirty," he laughed.

"Our special today is Denny's Grand Slam," announced the waitress and added, "Can I get you coffee or anything while you're deciding?"

"Coffee for me," Jason said.

"I'll have coffee also," Phil said.

Bill didn't want anything. Diane and Patricia both ordered Diet Cokes.

Phil studied the aging waitress. She had gray hair that was tied up in a bun. Her eyes had once been blue but were now nearly colorless. Her skin was splotchy and there were brown spots on her wrinkled hands and arms. She was short and stocky, without a waist. The uniform dress didn't do much for her either. She was the oldest person Phil had ever seen.

"Be right back."

They scanned the menus.

"I don't know about you guys," Jason said after a minute. "But I'm having the Grand Slam. I'm starving."

"You're always starving," observed Patricia.

"True." He shrugged and kissed her. "It's been a long day."

Daren hadn't said anything for sometime. He was sitting between Patricia and Diane. Phil was sitting across from him next to Jason. He was looking at each of them, remembering more pieces to the puzzle.

He recalled his arrival. He remembered seeing Washington across the

132

Potomac, Washington as it had been before it burned. Somehow he had hooked up with the very man he had come here to find. He evidently had been working with Jason Harding on the formula ever since. He must have tried to destroy it, but he had obviously failed. That had to be the only explanation. He had to ask. He had to say something. Phil knew who he was. Phil knew this man was *the* Jason Harding.

"I've got to say something." Daren said. "I can't go on pretending, not any more. I'm not Bill."

"What?" Jason looked at him from across the table.

"You heard me." For better or worse, he had said it. "I'm not Bill whatever-his-name-is. My real name is Daren Kosman."

Jason laughed, "You certainly did take a lick, didn't you?"

"Listen to him, Jason," said Phil. "He's telling you the truth."

Jason looked at him. "The truth? What truth is that?"

"I said I'm Daren Kosman," Daren repeated. "I remember now."

"Daren Kosman?" Patricia asked. "Since when?"

"You mean, you're one of them too?" Diane looked at him. She was sitting on the outside. She started to get up.

Phil took her hand and said, "Stay, Diane. It's time we got this all out in the open."

"I thought I could deal with this, but I can't. I just can't." She shook her head. "You guys can do whatever you want, but I've had enough." She stood and headed for the door.

"Wait, Diane!" Phil followed her.

Apparently they had become the center of attention. Everyone seemed to be looking at them.

"What was that all about?" Jason asked.

"I think she already knows about us."

"Knows? Knows what?"

"That Phil and I aren't who you think we are."

"Exactly who are you, then?"

"I told you. I'm Daren Kosman. I guess you could say I'm the instigator of this whole thing."

* * *

Outside, Phil caught up to Diane.

"You can't go, Diane. Not now. Don't you see? It's all coming together. I need your help. We all need you."

She kept walking toward the Cherokee. "No, you don't."

133

"It's almost over. Don't you want to be around when you get your Josh back?"

She didn't answer.

"Please stop." Phil grabbed her hand. She jerked it away.

"Don't touch me. Don't you ever touch me."

"I'm sorry." He held up his hands. "Please don't go. I need you. Josh needs you. You have to see this through."

"I don't have to do anything. You're going to kill that man, aren't you?"

He shook his head. "I don't think it will come to that."

"What if it does?"

"All of us were prepared to do whatever it takes. That includes Daren and myself."

"I won't be your accomplice. I won't be a party to murder."

"I wouldn't ask you to."

"Isn't that exactly what you're asking?"

"Please, Diane. You know how important this is. Stay and help us convince Jason. You can save his life. You know that, don't you?"

She unlocked and opened the driver's door, but stopped. She stood there looking at the empty interior, hesitating. Of course he was right. She had to stay. She loved Josh. She did love him, didn't she? Of course she did. He meant everything to her. If there was the slightest chance of getting him back she had to help. If this man killed Jason he wouldn't be the one who would be punished. He would be gone. No, Josh, her Josh, would be charged with the murder.

"Okay," she said without looking at him.

"You won't go?" He touched her arm. She jerked away again.

"I said don't touch me! The only person I want touching me is Josh Hamilton."

Phil held up his hands. "It's a deal. Will you come back inside? I promise I won't touch you."

She closed the door, but stood there with her back to him.

"What's wrong now?"

She didn't know. Diane turned around and looked at this man in Josh's body. Was it something he said? No. That wasn't it. It was Josh. It was all about Josh. She was suddenly feeling confused. Everything she thought she was sure of was starting to crumble.

She moved past him. Phil followed close behind. They sat without saying anything to each other or the others.

The waitress had brought the coffee and Cokes.

"What do you know about this?" Jason turned to Phil.

"Everything," said Phil. "I guess Daren told you I'm not really Josh Hamilton."

"That's right."

Patricia suddenly looked at Diane.

"I don't know what he told you," she said, "But I'm not part of this little conspiracy. I'm Diane Kimball, freelance photographer. I've been dragged into this thing just like the two of you."

"Do either of you have anything to do with those men who have been following us?" Patricia asked.

"To hell with them," Jason said. "What about the explosion?"

Phil looked around. Everyone was staring at them. This wasn't the place. They were attracting too much attention.

"We should go."

"No. I think we should stay right here until this is settled."

"I don't know anything about any men," Phil answered him. "There's just Daren and me and Lauren."

"Lauren? Who's Lauren?" Patricia asked.

"Daren didn't tell you?"

"She's probably the waitress, honey. This is the Twilight Zone and these guys are invaders from Mars."

"I caused the explosion, Jason." Daren admitted. "I remember now. I thought I was going to destroy the formula. I see now what I did was pretty stupid. Only you can destroy the formula."

Phil glanced at the waitress bent over the aisle table across the room and shook his head. No. She was too old to be Lauren.

The waitress finished wiping off the table and came back to check on them. "You ready to order yet?"

"No!" they all answered at once.

"Well, excuse me!" She stepped back. "Take your time. I got all morning." She turned to the next booth.

"Wait." Jason called.

"You change your mind?"

"Your name wouldn't happen to be Lauren by any chance?"

"Lauren?" she cackled. "Not likely, son. It's Evelyn."

"Are you sure?" Jason persisted.

"Sure as there's a God in Heaven, sonny. Evelyn Kellerman of Middletown. All my life I reckon. Something wrong with you folks?"

"No. Why?"

She laughed. "I've been listening to you, that's all. That fella has been saying some pretty strange things." She nodded toward Daren. He looked around. He seemed to be the only black man in the restaurant this morning.

"He does that sometimes." Phil attempted to laugh it off. "He was in an accident yesterday. Hit his head pretty hard."

"That's right." Daren agreed. "Don't mind me."

"We should be going, Phil. Why don't you bring us the check." Diane said to Evelyn without waiting for an answer.

"You ain't ordered yet."

"Diane's right. We should go. We can talk about this in the Jeep." Phil stood and took out his wallet. He handed Evelyn a ten-dollar bill. "For the coffee and drinks. Keep the change." He smiled.

"Thanks, son." She took the money and stuffed it in her apron pocket.

Evelyn and just about everyone else in the restaurant stared at the five strangers as they left. Strange things they were saying, strange indeed.

No one said anything else until after they had passed the Urbana exit on I-270.

"So where is this Lauren?" Patricia asked.

"I don't know." Phil answered. "She is supposed to meet us at the Lincoln Memorial on Wednesday, May tenth at six in the evening."

Jason looked at Daren in this black man's body. He had thought he knew this man, but suddenly realized he had never known him at all.

"We came back to plead with you, Jason. We have no proof we're who we say we are. And I have to agree with all those people back there at Denny's. It does sound hard to swallow, but we're asking you to trust us."

"You really have to trust them," Diane said. "Josh-I mean Phil-this man is telling the truth. Somehow he took over Josh's body. I can't get my Josh back unless you help them. That's why I came back. You have to believe him. He'll kill you if you don't do what he wants."

"Kill me?" Jason looked at Phil. Phil didn't say anything. "Is that true? You'll kill me if I don't help you?"

"I have no choice," Phil answered.

Jason shook his head. "This just isn't happening. It can't be happening."

"I know," said Diane. "I tried telling myself that. Tell him the rest of it, Phil. Tell him what you told me back at the cabin. How he's your father. How you'll do anything to stop him."

Jason held up his hands, laughing in spite of everything. "Whoa here. Father?" He put his arm around Patricia. "Honest, honey. I don't have any children."

"I certainly hope not," she said.

"Listen to us. It's a long story. It all starts a month from now. We think it began on July fourth of this year. We hope that date is correct. We're gambling everything that it is."

Jason forced a laugh.

"What's funny now?" Phil asked.

"Nothing." He shook his head. "Go ahead. I'm listening."

# Chapter Fifteen

**Sunday, May 7, 5:30 a.m.**

They were on I-270 somewhere between Germantown, Maryland, and the Washington Beltway. The sky had gotten lighter and the sun was coming up, painting the sky a thousand colors, but no one in the Cherokee noticed or appreciated the splendor that was unfolding.

Jason looked over at Daren. "I need to know something, Bill--or whatever your name is. Did you kill Rob?"

"Who?"

"Rob. Robert Williams. The man you so conveniently replaced. Did you have anything to do with that accident?"

"No. I've never killed anyone. Ask Phil."

Jason laughed. "Sure. You're here in another man's body, and you're telling me you've never killed anybody."

"It's true," Phil turned from the front seat and looked at Daren first, then Jason. His eyes met Jason's briefly.

Patricia sat between the two men, but she wasn't saying anything. She squeezed Jason's leg and smiled at him. She suddenly didn't feel comfortable sitting this close to a man who had suddenly become a stranger.

Jason and Rob had been as close as brothers, and Bill had come into the picture two weeks after Rob's death. Jason seemed to resent him, but he wouldn't talk about it. Before this weekend, Jason never talked much about his work. Exactly what he did had always been a mystery. He said he preferred to leave his work at the office. He told her it wasn't fair to her for him to bring it home, but when something went really well or drastically wrong, it managed to find its way into their conversations when they were walking and running or just talking in bed at night.

Bill was quite likable, liked to kid around a lot. She recalled when she first met him. It had only been three weeks ago, but it seemed like a lifetime. He came over one evening with two bottles of wine. The three of them sat around, talking and laughing, and finished off both bottles. She realized now that it had all been an act. Usually she could tell when someone was lying. She had been fooled completely. It had all been a very good act. This man wasn't Bill at all, just a person pretending to be someone he wasn't. He may not have killed Rob, but what about Bill Dodds? Where was the real Bill Dodds? She tried to move a little closer to Jason. Suddenly, she wasn't at all comfortable being this close to Bill-or Daren.

"Daren built the device that brought us here. He's head of the movement, but he couldn't kill anyone. That's why Lauren and I had to come. There was supposed to have been just the two of us, but things changed at the last moment."

"So you're an assassin? A hitman? You really did come to kill me."

"I prefer to think of myself as a soldier," smiled Phil. "And killing you would have been our last resort."

"You came here to kill me?"

"No one wants to kill you, Jason," said Daren.

"You're going to kill me, though. If I don't cooperate. Right?"

Phil nodded.

"We never thought it would come to that," continued Daren. "But that's why Phil, and Lauren, and Sandy were supposed to be here with the rest of us."

"Sandy? Who the hell is Sandy?"

"My sister. Your daughter," answered Phil. "I killed her."

"My daughter?"

"You killed her?" asked Patricia.

"I had to. She didn't give me a choice."

"So if I refuse to destroy the formula-" Jason began, but he decided he wasn't ready for the answer to the question he was going to ask. Instead, he asked, "Tell me. Did either of you have anything to do with that freaky accident that killed Rob?"

"I don't know about any accident," said Phil. "And I don't know anyone named Rob."

"Something's wrong with the formula, Jason," said Daren. "You've created a mutated strain of bacteria, and that mutation does some wonderful things. It would be great if it stopped there. It really would be the answer to the world's pollution problems, but it doesn't stop there. It never stops mutating."

"That's not true. I would have noticed. I've worked with this bacterium for years. It doesn't change."

"I don't understand why you haven't noticed it," wondered Phil.

"Maybe it doesn't," said Daren. "I was studying this strain Jason has created. I was testing it in every way that I could come up with. It doesn't change. It's not like anything we know."

"What are you saying, Daren? That you were wrong? It wasn't the bacteria after all?"

Daren laughed. "Of course it was the bacteria. We're living proof. All I'm saying is that the bacteria appear to be stable. That's probably why no one detected the mutations. Sometime after the July fourth introduction into the water supply the bacterium may come into contact with something, another strain maybe, that starts the chain of mutations. I don't exactly know what or when it happens. I wish I did. Jason, you've created a wonderful thing here. It does everything you want it to, but something else is at work. You're not ready to introduce the bacteria into the water just yet. We need to study it."

"We don't have time, Daren," cautioned Phil. "You of all people know that."

"I know we don't. Jason-you can't do it. You have to destroy the formula."

Jason shook his head. "I can't do that. Everything is set for the big day."

"The test site was totally destroyed," said Patricia. "They can't possibly have the ceremonies on July Fourth."

Jason laughed, "You'd be surprised what Fenwick can get accomplished. No. It's going to happen as scheduled. It's out of my control."

"Does anyone else have the formula?" asked Phil.

"I'm not so sure I should answer that."

"Not that I know of," Daren answered for him. "Containers of the solution aren't even scheduled to be mixed until next month. Most of the formula is still in Jason's head-- as far as I know."

"Can you really be certain of that?" Jason asked Daren.

"I think so."

"Listen, Jason," Phil turned around in the seat and looked at him. "We came here to convince you to destroy that formula before it destroys all of humanity as you know it."

"You haven't showed me any proof. All I have is your word. Quite frankly, I don't know you that well. How do I even know you're who you say you are?"

"Jason's right," agreed Patricia. "You two could be a couple of crazies. How do we know you're telling the truth?"

Phil shrugged. "The truth is out there, but by the time you find it, it will be too late."

"What if I don't cooperate? Are you going to kill me?"

Daren looked at Phil. Phil didn't answer.

"That's your back-up plan, isn't it?"

"We seriously didn't think it would come to that. We still don't, but that's why I'm here."

"Too much is at stake," said Phil. "We've risked everything. Eight of our friends sacrificed their lives for this mission. The future is being destroyed because of what you are about to do. We can't let that happen."

"Don't you see? We can't let even a trickle of that formula into the water supply. You just don't know what you have created here."

"Say you're right," agreed Jason. "All I have is your word. I don't have any proof that what you have told me is true."

"There's no way to show you. You'll just have to believe us."

Daren said, "The first real incident won't be recorded for another six years, sometime after the year 2000. Babies will be born with severe deformities, deformities like you've never seen before. It won't be just a few, either. At first, it will be approximately ten percent of all births, but that number will quickly increase, dramatically increase. In fact, it will snowball. There won't be anyway to stop it once it begins. You must believe that."

It was after six, going on seven, when they reached Georgetown, and still nothing had been settled, but Jason had a lot to think about. There was very little traffic, but there never was on Sunday morning, especially this early. Jason kept reminding himself it was really Sunday. He had just had the longest night of his entire life.

He had too many questions and not enough answers. The story Bill and Josh (or was it really Daren and Phil?) told was just too unbelievable to be real, but too fantastic to be fiction. Things like this just didn't happen-- couldn't happen. People couldn't really travel through time. They didn't take over other people's bodies. That happened in science fiction movies, not in real life.

Patricia guided Diane through the back streets to the dead-end court where Jason's townhouse was located. The red Cherokee pulled up to the curb in front of the townhouse and stopped. As Fenwick had said, a tan sedan was parked out front. Two men got out and met them.

"Mr. Harding?" asked the taller of the two. He was a big man with an athletic build and bushy brown hair. He was wearing a gray suit, white shirt, and yellow tie.

"I'm Jason Harding," said Jason. "You must be the FBI."

"Special agent Johnson. This is my partner, Agent Bricker." He indicated his companion, who was shorter, with a smaller build, bald, and wearing glasses. He wore a tan suit, yellow shirt, and no tie. "We've been assigned to watch you."

"We were told to watch out for you."

"May we offer a hand? You look a little battered."

"I've seen better days. Yes, please. I would appreciate that."

"I'll unlock the door," said Patricia.

"Wait," Johnson stopped her. "If you don't mind, Ms. Everest, let me get the door."

"Sure," she shrugged and handed him the keys. "Do you think there may be a bomb here too?"

"You can't be too careful. We never know what we might find," said Bricker.

"It will just make us feel better," added Johnson. He inspected the door before unlocking it and slowly swinging it open. Then he drew his gun and went inside. A few minutes later he reappeared and gave them the all-clear wave.

Daren insisted he was okay and didn't need assistance. Phil and Bricker helped Jason inside and to the sofa in the living room. Patricia retrieved the crutches and she and Diane followed.

"I'll be right back," said Johnson, and disappeared. A few minutes later he returned and tossed a tiny electronic device to Jason. "Recognize this?"

"What is it?"

"A listening device."

"A bug?"

"That's right. Looks like your phones are tapped also. I found that under your bedside lamp. Pretty hi-tech stuff. You can't get those things just any place."

"Can I see that?" asked Bricker. He took the tiny device from Jason and examined it closely. "This is one of ours, Johnson."

"I thought it was."

"You mean the FBI planted these things?" asked Patricia.

"No, ma'am," said Bricker. "The FBI didn't have anything to do with it."

"But you said it was one of yours?"

"It is. You better call for a clean-up crew, Johnson. We should sweep the entire house." He turned to Jason. "Looks like someone is very interested in you, Mr. Harding. Hope you didn't give away any national secrets."

Jason laughed. "I don't know any national secrets."

"We should check the Accord out front also."

"That's my car," informed Patricia.

"We know," said Bricker. "I had your tag run before you arrived, just to make sure it belonged here. It would be a good idea to sweep Mr. Harding's office, also."

"My office? You think they bugged my office?"

"Just a precaution, sir."

"I feel like I've been violated," Patricia sat down next to Jason and held her hands in her lap. He put his arm around her and pulled her close to him. "It was bad enough knowing someone was following us, outside watching-- but listening to everything we said? Why?"

Johnson pulled out a dining room chair and set it between the sofa and the chair where Daren was sitting. Phil and Diane were still standing in the entrance foyer. Johnson looked at the two of them. He seemed to be studying them. Phil watched him closely.

After a lengthy pause, he said, "That's why we're here, Ms. Everest. To find out."

"Mr. Harding, looks like you have friends in pretty high places," stated Bricker. "I understand the President himself is being kept informed. What exactly is it that you do, if I may ask?"

"I'm a research scientist. Bacteriology. I'm surprised they didn't fill you in."

"Makes a little more sense, now. You work for the EPA, right?"

"What makes more sense?"

"Something to do with solving the pollution problem. I've heard about your research."

"Yes. What makes more sense?" Jason repeated.

Johnson looked at Diane and Phil.

"We were just in the neighborhood," said Phil.

"I'm Diane Kimball. This is Josh Hamilton."

Johnson studied their faces for a moment.

"They saw the explosion," said Patricia. "Diane called the fire department and then came to help."

"Like I said. We were in the neighborhood," repeated Phil.

"Real heroes, huh?" asked Johnson.

"Not really, detective."

"I'm not a detective, Ms. Kimball." He smiled at her. "Just a field agent."

"Well, Agent Johnson, we were just trying to help."

"Like I said. You were real heroes. I understand you prevented a potentially major forest fire."

"Then you already know who we are?" asked Phil.

"Sure. We checked you out this morning. Your father was Olin Hamilton. He made a fortune in land development and left it all to you when he was killed in a plane crash. You don't do much of anything, except live off the old man's money." He laughed. "Can't say I blame you, though. I guess if my old man left me thirty million bucks I wouldn't be doing this. As for you, Ms. Kimball, we know you are a freelance photographer for several magazines. You take some pretty good pictures, too. I understand you even had a show once. I bet you didn't know Mr. Sayers has one of your photographs hanging in his office."

She shook her head. "No, I didn't know that."

"I don't know if you even remember taking it. You caught the President and Mr. Sayers walking on Pennsylvania Avenue surrounded by Secret Service agents. Good stuff. Mr. Sayers got the photo from *Time* magazine. They even enlarged it up and had it framed."

"If you know all that, then why did you ask us who we were?" asked Diane.

Johnson winked and laughed. "I guess it's just the detective in me wanting to get out."

# Chapter Sixteen

Lauren sat on the edge of the sofa and stared at Dan, sleeping soundly in the king-sized bed. This should not have happened, she told herself again and again. She should never have let it go this far.

It was still dark outside when she had gotten up and moved to the small sofa opposite the bed. Now, the sky was beginning to get lighter as layers of the night slowly dissolved one by one. When they came back to the hotel after walking for miles on the beach, Dan had asked her to come up to his room. Like the fool she was, she said yes. That was the final mistake.

Dan's room was big, a suite on the seventh floor facing the Gulf. He closed the door and kissed her, and they had sex. Just like that. They kissed. They had sex. One minute she was leaning against the door, and the next they were naked and in bed.

She felt as if she had been drugged. None of it seemed real. It was like she had dreamed it, but how could she? She had had no idea what sex could be like. She could never imagine that two people coupling like that would be so fantastic. It had been the most extraordinary thing she had ever known. She had read about the act, of course. She knew it was necessary for reproduction. She had guessed what was expected from her, what she was supposed to do, but actually doing it was something else entirely. The feel of him inside of her was like nothing she had ever experienced. Susan's body seemed to have a mind of its own. Lauren told herself it was Susan, and not her, that lost control, but once they started, she couldn't get enough of him. Sure, blame it on Susan, she thought. The poor woman can't even defend herself. Why don't you admit it--you wanted him? You wanted to experience the pleasure of sex. Once you did, you couldn't stop.

She looked at Dan. He must have felt she was some kind of sex-starved maniac or something. The first time had been too quick. The second time, though, had seemed to last for hours. He kissed her all over, whispered what he was going to do before he did it. She didn't understand the multiple orgasms that thundered through her body. She forgot who she was, what time it was, even The Mission. It became only the here and now. Their two naked bodies becoming one, limbs entwined. Her mouth sought his mouth, his body, and his throbbing erection. She never wanted to leave this bed. She never wanted to stop what they were doing. Please God, don't let it end, she had pleaded. But she knew that if it didn't end, she would go insane. Her

147

brain couldn't take the emotions that were rushing through it. Her head would just explode.

It did eventually end, and they both had fallen asleep, exhausted.

Sometime later she woke up. She wasn't sure how long she had been asleep. She wasn't even sure what day it was. She slipped out of bed and went out on the balcony. The cool breeze off the gulf felt surprisingly good against her body. She stood there for a long time, trying to sort things out. Phil was out there someplace, waiting for her. He was her companion, fellow soldier. He needed her-and she needed him. She *did* need him, didn't she?

She went back into the dark room and looked at Dan's peaceful, sleeping face. It wasn't fair. It wasn't fair to Dan, it wasn't fair to Phil, but most of all it wasn't fair to her. This life she had been given wasn't fair. Nothing about any of this was fair. She had to tell Dan. He deserved to know, but wouldn't he think she was crazy? Sure. How could he not? But it was the right thing to do.

She wanted to have sex with him again. Just one more time, one last time. She slipped between the covers and snuggled against Dan, lightly stroking his hard body. Her fingers played through his pubic hair and raked his enlarging shaft. She smiled, grasping it firmly.

Dan groaned and turned toward her. They kissed for a long time before she climbed on top of him and guided his erection into her. They made love again, slowly, savoring every delicious second.

* * *

### Sunday, May 7, 10:15 a.m.

"What are you writing?" Patricia asked when she came into the bedroom.

Jason was sitting up in bed and writing in a notebook. He looked up and smiled, "Are we going someplace?"

She was dressed in a conservative powder blue suit, the skirt a nice two inches above her knees, a white blouse with a pale pastel flower print, and conservative blue heels. Her hair was pinned up from her ears and shoulders. She was carrying a tray with coffee and toast on it.

"Not you. You're going to stay right here in this bed. I've got to go to the store for a few minutes. I'll get your prescription filled while I'm out."

"You're supposed to be off until Monday."

"I know." She set the tray on the bed. "So. Are you going to tell me what you are writing?"

"Nosy, aren't you."

"Sometimes."

148

I was just making some notes, trying to make some sense out of all this," he said. He closed the notebook and put it on the table. "What's this?"

"Breakfast in bed. My turn to serve you," she laughed.

"I didn't think there was anything left in the house to eat."

"There isn't. Toast and coffee. That's the best I can do. Besides, I didn't have much time. I need to be going."

"You didn't have to do this."

"I know. So, what are you writing?"

"That FBI agent, the one with the glasses."

"Bricker."

"Yeah, him. He asked me to think back for the last several days and try to remember anything out of the ordinary. He suggested I make notes."

"Remember anything besides those men that have been following us?"

"You know, it's funny. I can't even remember their faces. When Bricker asked me to describe them to him, I drew a complete blank."

"I was the same way. They scared me so much, and yet, I can't remember what they looked like. I can picture exactly what they were wearing, but their faces are completely blank."

"It makes sense you'd notice their clothes," he laughed. "Can't Julie or one of your managers handle things at the store just for today?"

"I won't be gone long, I promise. You won't even have time to miss me."

"Do I get a good morning kiss?"

"Sure." She sat on the edge of the bed, leaned over and kissed him.

"Johnson and Bricker still outside?"

"Yes. I asked them in for coffee about seven this morning. You were still sleeping."

"Have they heard anything from the Berkeley Springs police yet?"

She shook her head. "Not much. They said Albert Fenwick's men are assisting the FBI and the Berkeley Springs police with the investigation. They began sifting through the debris this morning."

"They won't find anything," Jason said.

"Why do you say that?"

"We know who caused that explosion, and we know why. He's smart enough not to leave any clues."

"People make mistakes."

"I don't think these people do."

"Are you saying you believe them?"

"Don't you?"

"I find it a little hard to swallow. People traveling through time? Come on."

"I don't know. There's been a lot of research in that field. Many scientists believe it's possible, even probable. There's the theory of relativity and quantum mechanics. Relativity deals with space-time curvature. I believe Einstein himself may have believed in time travel, although he never came right out and admitted it. Could you get the phone for me, please."

"Who are you calling?"

"Josh Hamilton--I mean Philip Rollins. I think we need to talk to him and Bill. I mean Daren Kosman. This is taking some getting used to."

Patricia went around the bed and set the phone next to him. It rang suddenly, and they both jumped and laughed at the same time.

Jason picked up the receiver. He was still laughing when he said, "Hello."

"Good morning, Jason. How are you feeling?"

"Oh, just swell, Albert. How are you?" He covered the mouthpiece and said to Patricia, "It's Albert Fenwick."

"I'm not the one with the injured leg," laughed Fenwick.

"You seem cheerful this morning. What's going on?"

"Some good news. The Fourth of July ceremonies will go on as scheduled."

"How is that possible? The place was demolished."

"It wasn't that bad. Sure, the building was destroyed and there is going to be considerable cleaning-up involved. That just means we will just have to assign more personnel to the project. The open-air theatre hadn't been built yet. We weren't going to start that until this week anyway. Construction is scheduled to begin tomorrow. They tell me they can have the place cleaned up and ready to go in three weeks. At least that's what they tell me."

"Maybe we should postpone the ceremonies."

"Nonsense. Dignitaries from all over the United States and several countries have made plans to be there. It must go on as scheduled."

"What if something else happens, Albert?"

"Relax, son. Nothing will happen. You wouldn't believe how many people are involved in this now. I finally convinced Sayers just how important this project is, and he relayed it to the President. We have the FBI, the Secret Service, the local police, and our own people working on it now. Nothing goes into that site or comes near your lab that we don't know about. The NIH has even set up a staging area where the formula can be mixed and packaged for transport."

"I thought they only dealt in infectious diseases?"

"I think they just want to be in on it. Everyone is suddenly wanting to jump on your wagon, Jason." He laughed again. "Could have something to do with a certain someone letting it leak that the President has taken a personal interest in this."

"I wonder who that person was?" chuckled Jason.

"I have no idea, but it's about time the EPA received proper recognition. Don't you think?"

"You've been busy. I feel guilty. All I've been doing is sleeping."

"That's okay. You needed it after what you went through yesterday. Besides, someone needs to give Washington a kick in the ass sometimes." He laughed, "I've got to go. I'm supposed to attend a briefing with the President this afternoon. I wish you could be there, also."

"The President, huh?"

"Damn straight. Everyone thought we were just wasting the taxpayers' money. I think they're finally beginning to see just how important this is. I know you can't attend that meeting, but how about Bill Dodds?"

"No," said Jason, a little too abruptly.

"I was just thinking it might be good to have a representative present. Someone who knows how this thing works. I assure you I won't allow him to steal any of your thunder."

"I'm not worried about that, Albert. It's just that Bill's not up to it, either. His head, you know."

"Of course. That's right. I forgot about that."

"Call me after the meeting, okay? I want to hear all about it."

"Call you? I'll come by. I need to make sure Patricia is taking care of my boy."

"I assure you, she's doing an excellent job," Jason grinned. He winked at Patricia and squeezed her hand. "Good-bye, Albert." He hung up the phone and said to Patricia, "Looks like everything is still on schedule."

"I've got to go, honey. I'll see you in a couple of hours."

"Do you really have to?"

"Comes with the territory." She smiled and kissed him again.

He picked up the phone again and dialed the number Diane had given him before they left.

* * *

"Hello," a woman's voice answered after three rings.

"This is Jason. May I speak to Daren or Phil?"

"Just a minute. I'll get Phil. Daren is still asleep."

Jason straightened his leg. It hurt like hell. He could sure use some of those painkillers right now.

In less than four weeks, the formula was supposed to be released to the world. The press releases had already been written and approved by the EPA, the FDA, the NIH, the President, and everyone else involved.

He still was not completely convinced there was anything wrong with his formula. He had yet to see any hard evidence to support their story. The formula worked. The bacteria totally destroyed all pollutants. There were no visible side effects, nothing to confirm this fantastic story Phil and Daren told them.

His formula was the biggest breakthrough in the EPA's history, in the history of the world. How could he keep something like this from the world? It solved everything. No more pollution. It was a dream come true. But what if everything they said was true? He could be condemning the human race to something worse than anything he could imagine. Could he really take the chance they were lying, making all this up? Should he gamble everything on that assumption? He needed more time, and that was one thing he didn't have.

Diane found Phil standing on the balcony, leaning against the railing. He was drinking coffee and appeared to be watching the progress of the morning rush-hour traffic along New Hampshire Avenue ten stories below. Cars and vans and trucks were bumper to bumper in both directions, and amazingly no one had hit anyone yet. Pedestrians challenged traffic to get from one side of the street to the other.

The sun was already up when he had gotten out of bed this morning. He found a change of clothes and dressed in jeans and a tan cotton shirt. The place was furnished as if Josh and Diane spent a lot of time here. There was a complete wardrobe of clothing, shoes, and accessories.

Diane was still asleep in the other bedroom of Josh's penthouse apartment. The door was closed. He hadn't tried the door, but was fairly certain it would be locked. Daren was asleep on the sofa in the den.

He sipped the hot coffee. He really enjoyed the taste of coffee and after several attempts, finally managed to make an acceptable pot that tasted almost as good as the first cup Diane had given him Thursday morning. Thursday morning. That seemed like a lifetime ago.

Phil heard the balcony door open and turned.

Diane handed him the portable telephone. "It's Jason Harding."

He took the phone and smiled, started to say something, but she turned and left.

He watched her go. She was barefoot and wearing a plain white cotton nightshirt--looking as if she had just awakened. Phil admired how naturally beautiful she was and had been about to tell her. He heard her bedroom door close a few seconds later.

"We've got to talk. Just you and me and Daren. Can you come over?"

"I'll be there right away." He disconnected the portable and went inside. Diane met him in the kitchen. She had gotten dressed in a cream-colored cotton shirt and faded jeans.

"Well?" she asked.

"How's Daren?"

"Sleeping on the sofa. What did Jason want?"

"He wants to talk. That's a good sign."

"When are you meeting?"

"As soon as I wake Daren and can get there."

"I'll drive you."

"I appreciate it. I'm still lost around here."

"I'm not doing it for you. Nothing I do is for you. You must know that."

"I suppose. It would be nice to think you cared about what was happening though."

"Oh, I care. You better believe I care. Has he made a decision?"

"Maybe."

"Then it's almost over."

"You can't wait to see me leave, can you?"

"I can't wait to have my Josh, my real Josh, back."

# Chapter Seventeen

**Sunday, May 7, 11:57 a.m.**

Sunlight flooded the room through the open balcony doors. Dan buried his face in his pillow. The sunlight was so bright it was almost painful. Something had awakened him. What? It wasn't the sun. It was a sound. A click, like a door closing. He covered his head with the pillow. The balcony doors were still open and the cool gulf breeze whipped the drapes and filled the room with a salty dampness.

Dan tossed the pillow aside and sat up.

"Susan!" he called.

The bathroom door was open, but he couldn't see inside. He turned toward the balcony. There were two chairs on the narrow balcony, but no Susan. He could hear beach sounds far below.

"Susan!"

She didn't answer.

He got out of bed and went to the bathroom. It was empty.

Dan came back to the bed and sat down. She was gone. She left without even saying goodbye. He closed his eyes and remembered hearing her say, "I love you." She *did* say it, didn't she? He picked up the sheets and put them to his face. He could still smell her.

He had to get dressed and find her. Calm down, Dan, he told himself. She hasn't left, she's just not here. When he leaned across the bed to pick up the phone, he saw the note on the pillow. He picked it up and tried to focus on the handwriting. "Forgive me, Dan. I was being selfish. I never should have let any of this happen. I'm sorry." It was signed, simply, Susan.

He dialed the hotel operator; "Can you ring Susan Hensley's room, please?"

"I'm sorry, sir. She's checked out."

Dan looked at his watch. Twelve-fifteen. Sam Collard, the Mid-Atlantic regional sales manager, was supposed to fly in today. He picked up the phone and dialed the operator again. "Can you page Sam Collard, please? He's with the ARCO group."

"Yes, sir. Just a minute."

A moment later Sam answered, "Hello?"

"Sam, this is Dan. I wasn't sure if you would be here yet."

"I'm at the front desk now. Listen, I sat with Kilpatrick on the flight down. He's joining us for dinner tonight. He wants to personally congratulate you on the Norfolk sale. I wouldn't be surprised if you're named Salesman of the Year."

"I can't make it, Sam. That's why I'm calling."

"What's wrong?"

"There's been an emergency back home."

"What kind of an emergency?"

"I can't say right now. Trust me. I have to fly back to Washington immediately."

"You can tell me, Dan. What's going on?"

"I can't. Not right now. Later. I'll call and explain. Okay?"

"Listen, Dan. I'm in the lobby. I'll come up if you want to talk about this. You need to tell me what's going on."

"I can't, Sam. I have to do this. Offer my apologies?"

"Okay, but this better be good. Call me when this emergency is over."

"I will. I promise." He hung up the phone.

He sat there on the edge of the bed and thought about what he had just done. He didn't even know Susan, not really. Before Thursday, he hadn't known she even existed. Three days later he was willing to flush his entire career just to be with her. But he had to have her. He needed her more than anything on earth.

Was this what love was all about? He had never felt anything like it before. It had surprised even him when he first laid eyes on her in the plane. He picked up the phone and dialed USAir. By the time they located her flight, the plane had left the gate. She was on her way back to Washington.

* * *

### Sunday, May 7, 10:30 a.m.

Patricia left the front door unlocked intentionally. If the two agents needed to go inside for some reason, Jason wouldn't have to let them in. She didn't want him coming down those stairs on crutches if he didn't have to.

"I'm leaving the door unlocked," She called upstairs. Jason didn't answer. He must be on the phone, she thought.

She went to her white Honda Accord. The car was three years old and had almost a hundred thousand miles on it, but was still running perfectly. In fact, she had never had any trouble with it, not even a flat.

She unlocked the driver's side door and opened it. Before getting in, she looked around. No unfamiliar cars or people anywhere. The tan FBI car with Johnson and Bricker in it was still parked out front. She thought about going over and telling them where she was going and that the door was unlocked.

156

Maybe she should ask them if they wanted coffee or anything. She decided they were big boys. If they needed anything they could ask Jason. They probably already knew where she was going anyway.

She backed out and waved to them as she drove past. The two men didn't look up or even acknowledge her. She thought, how strange. They must be studying something really important. They almost looked like they were asleep, but she knew that was impossible. FBI agents would never fall asleep on the job.

\* \* \*

### Sunday, May 7, 1995, 2:07 p.m., Washington, DC

"What's going on, Susan?"

"What do you mean?"

"I'm not blind, girl. I can see when something's not right. What's wrong with you?"

"I don't know what you mean, Hill. I'm perfectly fine."

"Well, if you're so fine, then tell me where we're going."

Susan didn't answer right away. She turned toward the window and watched the scenery slide past as the taxi maneuvered its way through the heavy traffic on the busy thoroughfare. The skyline was crowded with tall glass and metal buildings. They were crossing an intersection, she read the street signs: Jefferson Davis Highway and Army-Navy Drive. The taxi crossed the intersection and went under an overpass. When it turned left and went up the ramp, she saw another sign, I-395 South. To the right she saw the ancient Pentagon building. Only it wasn't so ancient, was it? It was on the west bank of a wide, slow moving river. The Potomac? Across the river was Washington, DC. She could see the Lincoln Memorial, the Washington Monument, the dome of the Capitol Building with Liberty standing tall on top. She recognized all the landmarks from pictures and video clips she had seen. The city didn't exist in her time. The capital of the United Cities was Atlanta, the largest of the twelve cities.

"Susan?"

"What?"

"I asked you a question."

"I don't know, Hill. Maybe I do need to see a doctor."

"Or maybe you just screwed your brains out in Florida. Forget about him, baby. I don't trust salesmen anyway. They all got a pile of bullshit about ass deep."

"He was really wonderful, Hill. I've never met anyone like him before."

157

"Well, you don't know anything about this character."

"I'm sure I know more about him than he knows about me."

"That may be true, but these days, you can't be too careful. There's a lot of real bastards out there."

\* \* \*

Patricia was less than a mile from her exit on I-66 when the car engine began to skip. She patted the accelerator several times, but it didn't seem to do any good. The engine coughed, cut out, coughed, and then died altogether. She guided the car to the emergency lane and turned on the flashers.

Patricia checked the fuel gauge. She had three-quarters of a tank. She wasn't out of gas, then. She would just have to call AAA. She had had the service for years for just such an emergency, but had never used it.

Patricia bent over and rummaged through her purse on the passenger seat. She found her cell phone, flipped it open, and started to dial the number when she noticed a black Chevrolet Impala stopped behind her. The two men inside got out and approached the car. They were wearing masks.

# Chapter Eighteen

**8:00 p.m., North Nashville**

Richard Levi had never really given the process much thought. Before today, he had never thought much about how he had been formed, what made the parts of his body work, who his biological parents were, or what it had taken to make him what he had become. What exactly had he become anyway? The answer was simple, a hired assassin who went by the title UCCIA agent. What was a UCCIA agent anyway? It was just another title for Contract Assassin.

He stood on the observation deck and looked down at the doctors in the operating chamber below. They were performing miracles on the two babies that had just been born, but the procedures were no longer considered miracles. They were just necessary operations required to bring another child into this world as a productive and contributing being.

He looked at his hands, turning them first one way and then the other. He had always thought of them as his hands, his arms, made of the flesh that God had given him. This was his body. It had always been his body. He studied the doctors in the chamber below. They were attaching the infant components. This was just the first step of many that would be performed on the children before they became adults. The infants didn't even remotely resemble what they would become. In a world where perfection was the normal, these children didn't belong, but what they would become did. Over the next several years, and dozens of operations later, they would become part of a productive society. A beautiful, perfect shell would hide their deformities and ugliness. They would never remember any of this. One day they would walk out of the institute and become productive humans in jobs they had been trained for since birth. He knew all this because more that once he had lain on that same table. But they were luckier than he was. They would never know what it was like to be real. He cherished that memory.

The sperm and egg banks were nearly depleted. Just how many more of these operations would there be? A dozen? A hundred? Maybe as many as five hundred? Certainly not many more than that. What then? He was one hundred and twenty years old. That was still young by today's standards. Long ago scientists discovered the brain didn't age like the rest of the body. It even seemed to grow stronger with age. He knew it was possible for him to live forever. There were already many others that were older than he was, some even approaching two hundred. Jerrell Hardman was one of those.

159

How much longer would he live? Would any of them live? Forever? He knew it was possible, but did he really want to live forever? This was the first time he had asked himself that. He suddenly realized he didn't know or want to know the answer.

Later that evening, Richard returned to the caverns. He told everyone to take the night off. They deserved it, and he wanted to be alone. After everyone left, Richard went to one of the offices and sat behind a desk that had been used by one of those people who called themselves the Disciples. Richard studied the papers piled there.

He recalled ancient videos he had watched long ago. At one time man had seemed obsessed with creating artificial beings, robots, androids, or whatever one chose to call them. More than three centuries ago, Mary Shelley had created a character within the pages of her famous book, *Frankenstein*. Dr. Frankenstein had created a monster that was made of body parts robbed from graves. From the pages of that book, that monster had become the subject of innumerable movies and had given birth to dozens of others, monsters to perfect beings that spanned hundreds of years.

He wondered if the authors of those forgotten novels and movies ever realized that one day man would be forced to create real Frankenstein monsters to insure the continued existence of the human race.

Richard studied the backs of his hands lying on the papers. They were so perfect. Was he a monster seeking perfection? Did he really want to continue this existence? He wasn't sure anymore. In Mary Shelley's novel the monster had slipped from the control of his creator and stood grimly over the doctor's death. Wasn't that exactly what was happening now? The monsters had gone back to destroy their creator?

He looked out past the large window across the front of the office. The great cavern was filled with machinery and computers. They could still only guess how much of it worked. None of them really knew how or why the process worked. They knew it just did. They could make slight changes, even call them improvements, but the fact remained they still didn't know how or why any of it worked. The mind that had created this process was a genius.

Tomorrow Jerrell Hardman was going to send somebody back, probably himself. Richard knew this. Wasn't that what it had been about since the beginning? The ones who got away had to be stopped, didn't they? They couldn't be allowed to change things. It would mean the end of Utopia, the end of them all? Would that be so bad? If things really were changed, it might possibly mean none of this would ever happen. But did that necessarily mean the end of his existence? Maybe he would still be born. Only this time he would be a normal baby, from normal parents. He rotated his hands and studied the palms. Perfect. And these hands would be real. Maybe they would even be the hands of a famous artist.

Richard reached a decision. He leaned back in the chair and closed his eyes. He realized he felt better than he could remember ever having felt. It was the right thing to do. It was the only thing to do.

\* \* \*

### August, 1959

"Hey, Sam. Are you going to stand there all night?" someone shouted.

Someone else yelled, "What are you waiting for? Hang the bastard."

Was he dreaming? Had he fallen asleep?

It was dark and there was a stiff breeze blowing. There were a dozen or more shapes wearing white robes and pointed hoods. Shadows danced throughout the gathering while the house and barn burned in the distance. A great wooden cross blazed in a clearing between them and the burning structures.

Richard looked at the black man and then at the rope in his hands. He saw fear in the man's eyes, but there was something else there too. Hate? Rage? Whatever it was caused chills to run up and down his spine. It was a strange feeling because he had never felt anything like it before.

"Hang the nigger," someone else shouted. "Hang them all."

There were other shouts of agreement. Richard heard the excitement in their angry laughter and jeering.

"If you don't have the guts for this, Sam, then give the rope to Eddie."

Richard stared at the hooded man whom had spoken to him in a low, controlled voice. All he could see were the man's eyes, but they were familiar. He realized he had looked into eyes just like these before. Only that other time they had belonged to Jerrell Hardman. For a moment he thought he saw his own reflection in those eyes.

He looked down at his hands holding the rope and then back at the hooded man again. He lifted the rope and started to place it over the black man's head, but he hesitated. No. He couldn't do this. This was not why he went back. This was not why he chose this time period.

"No!" He threw the rope down. "I won't do this. This is wrong, and I'll not be a part of it." He started to untie the black man's hands. He felt this huge muscular man trembling.

With no warning, the one called Eddie struck him with his fist. Richard fell backwards, the dust rising in a dirty cloud. He felt his jaw. He had never experienced anything like that before. Was it broken? It hurt like hell, but there was something about it that felt good.

Eddie picked up the rope and put the noose around the young black man's neck. He was hardly more than a boy. Richard realized what they were going to do. Four other hooded men picked up the rope and started pulling on it. The black man was lifted from the ground. His hands were still tied, but he kicked and fought the tightening noose.

A gunshot exploded out of the darkness. Eddie suddenly released the rope, clutching his chest as he fell in the dirt in front of Richard. A dark red stain had begun to blossom on his chest. Blood came out of his mouth and nose, and he clawed at his chest, gasping for breath. It only lasted a few seconds, and then he was still.

"Put down your guns!" someone in the darkness shouted. "You are surrounded!"

"Like hell we will!"

There was more gunfire. Richard started to get up. The black man held him down with his strong body.

"Stay down!" he warned. "You'll get your sorry white ass shot! The woods are full of crazy whities trying to kill each other."

"Thanks."

There was a battle going on. Richard could see the new arrivals in the light from the burning buildings. It was clear which side he wanted to be on. The men in the white sheets were searching for cover. The fire roared behind them. He and this black man were right in the middle of it all.

"I wasn't going to do it," Richard said.

"What did you say?"

The muscular man was pinning him to the ground, actually shielding him with his own body.

"I wasn't going to put that rope around your neck."

The black man laughed. "Sure you was. You whities are all alike."

"No, I'm not like them. I don't know what's going on here, but that's not what I came back for."

"Where you been all night, man? You whities done kilt everybody in the house. They kilt my sister Sarah Jane, too. You tellin' me you had nothin' to do with that?"

"I didn't," Richard insisted. "I know you have a difficult time believing me, but I don't know what's going on here. I-"

"What's goin' on?" The black man interrupted. "Let me tell you what's goin' on. Them guys in the suits are Feds. Them in the sheets are the good white folk of Selma, Alabama. They don't want us here no more. Them men warned us what would happen if we didn't leave."

162

"Who are they?"

The black man laughed, harder this time. "Look at you, mister! You see what you're wearin'? You're one of them!"

"No," Richard shook his head, "I'm not."

"Then why you wearin' that sheet? Why you helping them hang me?"

"I told you I wasn't going to do that!"

"Sure, and I believe in the Easter Bunny."

Richard tried to get up again. A bullet hit the dirt less than a foot from where they were lying.

"I don't care what you believe! It's the truth. Now, let me up. We have to get out of the line of fire before we get shot."

"Stay down!" ordered the black man.

"You're a yellow-bellied coward, Tingeley!" yelled someone. "You gonna let that nigger tell you what to do?"

"Let me up!" ordered Richard. "We're both sitting ducks out here."

"The name's Talmadge Hollister, and I ain't no nigger."

"I never said you were."

"I ain't."

"Well, it's nice meeting you, Talmadge. What do you say we try to get to that tree over there?"

"I s'pose you' right. Stay low and follow me." Talmadge started to crawl on his hands and feet. Richard followed. When Talmadge reached the tree he looked back. "Come on! Move your sorry white ass."

Richard stood and ran.

"No!" Talmadge yelled. "Get down, you fool!"

Richard heard the gunshot before he felt it. The bullet exploded into his back, the force of it spun him around and threw him to the ground. White pain blasted every nerve in his body.

More shots exploded from all directions. There were flashes in the darkness like lightening in a summer storm. Someone had his arms and was pulling him.

"Hang in there, mister!"

"The name's Richard Levi," coughed Richard, his mouth filling with blood. He tried to laugh, "I guess that was stupid, huh?"

"You got that right," answered Talmadge.

They reached the tree and Talmadge propped him up against the ancient oak. A bullet splintered the bark just above their heads.

"I can't feel my feet, Talmadge."

"Be still. You gonna be alright."

"No," Richard shook his head. "I'm cold and I can't feel anything in my legs. I think I'm dying. This is what it feels like, isn't it?"

"Never died before," laughed Talmadge.

"Look. I don't understand what's happening here." He coughed and spit up a mouthful of blood. "I thought the Fifties were supposed to be a wonderful time. It was after Korea and before Vietnam."

"A good time for white folk, maybe. What's Vietnam?"

"A crazy war that should never have happened. I thought it would be the perfect time. I could come here and start over." He started coughing, and more blood spilled from his mouth.

"Where you from, anyway? You don't sound like you from around here."

"I'm not. It's a long way from here, a very long way." He tried to laugh. It hurt like hell and he only succeeded in coughing up more blood. He tugged at the sheet and asked, "What does this mean, Talmadge? Why am I wearing this sheet? Why are those men wearing sheets and hoods?"

"You really don't know, do you? Them are Klan. Ain't you ever heard of the Ku Klux Klan? The KKK? You one of them, mister."

Richard shook his head, "No. I'm not."

"Then why you wearing the sheet?"

"I can't explain. Do me a favor. Take it off. I don't want to be remembered as being one of them."

Talmadge tugged at the sheet, pulling it over Richard's head. The sheet was soaked in his blood. He tossed it and the hood away.

"It's so cold, Talmadge," he shivered. He wasn't feeling any pain. He wasn't feeling anything except this awful cold.

"Just hang in there."

"This is the FBI!" shouted someone. "Throw down your guns and no one else will get hurt!"

More gunfire answered the request.

"Talmadge?" Richard tried to say his name, but all he could do was whisper. "I'm dying, and I know it."

"I told you you're gonna be okay. Just be still."

"No," he shook his head. "I can feel the numbness and cold creeping up on me," he whispered, finding it very hard to make the words come out. "Before I die, I have to tell you something. I just remembered what's going on here." He coughed again. It was becoming harder and harder to talk. He prayed to God to let him finish what he had to say.

"A lot's going to happen in the future that's going to change what's happening here tonight."

Talmadge started to say something.

"No. Just listen to me. I don't have much time. Things are going to change, Talmadge. Take my word for it. Your people will overcome this prejudice. One day a black man will even be elected president."

Talmadge laughed.

"It's true. When that day comes everyone will look back and wonder what this was all about. Do you know why, Talmadge?"

Talmadge just shook his head.

"Because when that day finally comes, people won't be concerned about what color, what nationality, what religion they are because they'll all have a common enemy. Something is going to happen that will change everything, unless one man is stopped. Listen to me, Talmadge, and remember this. His name is Jason Harding. He hasn't been born yet, but he has to be stopped. He's a scientist. The year is 1995. He's your real enemy. He's going to put something in the water that will destroy everything. Don't let it happen, Talmadge. Promise me you'll remember!"

"I don't know what you're talking about."

"Promise me!"

"Don't let what happen?"

Richard coughed. More blood. He was choking. He couldn't suck in air. He gripped Talmadge's arm as yet another spasm worked its way through his body.

"How will I know?"

"You'll know. Listen to the news. Read the newspapers."

"Oh, man. You got to see this." Talmadge lifted him up.

The Klan members had thrown down their guns. The were holding their hands up and slowly coming out of the darkness. A couple of them had to be carried by the others.

"You fellows okay?"

Talmadge looked up at the man in the dark suit. He was black! A black FBI agent? The world really was changing.

"I am, but this man is in pretty bad shape."

The FBI agent knelt and put a hand on Richard's shoulder. "Help is on the way, buddy. Just hang on."

"That's what I been tellin' him."

Richard looked at Talmadge and smiled. Talmadge was still holding him in his embrace. He saw something in the big black man's eyes that he had never seen before. It was compassion. That was what had been missing. Somewhere along the way, they had lost it. Without compassion, how could the human race survive?

"Stop him, Talmadge. Promise me."

Talmadge nodded. "I promise."

Richard exhaled, but could not make his lungs bring in more air. He looked at the black man in the dark suit and the gentle black man who still held him in his strong arms. His eyes began to cloud over. He could still hear them talking, but he knew he had died.

# Chapter Nineteen

**Sunday, May 7, 4:00 p.m.**

Diane parked the Cherokee in the space vacated by Patricia's Accord, and the three of them got out. She waved to the two FBI agents, but they never looked up. They looked as if they were asleep. Swell bodyguards, she thought.

Phil knocked on the door and heard Jason call out, "Come on in. The door's not locked."

Jason was standing at the top of the stairs, holding onto the banister for support.

"What are you doing out of bed?" Diane asked, and without waiting for an answer she said, "Help him, Phil."

"I have to go. I have to get the disk."

Daren and Phil went up the stairs. They each took an arm and attempted to help him back to the bedroom.

"No!" he resisted, shaking his head. "You don't understand! I have to go now!"

"Don't you think you're a little underdressed?" asked Diane, indicating his gym shorts and the blue undershirt.

"What's wrong, Jason?" asked Phil. "Where do you have to go?"

"They have Patricia. They told me they'd kill her if I don't give them the disk. I have to meet them in one hour."

"Who has Patricia?" asked Diane as Daren asked, "Who are they?"

Diane went to the window and looked out. She should wake up those two stooges down there. They needed to hear this.

"I don't know. Probably those two men that have been following us." He sat on the edge of the bed, the pain in his leg forgotten.

"Are you sure?" Phil asked.

"Who else could it be?"

"Are you sure they have her?" asked Daren. "It could be a trick."

"They let me talk to her. They did something to her car, and it broke down on the expressway. That's when they got her."

"Is she okay?" asked Diane. "Have you told anyone about this?"

"No," he shook his head. "I can't. They said they'd kill her if I told anyone. I have to help her, guys. I have to give them the disk."

"Listen, Jason," Phil sat on the bed next to him and put a hand on his shoulder. "You can't give them the disk."

167

"He doesn't have a choice, Phil," said Diane. She came across the room and stood in front of them. "You don't understand what it's like to love someone, do you?"

"That's got nothing to do with it, Diane. He can't give them that formula. We can't let anyone have that disk. You know that. It has to be destroyed."

"Weren't you listening? He said they will kill her if he doesn't give it to them."

"There may be a way around this," said Daren. He had turned on Jason's computer at the desk near the door and was waiting for it to boot up.

"It's not in the computer, Bill--I mean Daren."

"I guessed that, but I can give them what they want," he grinned.

"How? No one knows the complete formula. I used a special EPA program to write it, and I've never shown it to anyone. Not even you, thank God."

"I know," he laughed. "You never trusted anyone, did you?"

"I trusted Rob-and now he's dead."

"I don't need your formula, Jason. I'll write one of my own. They'll believe they have the real thing. Trust me."

"Trust you? This is Patricia's life we're talking about. We can't take the chance of giving them a phony formula. They'll kill her."

"I never said it would be phony," he said as he began to type.

"I don't understand. The real formula is in my head and on a disk that's safely locked away."

Daren continued typing. Jason watched from the bed as strings of equations spread across the seventeen-inch computer screen.

"Jason, you have to tell us," Phil said. "Where is the disk with the real formula?"

"I'm the only person who knows where it is. I'm the only one who can get it."

"Where's the disk?" Phil asked again.

Jason shook his head. "I can't tell you. I won't."

"We have to help, Phil," insisted Diane as she went to his closet to get him some clothes.

"No. We can't," Phil was shaking his head. "We've sacrificed too much, too many lives already. We can't let anyone have that disk."

"Thanks, Diane," said Jason, "But I have to do this alone. They might be watching us right now."

"I won't let you do this, Jason," warned Phil.

"What are you going to do? Kill me?"

Phil didn't answer and Jason suddenly knew. Of course they would kill

168

him. It was really the only way.

"No one has to die," said Daren. "Not today, anyway."

"What are you doing?" Phil went to the computer and studied the screen over his shoulder. "I've seen this before. Isn't this the-"

"That's right," grinned Daren.

"They'll know your formula is a fake," stated Jason. "I don't care what you do or say, I have to give them the real formula."

"What makes you think they won't kill her anyway?" asked Phil.

Jason stared at Phil. "I won't give them that disk until she is safe."

Diane crossed the room and looked out the window again.

"What's wrong?" Phil was watching her.

"Something's been bothering me. Those two FBI agents haven't budged since we've been here. They can't be asleep. Something's not right."

"Look. Albert is going to show up in a few minutes. I can't tell him about this. I know him. He'll call the FBI, the CIA, the DC police. Hell. He'll probably even call the President."

"I think you should tell him, Jason." Diane turned from the window. "I think all of us should go down right now and tell those two agents everything."

"No," Jason shook his head. "I won't do that. I can't."

"That's right. You can't," said Phil. "Tell us where the disk is, Jason."

"No. The formula isn't worth Patricia's life."

"Why do you think they want this formula so badly?" asked Daren.

"I don't know. I haven't really thought about it."

"My guess is they want to sell it," answered Phil. "To the highest bidder."

"They'd never get away with that."

"Maybe not in this country."

"Take a look at this, Jason." Daren leaned aside so Jason could see the screen. "What do you think? Look familiar?"

Jason got up from the bed and made his way to the computer. He scanned the formula Daren had written. It *did* look familiar. It was very similar to his, only with a few major differences.

"Yes. How do you know all this? I never showed you any of this."

Daren didn't answer.

Jason studied the formula and started asking questions. "What have you done here? How does this work? Why didn't I think of this?"

"It's basically still your formula, only with a few minor changes. This version doesn't depend on bacteria to do its thing."

"Then how does it work?"

"Trust me. It works, and it's safe."

"You can't give them this, Daren," insisted Phil.

"Why not? We *know* this works. Won't it accomplish the same end?"

"We can't give those men this formula."

Daren's expression became serious. "This is what they want, Phil. I don't believe we can fool them with something bogus. This will satisfy them and complete our mission at the same time."

Phil studied the computer screen again. Something about the formula was different. He had seen this exact formula years ago, but something about this was different.

"I still think I should give them the real formula," said Jason.

"No," answered Phil. "You can't do that. You can't ever do that. Daren, you're the smart one here, but you must know we can't give those men this formula. They'd hold the world hostage with it."

"What do we care? If they use it our problem is still solved."

"Is it? If the wrong people get this, how's the future going to be affected?"

"I made a few changes."

Phil studied the formula again. "Here," he pointed to the seventh line on the screen. "That's what is different. What did you do here?"

"The chemical compositions will begin to breakdown in approximately ten hours. After that, it will simply disintegrate. In other words, it will cease to exist. They will have nothing." He laughed. "The formula will be worthless."

"Something's going on outside." Diane had gone back to the window and pushed back the window curtain.

Phil moved across the room and joined her at the window.

"See that boy across the street? A moment ago, he stopped at the car and looked like he was going to say something to agent Johnson. He reached in the window and touched him. Johnson fell forward and the boy bolted and ran. He looked like he had seen a ghost."

The boy was pounding on the door of the townhouse. It opened. He started crying and saying something to the woman in the doorway. He pointed at the FBI car. The woman put her arms around him and pulled him inside. The two agents still hadn't moved.

"You're right. Something *is* wrong!" Phil agreed. "Daren? Finish up that formula and put it on a disk. Diane, help Jason get dressed. I'll be right back."

"What are you going to do?"

"Check on those two agents."

"Phil?"

Phil stopped at the door and looked at her. She was almost silhouetted against the bright light from the window behind her.

"Be careful."

He smiled and winked.

Phil went down the stairs and outside. He didn't say anything as he approached the car from the passenger side. He checked the house across the street. No movement there. The car's front windows were open. Neither man was moving. Johnson was still slumped over the steering wheel. Bricker was facing straight ahead.

The street was quiet, and there was a slight breeze blowing as he approached. Phil carefully reached in and tapped Bricker on the shoulder. The man fell toward Johnson. That was when Phil saw it. The car and the men were covered in blood. Both men's throats had been cut. He felt Bricker's neck. Of course there was no pulse. He was cold as ice. The man had been dead for hours, probably all day.

Phil looked around. No one on the street. He looked at the house across the street again and saw the curtains in a front window move.

He turned slowly and causally walked back to the townhouse, resisting the temptation to run. Opening the door, he went inside and closed it behind him. He leaned against it, breathing hard.

Think, he told himself. You've got to think. What do you do now?

Phil went upstairs.

"We have to get out of here."

"What's wrong?" asked Diane as Phil came into the room. She had just finished putting tennis shoes on Jason's feet. She had had to cut the pants leg off to get the jeans over his bandaged right leg. He was wearing a plain green pullover shirt.

"Johnson and Bricker are dead. Their throats have been cut."

"We have to call the police." Diane went to the phone.

"No." Jason put his hand over hers. "We can't do that."

"My guess is the woman across the street has already done it for us."

"Finished," said Daren and ejected the disk from the computer.

"Good. Now let's get out of here."

"We can't just leave," said Diane. "What about the police? The FBI? What are they going to think?"

"We don't have time to worry about that," answered Phil. He helped Jason to stand. "How about it? You think you can make it to the Jeep?"

"No problem." He looked at Diane. She was hesitating. "I have to go, Diane. I have to do this for Patricia."

"Okay. I'll drive."

Phil and Daren helped Jason down the stairs. Diane opened the door and looked around. She didn't see anyone. She motioned for them to follow and they went to the Jeep and got in. Why did she feel like they were the criminals here? They hadn't done anything wrong. She started the engine and backed out, then put the Jeep in drive. She saw the front door of the house across the street open just as she turned onto the main street and guessed the police probably weren't far away.

"Now, what do we do?" she asked.

"I was told to take a taxi to Haines Point. They told me to come alone and wait by the Sleeping Giant statue. They said to bring the disk. After they have confirmed its authenticity, they told me they would release Patricia."

"Do you believe that?"

"I have to."

"I thought you said you weren't going to give them the formula until you were sure Patricia was safe," said Diane.

"I know what I said. You better pray your version of the formula fools them, because if it doesn't, I'll give them the real one."

"It will," asserted Daren.

Diane stopped at the next intersection, waited for a break in traffic, and turned left. The next light at Thirty-First Street changed to red. She was in the right hand lane. A police car pulled up next to her in the left lane. There were two policemen in the car. Diane smiled at the one nearest her. He was a handsome man, with a tanned face and was wearing dark sunglasses. He glanced at the passengers in the Jeep out of habit. Jason was sitting in the back next to Daren. Phil was in front, holding his breath. This was it, he thought. Busted. Any second now they were going to ask them to pull over and get out.

The light changed. The policeman nodded and smiled back at her as Diane pulled away.

"We have to get out of town," she said. "The police are going to be looking for this Jeep. What if we're not as lucky the next time?"

"Drop me off. I'll hail a taxi. Get out of here while you still can."

"You can't go there by yourself, Jason," said Diane.

"Diane's right," agreed Phil. "You can't trust these men."

"I don't have a choice. Can't you understand? They've got Patricia! The formula just isn't worth her life."

"I understand." Daren handed him the disk.

"Are you sure this is going to work?"

"Positive."

"What if they ask me to mix it for them?"

"Then mix it. I'm sure you're going to be amazed how simple it is."

"Pull over here," Phil said to Diane.

"Why?"

"Just pull over. Jason is right. He has to go alone, and we have to get out of the city."

She didn't argue, pulling over to the curb near the intersection of L and Twenty-fourth Streets.

"What makes you think you can trust those men?" she asked.

"I don't trust them." He studied the disk before putting it in his shirt pocket. "I'll tell them the disk is worthless if I don't show them how the formula works."

"But that's not true," said Daren.

"I know that, but they don't."

"I don't like it, Jason," argued Diane. "These two men don't care what happens to you or Patricia or any of us. They don't give a damn if you get killed."

"That's not true," Daren said from the back.

"Isn't it? Why don't you just tell us the truth? You don't really give a shit what happens to any of us."

"It doesn't matter, Diane. I'm doing this for Patricia." Jason opened the car door.

"Well?" asked Diane. "Aren't either of you going to help him?"

Phil got out and helped Jason to a nearby bus stop bench.

"Do you think you can handle this?"

He shook his head and laughed. "No. My leg hurts like hell and I'm scared to death. They said they would let me go in three days. After they verified the formula. That would be Wednesday. Why don't I meet you on the Mall in front of the Air and Space Museum that evening at seven?"

"What if they don't keep they're end of the bargain?"

"Then you win. Your mission will be completed." He handed Phil a folded piece of paper.

"What's this?"

"Give it to Diane. Chances are if anything happens to me, you're not going to be around for long."

Phil hadn't considered that possibility.

"Tell her to give it to Fenwick. He'll know what to do."

"Nothing is going to happen to you, Jason. We'll see you there," said Daren.

"Why don't we meet you at the Lincoln Memorial? A friend of ours is supposed to meet us there at six on Wednesday."

"Would that be your friend Lauren?" he asked.

"Yeah."

"I'd like to meet her. Tell her how she missed all the excitement."

Phil laughed. "You just be there."

"I will. If I'm not, I guess that's okay too. At least I died for a good cause."

"No one's going to die." Phil got back in the Jeep, lowered the window and said, "Don't do anything stupid, okay?"

Jason just grinned. He sat on the bench until he was sure they were gone. Then he hailed a cab and told the driver to take him to the Trailways bus terminal in Silver Spring.

Twenty minutes later he was standing in front of a wall of lockers near the back of the terminal lobby. He opened one of the lockers and removed a brown envelope. Inside the envelope was a computer disk.

He bent the disk until it cracked and split. The metal protecting the film inside fell off. He pulled the casing apart. Inside was a thin piece of plastic. He tried to tear it, but couldn't, so he crumpled it. He looked around and noticed two young black men standing next to the men's restroom. They were talking and smoking cigarettes. He went up to them and asked, "You got a light?"

"Sure man." The one closest to him took out a lighter and flipped it open.

"May I?" He took the lighter from him and set the plastic from the disk on fire. The two teens watched as he let the disk burn almost to his fingers before letting it drop to the sidewalk. "Thanks." He handed back the lighter.

"What was that about?"

Jason didn't answer. He went outside and hailed a cab. He told the driver to take him to Haines Point.

Now the only copy of the formula was inside his head. If these men somehow found out the formula were a fake, he still had something to bargain with. He briefly wondered if by destroying the real disk he might have sent Phil and Daren back to where they came from--or even wiped them out altogether.

174

# Chapter Twenty

Patricia wanted to wake up, but her mind swam in a foggy mess of memories and nausea. She fought the bile that was coming up in her throat and forced her eyelids open, but they were too heavy and kept closing. She knew she was waking up, and this sick sensation would soon pass, but everything was still a dream. The dream was like quicksand. The closer she seemed to being awake, the deeper into the dream she sank. Her stomach churned. She knew she was going to be sick, but she could do nothing.

The memory of what happened was still deeply submerged in a cloudy dream. She recalled the two men in masks. She remembered one of them pulling her from the car, while the other one gagged and blindfolded her. She remembered the sound of passing cars and how no one had even stopped to help. She wondered if anyone even bothered to call the police? Probably not. People just didn't want to get involved. The two men forced her into their car, and they drove for a long time. She listened for sounds she might recognize. For some reason this seemed important. She had been in the car for quite a while, when the two men suddenly stopped and removed the gag from her mouth.

One of the men held her, and the other one said, "It's time to call your boyfriend."

She heard him punch in the numbers on a cell phone. Before it started to ring, he said, "Tell him only that you have been kidnapped and that you haven't been harmed. Got that?"

The phone was put to her ear just as Jason said, "Hello."

"Jason!" she cried.

"Patricia? What's wrong?"

"Two men. They-"

The phone was jerked from her ear.

"You don't listen very well, do you, lady?" said a different voice. To the other man he said, "Put the gag back on her." Then she heard him say into the phone, "Your girlfriend is okay for now. Do as we say, and you'll get her back in one piece. You go to the cops or the Feds or that boss of yours, and you'll get her back one piece at a time."

There was a brief silence.

"What do we want? I think you already know. Bring the formula with you to Haines Point. Come alone."

There was another silence.

"How long? You just wait. We'll be there." He hung up the phone.

They pulled her out of the car and put her in the trunk before covering her nose with a cloth. Patricia quickly recognized the smell of ether, remembering that awful smell from a childhood operation, back when they still used the stuff. It had a distinctive odor, something like brake fluid.

It took all her will power to keep her eyes open. She saw that she was in a place filled with shadows. Light was coming from somewhere, thin streamers of it, dust particles swimming and dancing in its path. Her head was so heavy she couldn't lift it. She watched the ceiling, studying it. The light danced across the dark, rough wood of the ceiling and down the walls. She imagined the dance of the brooms in a scene from Walt Disney's "Fantasia." The room was in twilight, but there was enough light to see that its walls were made of logs and it was empty of all furniture. She was lying on the bare floor.

Patricia sat up and wrapped her arms around her knees. She rested her chin on her knees and tears suddenly flooded her eyes and cascaded down her cheeks. The floor was rough, cold and damp. Her stomach churned and she was feeling nauseous.

"Oh, God," she cried suddenly and clutched her stomach.

The sour taste of bile rose in her throat, and she knew she was going to vomit just seconds before she actually did. Patricia wiped her mouth with the back of her hand. She couldn't recall the last time she had thrown up. It was disgusting. The stench of it caused her stomach to churn even more. She had to get away from that awful smell.

Somehow she found the strength to stand on trembling legs she wasn't sure would support her, but they did. She remembered once, a long time ago, when she was very drunk. Waking up the next day had been similar to how she felt now.

She staggered backward and leaned against the wall, she looked around the dimly lit room. It was small; barely more that ten feet square. Patricia saw that the light was coming through a boarded-up window. She stayed close to the wall for support as she made her way around the perimeter to the other side of the small room. Boards loosely covered the opening, nailed across the window from the outside. Between the cracks, she could see tall grass and trees. Beyond the trees were distant green hills. The sky was dark blue, nearly cobalt, with piles of cottony clouds.

Where was she? Where were the two men that had brought her here? Maybe they were still out there. She looked between the cracks but couldn't see much of anything.

There was no glass in the window, only the boards covering it. She thought that if she could get her fingers between the gaps in the wood, maybe she could work the boards loose. She grasped one of the boards and worked it back and forth. It was old and rotten and came loose easily with very little effort. She let it fall and began working on another one. This piece wasn't as old and weathered as the first, and didn't budge. She quickly gave up on it and tried the one above, but with the same results.

With at least eight inches between the boards now, she had a better view of her surroundings. She surveyed the clearing around the house. It was overgrown and looked as if it had been deserted for sometime. There was a rusted-out shell of a truck with four flat tires parked by a huge old oak tree to the left of the clearing and an overgrown dirt driveway that looked as if it hadn't been used for sometime. The driveway disappeared from her line of vision to the far left of the truck.

Patricia listened. She didn't hear anything but the sound a light breeze was making through the grasses and the trees.

She turned back to the room and studied it. A door? Two doors. She hadn't noticed them before. She held the wall until she reached the first door. Turning the knob slowly, she pulled it open. A closet. An empty closet. Why should that surprise her? She tried the second door. The knob turned and the hinges screamed in protest as the door opened into the small room.

Patricia leaned against the doorjamb and surveyed the shadows of the large room. There was an old, tattered sofa in front of a huge stone fireplace and nothing else. All the windows were loosely boarded up, but enough light was getting through to let her see just how empty the place was.

There were footprints in the thick dust that coated the floor. Those would likely belong to the two men who had kidnapped her, she thought. There was another door directly across the room. That would probably be another bedroom, she guessed. To the right was a counter and what appeared to be the kitchen beyond. Where was an outside door? She followed the path of the footprints. Still using the wall for support, she made her way around the corner. At the end of a short, narrow hallway was a door. She could see where the dust had been pushed back when it was opened. Trying the knob she found it was locked. Of course. She almost laughed. Had she really expected it to be that easy? She tried it again anyway. No. It was definitely locked.

Giving up on the door, she returned to the big main room and looked around, studying the house's interior. She clutched her stomach again, and tears came to her eyes once more.

"Please God," she cried. "Don't let anything be wrong with our baby."

Patricia wiped the tears from her eyes. She was suddenly angry with herself for not having told Jason. Ever since she had taken that home pregnancy test, she had found one excuse after another for not telling him. She just wanted to be sure. She had convinced herself she should see a doctor first. She hadn't been going to the store the morning that she had been kidnapped. She was on her way to the doctor's office, to confirm what she already knew. Now, she might not ever get the chance to tell him.

"No." she proclaimed and gritted her teeth stubbornly. "I'm getting out of this place. I won't give up. I won't."

The nausea had subsided. Her legs weren't as shaky, either. From someplace deep within she was tapping a reserve of new strength. Adrenaline was flowing. She went to the kitchen, opening drawers and cabinet doors. They were all empty, nothing but rat droppings.

There was another small room just off to the side of the kitchen. The room was empty, but there was another door, a back door. With little enthusiasm, she turned the knob. She heard the click. It had only been locked from the inside. She was almost laughing as she pulled the door open, but boards had been nailed over the opening.

"No! No!" she cried and began banging the boards with were fists.

One of the old boards came loose and fell.

Patricia wiped the tears out of her eyes and studied the opening for a moment. Then she tested the other boards, but they seemed to be solidly attached. She put her head against the boards and was about to start crying again when something stopped her.

Anger swept through her body like a sudden summer storm. Anger at having been kidnapped and drugged. Anger at being imprisoned here. Anger at the two men that were using her as a pawn to get what they wanted from Jason. Anger for being weak.

"No!" she shouted and struck the boards again with clinched fists.

One of the boards loosened. She had felt it. She backed away and studied the opening and the remaining boards that were imprisoning her. She sucked in her breath and using all of her one hundred and fifteen pounds, she threw herself against the weathered boards. They splintered, broke, and came loose. She tumbled through the opening and down the three wooden steps, scraping the skin from her legs and banging her head as she fell.

She couldn't recall ever having felt so much pain, but the only thing she could think of was the baby. She clutched her stomach with bleeding fingers and cried.

"Oh, God! What have I done? What if I've killed my baby?"

In some way she couldn't explain, she knew the baby was alive and okay.

She sat up and looked around. The house was a rustic, ancient cabin, overgrown with ivy, vines, and weeds. There were two smaller structures, equally neglected, and a driveway that came out of the woods to her left and disappeared through the trees on the opposite side. The grass had been trampled in the clearing, but she couldn't tell from which direction the car might have come.

There were none of the sounds she was so accustomed to hearing, sounds that people and machines made, sounds of civilization.

She used this new reserve of strength she had discovered and began walking. She had a fifty-fifty chance of taking the right direction. She just prayed this was her lucky day. She hadn't gone more than a hundred yards when she stopped, removed her expensive shoes and broke the heals off. Slipping them back on, she smiled. It was the first smart thing that she had done.

"That's better."

\* \* \*

"Who was that?" asked Lockner.

"Talmadge Hollister," answered Bowerman, closing the cell phone. "It won't be long now, buddy. Oh, and he said Harding's friends found the presents we left them."

"How does he know that?"

"How the hell should I know? What difference does it make? A few more days and we're going to be millionaires."

"What about the girl?"

"What about her? She can't identify us. We were wearing masks."

"You're just going to let her go?"

"Sure. If she ever gets out of that place. Why not? She doesn't have anything we want, and she couldn't recognize us from jack shit. That cabin is so far out in the boonies, even if she gets out it'll take her weeks to find her way out of those woods. By then, Harding will be dead, and we'll be out of the fucking country." Bowerman started the engine and put the car in gear.

"How do you know you can trust this Hollister guy?"

"I know Talmadge. He used to run the FBI's Richmond field office before he got smart and went into politics. With a little help from a Saudi prince, he's made some pretty smart land investments. The guy is worth a fortune. Believe me, we can trust him.

\* \* \*

179

**Tuesday, May 9, 10:18 a.m., Somewhere in West Virginia**
Phil stood on the edge of the cliff with his eyes closed. A clean stiff breeze pounded his body and rustled through the trees higher up on the mountain. He opened his eyes and gazed out on the tranquil green valley with the wide river meandering through it like a lazy serpent.

This was how God had meant it to be, he thought.

After they dropped Jason off, they knew they should leave Washington. When the bodies of the two murdered FBI agents were discovered, there were going to be a lot of questions--questions they couldn't answer right now without jeopardizing everything. What could they say, anyway? The truth would be easy enough, but it would sound absurd to anyone in his or her right mind. They couldn't risk it, anyway. No. The only logical thing to do was to disappear for the next few days.

They couldn't stay at Josh's cabin, either. That would probably be the first place anyone would look. No. They had to disappear until after they heard from Jason.

Sunday night, before leaving Washington, Phil had gone to an ATM and withdrew the maximum cash available in a single day. That had been about three hundred dollars. They had to disappear for at least three days, and Phil had fifty dollars in his wallet. They had to get rid of the Cherokee and find another vehicle. Diane said there was cash at Josh's cabin, in a safe in the bedroom. He had, among other things, five thousand dollars in it.

They drove to the cabin later that night. Diane knew the combination. Apparently Josh trusted her with everything. Phil said something to that effect. She just said, "Why shouldn't he?"

They left the cabin at seven-thirty the next morning and drove to Martinsburg, West Virginia, where they parked the Cherokee in the mall parking lot. They locked it and walked to the McDonalds on highway 9 across from the mall entrance. There was a used car lot next to the bank across the street.

"I'll buy the car," said Diane. She had all the money in her purse. "I've never done this before, but it shouldn't be too difficult."

"Be careful," warned Phil.

"I can take care of myself."

"I'm sure you can. Just be careful."

"Oh, I will. I'm doing this for Josh, you know."

"Sure."

"I am."

"I know you are."

"I don't give a damn what happens to you."

"I know that too."

"You do?"

"You've told me often enough. You say you love him, and you hate my guts. I believe you."

She just looked at him. She was suddenly at a loss for words.

Twenty minutes later she returned. Daren and Phil hadn't seen her until she slid into the booth and laid the keys on the table.

"Any problems?" asked Phil.

"Why should there be? He had something he really wanted to get rid of, and I had the cash. I just pretended to believe all the crap he was giving me and didn't argue about the price."

"What did you get?"

"You'll see." She looked at the both of them across the table and smiled. "That man didn't even ask to see my driver's license. All he could see was the money. I bet he thinks he got the best of a woman trying to buy a car without a man along."

"I'm impressed. You're good at this," said Daren.

"I'm learning. Lately, I've been surprising even myself." She laughed. "I think we should get out of here now. I know a place where we can rent a cabin for cash. It's just west of Berkeley Springs. They have about a dozen cabins scattered on the western slopes. This time of the year they should have a few vacancies."

"We had coffee and a muffin while you were gone," said Phil. "Do you want breakfast before we go?"

"Just coffee. Order it for me while I go to the restroom?"

"Sure."

"With cream and sugar."

"Okay."

She met them at the door a few minutes later. Phil handed her the coffee.

"Careful," he warned. "It's really hot."

"That's the way I like it."

"So where's this car you purchased?" asked Daren.

"It's not exactly a car." She sipped the coffee and stepped down from the curb.

"What does not exactly a car mean?" asked Phil.

"That it's a truck. That truck."

She was pointing across the parking lot at a faded brown pickup truck with a cracked rear cab window. The truck was ancient, even by 1995 standards.

"The salesman said it's a 1963 model. A real classic. He said it was

181

owned by a little old lady on a farm."

Phil opened the passenger door and looked in. The paint on the metal dash was faded and peeling and the plastic upholstery was cracked and torn.

"You did good." He looked at her across the empty cab and winked. "No one will be looking for us in this. That's for damn sure."

"That's exactly what I was thinking," she smiled.

"I guess this means I sit in the middle," said Daren.

"The middle or the back, your choice." Diane sipped her coffee.

Daren looked at the empty bed and shook his head. "I'll take the middle."

"Then let's go." She climbed in and started the engine. It coughed, died, and coughed several more times before catching. The valves rattled, and the entire truck vibrated. "Purrs like a kitten, doesn't it?"

They rented the cabin at nine-thirty that morning. Three days, two hundred and twenty-five dollars cash, no questions asked.

* * *

Phil had left Daren and Diane sitting on the deck of the small cabin they had rented. He needed to be alone for a while. It felt good to walk, and the wind was cold and clean against his face.

For the first time he realized what it was that was bothering him. He had never given it any thought, and that was why it probably surprised him now. If-no, *when*-the formula was destroyed, what was really going to happen? Were they just going to cease to exist? Was his whole life going to be wiped out, just like that?

"What are you doing?"

Phil jerked and turned. Diane was sitting on a large rock about thirty feet up the slope.

"How long have you been sitting up there?"

"Not long. I was wondering where you had gotten off to, so I went looking."

Diane lifted her camera, aimed it at him, focused, and clicked.

"What was that for?"

"Something to show Josh. He's never going to believe any of this."

"Why tell him?"

"Why shouldn't I?"

"You're right."

"So, what are you doing?"

"I just needed some time to think."

"Don't tell me you're developing a conscience. Don't you think it's a little late for that?"

"I know you hate me, Diane. I don't blame you."

She was studying his face through the camera. She didn't say anything.

"I really do have a conscience, you know."

"Sure." She pressed the shutter and clicked off two more pictures.

"That's not why I wanted to be alone, though." He sat on a fallen tree and looked out across the peaceful valley. "I've killed so many people, it has become almost automatic. We kept telling ourselves it was something that just had to be done, it was God's work."

She put the camera down and laughed.

Phil turned and looked up at her.

"I know. I guess we were just using God to make what we did seem right. But someone had to do it, and we had all the necessary resources."

"It's always the same, isn't it?"

"What do you mean?"

"People are always using God to make something wrong seem right. You may fool other people. You may even fool yourself, but you sure as hell won't fool God. Personally, I wouldn't have the courage to even try."

"You're right, but that's not why I wanted to be alone."

Phil stood and walked a little farther down the mountain before stopping and leaning against a large maple.

"We say we believe in God. So when we die, we should go to Heaven. Right?"

"I'm pretty sure that's how it works." She stood and moved a little closer.

"What if we don't die? What happens then?"

"Everybody dies."

He turned and looked up at her. She saw that his face was wet with tears.

"Not everybody, Diane. Maybe you. Maybe Josh. But as far as Daren and Lauren and I are concerned, we're not going to die."

"That's stupid. We all die. And if we believe in God, we go to heaven, and if we don't, then we go to Hell. It's as simple as that."

"No, it's not that simple."

"What's not that simple? Dying?"

"We're going to cease to exist, Diane. Do you know what that means?"

"I don't understand." She was seeing a side of him she had never seen before, or maybe she just hadn't taken the time to look past what he had done.

"If Jason is killed, you will get your precious Josh back."

"So you've told me."

"Have you ever wondered what will happen to us?"

"Not really."

He laughed. "I guess not. Well, I never gave it much thought before, either." He turned away and seemed to study the distant, mountainous horizon. "I'm never going to see heaven. I just realized that today. The heaven we thought we believed in. Jesus and God. The true Disciples. We'll never see them or any of that."

"That really is stupid, you know. If you believe in God you go to heaven."

"If you die. If Jason is killed or the formula is destroyed, we will simply cease to exist. We will have never lived, so how can we die? If we've never lived, how can we go to heaven?"

"That can't be right." She came down to him, stopping less than a foot away. "We're missing something. There's got to be more to it than that."

Diane put her hand out and touched his. It was the first time they had touched since that first night. Phil wrapped his fingers around her small hand and squeezed it gently.

"No. That's just how it is. You know? If I had thought about this before, I don't think I could have gone through with it. I'm still tempted to go looking for Jason, to protect him, to let him go through with it. Put the damn formula in the water. I'll go on living. I'll keep on being a real person." He laughed. "Maybe not completely real, but at least I'll have a soul. Then I remember I only have ninety days here. The process is going to reverse itself and send me back. At least in the future, I have a chance to die and go to heaven."

Diane looked at her hand in his. When had Josh last held her hand? Had she ever seen him cry? Had he ever bared his soul to her like Phil was doing? Did he even believe in God?

She took her hand out of his and brushed his cheek with her fingers before kissing him lightly on the lips. Phil gently, hesitantly, embraced her and returned her kiss. It wasn't a kiss of passion, but of desperation. She put her arms around his neck and held him. Without realizing what she was doing, she heard herself whisper against his ear, "I love you."

Had she really said that? No. She couldn't have. She didn't love this man. She loved Josh.

Diane pulled out of his embrace, turned and went back up the mountain toward the cabin. She had gone only a few feet when she fell. Instead of getting up, she stood on her knees and began to sob. What was happening? What was she feeling? She suddenly felt Phil's hand on her shoulder, and his touch made her tingle.

"No." She brushed his hand away. She got up and continued on up the mountain without stopping or looking back. "It's not fair. You can't do this

184

to me."

Phil watched her go. If he had known what she was feeling he would have realized he was just as confused as she was.

He looked up at the sky through the canopy of big trees and cried, "My God! Why are you doing this to me... to us?" But he was sure God had nothing to do with what was happening here.

# Chapter Twenty-One

"How do I read this crap?" Bowerman asked when the file appeared on the screen of the portable computer.

"You don't have to." Jason said.

"So how does this fucking formula work?"

"First you let Patricia go."

"You're not in a position to be making requests." Bowerman stared at him.

"Give us how this works and we'll let the woman go." Lockner said. "You have my word."

"Why should I believe you?"

"You'll just have to trust us. Look, all we want is the formula. We don't want to kill anyone."

"What about the two FBI agents?"

"Don't know anything about it," said Bowerman.

"Sure. Look, you have the formula. I'll show you how it works after you let Patricia go. When I know she's safe-"

Bowerman laughed.

"I'm asking you," said Lockner. "Just show us, and I promise nothing will happen to her."

Bowerman said, "You're in no position to bargain. Like the man said, you have our word. Give us what we want and we let the girl go. What could be simpler than that?"

Lockner added, "Look, Harding, I don't want to hurt your Patricia. Mix up this formula of yours. We'll test it, and if it works we'll let her go.

Bowerman added, "If it doesn't, neither of you will be going anyplace."

"If I do this, what about me? What do you plan to do with me?"

"I suggest you don't worry about that right now," answered Bowerman. "All I will promise is no harm will come to the woman as long as you cooperate."

"Just do it," said Lockner.

Jason studied Lockner's face and realized he believed him. He really didn't have any intentions of harming Patricia. "Okay, but we're going to need a few things."

"Like what?" asked Bowerman.

"Give me some paper and I'll make a list."

Lockner handed him a small notebook, and both men watched as he listed the ingredients and other items that he needed.

"This is everything you will need in order to prepare a test sample."

"This is it?" Bowerman asked.

Jason just nodded. "What did you expect?"

"All the commotion this thing has been making, I expected a hell of a lot more than this."

"Sorry to disappoint you. It's really quite simple."

Lockner scanned the list just to make sure he understood everything he needed. "Where do I go to get this?"

Jason told him the different stores he would have to go to for the ingredients and the equipment.

\* \* \*

**Tuesday, May 9, 2:30 p.m.**

"Wait here," Hill told the cab driver. She opened the back door, got out, and went up the several steps to Susan's townhouse. She was dressed in a USAir navy pants suit.

She hoped Susan was ready to go, because they were late. Their flight was in one hour, a one-day turn-around to Atlanta. She rang the bell three times before Susan finally opened the door.

"What's this?" Hill asked when Susan appeared in a white terry cloth bathrobe. She wasn't wearing makeup and her hair wasn't even combed. She looked like she had just gotten out of bed. "Don't you know we fly in one hour?"

Susan shook her head. "No."

"We always go to Atlanta on Tuesday. You know that."

"I can't go, Hill. I'm sorry."

"Sorry. Tell it to Morse. What's wrong? You sick? Did you see that doctor like I suggested?"

"Not yet. I don't feel good, Hill. I don't think I should be flying today . . . maybe not this week."

"You know how Morse gets. You really should have called her."

"I know. I will. I promise."

"Well, it's a little late now. I'll try to cover for you. I've got to go, but I'll call you tonight. You go see that doctor, okay?" She went back down the steps and got in the cab. "National Airport, and hurry." She stuck her head out the window as the driver was turning the taxi around and called to Susan, "Don't forget to call Morse. Maybe she won't write you up. Hell, maybe she won't fire you."

"I will."

"Do it now. Okay?"

"I promise."

Lauren closed the door. She went to the sofa and sat down. She couldn't stop thinking about Dan. She remembered his touch, his kiss, how he laughed, and their wonderful sex. She couldn't think about anything else. She had let her feelings get in the way of the mission.

Why wasn't she acting like the soldier she had been trained to be? She was useless in this state. As long as she remained in this condition, she wasn't going to be of any use to anyone. She never placed the ad in the Washington Post, even though she had seen the other two in the Sunday edition. There was one for Phil and one for Daren, which meant they both would be there. Maybe she could just show up and tell them she couldn't get it placed in time.

Eighty-five days. She had grown up thinking she would live forever, now she had only eighty-five days. Maybe even less. She wanted to live. She wanted to see Dan again. She had to see him again.

The doorbell rang. Hill had come back to talk her into flying today, she thought. Or maybe just to make sure she called Morse. Who the hell was Morse, anyway?

Lauren opened the door. There stood Dan, grinning and holding an armload of flowers. She didn't know what to say, so she didn't say anything.

"Are you going to ask me in or tell me to take a hike?" He laughed.

She stepped aside and motioned for him to come in.

"I'll take that for a yes." He came inside and held the flowers out to her.

She took them, smelled them, and smiled. No one had ever given her flowers before.

"I know I shouldn't have done this. You probably never wanted to see me again," he began. "But you left so suddenly I didn't even get to say good-bye. I had to see you again, Susan. I had to."

Lauren dropped the flowers and put her arms around his neck. She kissed him gently, hesitantly, then harder. He returned her kisses, embracing her tightly.

"God, I missed you," he said against her neck. "I missed your smell, I missed your touch. Don't you know how much I love you?"

She suddenly stopped kissing him and backed out of his arms. There were tears in her eyes.

He tried to put his arms around her again, but she pushed them away, shaking her head.

"What's wrong? What did I do? I shouldn't have come. I knew it, but I came anyway."

"You didn't do anything, Dan. You did everything. You made me fall in love with you."

He laughed. "Then nothing's wrong."

"No." She shook her head. "Everything is wrong. You don't know. You can't know. I love you, but that's wrong because it's not fair to you."

"I don't understand."

She went to the sofa and sat. Dan followed and sat next to her. He started to take her hand. She moved away.

"I have less than three months, Dan," she said suddenly. She looked at him, the tears flowing.

"What are you saying? You're dying?"

"If only it were that simple." She looked away.

Neither of them said anything. The silence was long and heavy.

Lauren wiped the tears from her eyes and faced him again. "I want you more than I've ever wanted anything, but it's too late. It was always too late for us."

"No. I-"

"I'm not Susan, Dan," she said suddenly. "I'm not the person you think I am."

He laughed. "You're joking, right?"

"No. My real name is Lauren Jefferson, and in three months I'll cease to exist."

"I know. It's some kind of witness protection? That's it, isn't it?"

She shook her head.

"Cause if it is, I'll go with you. I can change my name also. We can become Mr. and Mrs. Smith. I don't care. I just want to be with you, Susan. Lauren. Whatever you want to call yourself. I want to marry you."

"I know you do."

"You do?"

"Hill said you told everybody in Florida." Lauren had to laugh.

He grinned. "What's the problem then? You said you loved me."

"You can't go with me, Dan. The Susan you see here will still be here, but what's me, what's in here-" She touched her forehead, "will cease to exist. I'm Lauren Jefferson, Dan. As crazy as it may sound, I come from another time. I'm a soldier, and I'm on a mission to save the human race."

"You're right." He stood and walked around the room. "That sounds pretty damn crazy. Beats anything that I could come up with." He laughed.

"Sometimes truth is stranger than fiction," she said. "Now that you know all this, you must understand why I can't let this go on."

He sat in the chair on the opposite side of the room.

"So? This mission. You say you're here to save the human race?"

She nodded.

"What are we going to do, blow ourselves up? Is the Earth going to be hit by a giant meteor? I know. There's going to be a great flood." He shook his head and laughed. "No. God said he'd never do that to us again."

"It's something much more subtle, Dan." She got up and went to him. She knelt, put her hands on his knees, and looked up at him. "We're here to stop a man from doing something that the people of this time will praise him for. In my time, the same man is cursed the world over."

He shook his head. "I'm having a hard time with this, Susan."

"Lauren. My real name is Lauren."

"Okay, Lauren. You need any help? I can help you."

She laughed. "I told you that you would think I'm crazy. I don't blame you."

"What am I supposed to think?"

"I'm not asking you to think anything. I'm not even asking you to believe me, Dan. What I have told you is true. If you want proof you can come with me Wednesday night."

"What's happening Wednesday? The "People Not of This Time" meeting?" He laughed.

"Something like that." She looked into his eyes. She didn't smile.

He suddenly had this terrible feeling everything she had said was true.

# Chapter Twenty-Two

Mammoth Cave echoed his rage, intensified his curses through its vast corridors. Jerrell Hardman was demolishing the office most recently occupied by Howard Levi, the office he had used until last night. No one had ever seen this man, the head of the UCCIA, lose control like this. He was screaming and cursing and throwing anything he could get his hands on. The fifteen technicians and scientists that had reported in this morning cowered in the recesses of the mammoth chamber that housed the transference equipment. Not one of them wanted to get too close to this man. Even when he was in control of his emotions no one knew what to expect; they certainly didn't trust this current state he was in.

The doors of the restored elevator slid open and a technician in a long white lab coat stepped out. He heard the commotion from the Transference Chamber and immediately ran in that direction. A wall of scientists and techs in white lab coats blocked the wide entrance. He put his hands on the shoulders of two men and asked, "What's going on? Has something happened to the equipment?"

There was a muffled explosion in one of the offices followed by the hiss of electricity. The chamber lights flickered briefly.

A man turned and said, "Haven't you heard? Mr. Levi took a trip last night."

"So? What's going on here?"

"Not just any trip. *The* trip."

"You're kidding."

"Look for yourself. That's him over there on table five."

The man turned his body sideways so there was a break in the wall of coats. The tech slid through so he could get a better view. There were two bodies lying next to each other, the woman Levi had enticed with promises of wealth on table four and next to her was Richard Levi. The three tables with the Disciples had been removed from the room earlier the day before. Twelve tables remained.

Hardman came out of the demolished former office of the Disciples. The room was in shambles. Nothing but the desk remained recognizable. He went to table four and five and paced back and forth in front of the two motionless bodies. No one dared approach him or say anything to him. They just waited, fearing for their immortal lives, for this storm to pass, as it surely must.

Hardman abruptly ended his pacing and stood in front of Richard Levi's body. He bowed his head, stroking the still face.

"What do you suppose he's thinking?" someone whispered.

"You don't want to know," someone else chuckled.

The new arrival leaned forward to see who had made that last remark, but all the faces were wearing the same expression.

Hardman gently stroked Richard's face, first with one hand and then both. Now, he cupped Richard's face in his hands and said too softly for anyone to hear, "You disappointed me, my old friend. You are the only one I ever trusted." With those last words said he suddenly snapped Richard's neck. The sound of the artificial spinal cord and the plastic vertebrae in Richard's neck breaking seemed to explode through the silent, endless caverns of Mammoth Cave.

"Now, you can lie here forever, Comrade. This body we gave you will never answer another command."

"There's your answer," said someone.

The new arrival watched, silently observing the perfect faces of the technicians.

Hardman stroked Richard's face one more time, turned around, and looked at the faces of his audience. Suddenly he smiled, his entire mood seeming to change instantly. He pointed to two of the techs in the middle of the wall that blocked the chamber entrance.

"You two. Come here."

They instinctively stepped backward.

"Remove these worthless pieces of trash. We have work to do."

The two techs knew exactly what to do. Hardman had unintentionally chosen the same two that only a few days ago had taken away the other three, the ones who had called themselves Disciples. They disconnected all the apparatus and wiring from the two bodies. Since the tables were on wheels, they each rolled a table across the big room to the exit. The white coats separated and let them through.

Hardman seemed to study the remaining ten tables. He moved past them, checking the computers and monitors. When the two men returned a few minutes later, Hardman moved toward the loosely gathered group and stopped a few feet in front of them.

"First, I want all but one of those tables disassembled."

"We shouldn't do that sir," said a senior tech. "We're still learning how they work."

Hardman ignored him. "All monitors and computers, all devices associated with those tables, will be disabled also."

"That would mean over half this equipment would have to be disabled," added someone else.

"There will be only one more trip taken from this room."

"Sir? May I say something?" asked a group leader.

"Make it brief."

"It is not wise to disable the other tables. We can not recreate this technology as yet. Give us another week. I beg you."

"Maybe you do not understand." His smile was menacing, deadly. This man was unpredictable. "This equipment will not be used again after today."

"What if something goes wrong with the last table?" he added. "There won't be a back-up."

"I don't care. There is one last opportunity to set everything straight again." He looked at them, studying their faces. "Someone tell me. How many of you are actually needed to operate this equipment?"

"Just one of us," said someone.

Hardman walked within the gathering, studying the perfect artificial faces. "Who said that?"

A man nervously stepped forward. "I did, sir."

"You will stay then. The rest of you may now leave."

No one moved.

"Well. What are you waiting for? I said leave us. Now."

The techs and scientists exited the large chamber and gathered in front of the elevator. The chosen one didn't move. He watched the others go, some whispering their protests. The elevator was summoned, the doors opened, and the fifteen men entered. The doors closed, the elevator hummed, and ascended the restored shaft.

"What is your name?" asked Hardman.

"Reynolds, sir."

"I counted fifteen. Was that everyone?"

"Yes, sir. Mr. Levi dismissed the others two days ago."

"Well, Reynolds. It looks like sixteen is going to be your lucky number."

Reynolds wasn't feeling very lucky.

"Are you just going to stand there? We have work to do. I want these other tables disassembled immediately. There will be only one left operational."

"That would mean no one else would be able to transfer."

"I am aware of that." Hardman smiled.

"What if something goes wrong?"

"We have been through this already. I'll take that chance. I will not allow anyone else to tamper further with the past."

"Very well." He saw that arguing with Hardman was futile. "I am prepared to go whenever you say."

Hardman laughed. He went to the man and slapped him on the shoulder.

"What makes you think you're going anywhere?"

"I thought that was why you asked me to stay. That was why you said it was my lucky day."

"I am the only one going anyplace. I merely need your assistance."

"Sir?"

"You heard me. Someone has to clean up this mess. Someone a long time ago once said if you want a job done right, then do it yourself."

"Are you aware this is a one way trip, sir?"

"I know that."

"If we disassemble all the other tables, no one else will be able to go back. What if something happens during transport or after you arrive?"

"Nothing will happen. But if it does, so be it. I am prepared to make that sacrifice. For every person that goes back to the past, our present is altered to some degree. We'll never know just how much has been changed already." He smiled again. "Well, Reynolds, shall we get started? We have some work to do here."

"Yes. Of course, sir."

"This body of mine, as is yours, is almost entirely robotic. The only thing left that is real are the eyes and the brain. When I go back I'll be an immortal among mortals. After I have set things right again I can simply relax and enjoy life for the next two hundred years."

"Not really, sir."

"What's that?"

"Your immortality doesn't accompany you during the transfer."

"Of course it does."

"No, sir. Only your thoughts, your mind, are transported. Your body remains behind. Just like the others."

"Are you saying I'll be just like one of them?"

"You will be exactly like one of them. According to what we know you will be transported to a man's body between thirty and forty years old. We can't even control the location. About the only thing we can control is the time. We can transport you to an exact year, month, even down to the minute."

"But you will know where I appear."

"Yes, but we can't do anything about it. There are so many things that might go wrong. What if you appear in a man's body that is about to have a fatal accident? Perhaps it may even be a man who is paralyzed or has cancer. You really should consider letting me take this trip in your place. Just tell me what to do."

Hardman laughed. "I don't think so. I'm the only one left who I trust to do the job right. Show me which machines are not necessary."

Reynolds went to one of the monitors. "This one is connected to table six. The other six monitors are wired independently to the other tables. They may be disconnected. The computers are all necessary for the transference process."

"Then we will disconnect those monitors and unassemble the other tables."

An hour later they were finished. All unnecessary equipment had been removed from the chamber and piled in the elevator lobby.

"It's time to prepare the transport," Harding said. "Calibrate my arrival time for the first of February, 1995. That gives me five months to locate Jason Harding and help him along. Since my body is going to be real, I would prefer the summer, but I guess that will be just one more sacrifice I'll have to make."

"Everything is set, sir." Reynolds went to the only remaining table. "When you lay down on the table, this gold band will move forward encircling your head. A force field will support your head inside the ring, so don't worry about the needles. They never actually touch you. When you press this button, the transfer will begin. This other button is the abort."

"What exactly what will you be doing?" Harding asked.

"Nothing, actually. I will be monitoring the process, but I don't need to do anything else."

"Then everything is ready to go?"

"Yes, sir."

Hardman removed his laser gun and shot Reynolds between the eyes. It happened so fast that Reynolds didn't even have time to react. He crumpled to the floor, brain dead.

Hardman went to the elevator and blasted the controls. He changed the intensity of the laser beam and fired at the doors. The metal melted and fused together. He looked at the pile of components that had been the tables and monitors. Without changing the setting on his gun, he fired at the pile until it was a melted, shapeless mass. He went back to the entranceway. He changed the setting of the laser again and fired at the ceiling. The stones collapsed and filled the elevator room with dust and debris.

Even if they got the elevators working and somehow got the doors open, all they were going to find was a mass of rocks. It would take anyone some time to get past this, if ever. He seriously doubted if anyone would put out the effort. Even if they did, all the tables but one had been destroyed. He had

197

been told each of the tables could only be used once. The time traveling would end here.

He went to the table, laid down, and the wide gold and copper band moved forward. He felt the electricity tingling around his scalp. He put his hand over the button.

He looked around the deserted room one last time before pressing it.

# Chapter Twenty-Three

**Tuesday, May 9, 4:30 p.m.**

Even before she left the house, she had a nagging feeling she was choosing the wrong direction. The farther she walked, the stronger that feeling became. The dirt road had become barely more than a wide path. Patricia thought she was keeping to the main road, but with each split the road had seemed to become narrower and less used. She had been walking since early morning, thinking she was staying on the main road, but somewhere along the way, maybe more than once, she had chosen the wrong direction. Maybe there had never been a right direction.

She came to a section of the road blocked by several fallen trees. Looking for a way to get around the trees, she noticed for the first time how overgrown the road had become. Her first thought was to turn around and go back in the direction she had just come, but she quickly decided that would be foolish. She had no idea how far in the wrong direction she had come, or how many wrong turns she had made. She decided the only logical decision was to continue on in the direction she was going. She had to come out someplace. A highway and civilization might be just up ahead. On the other hand, she might be miles from anything and just going deeper into the woods.

She listened to the wind blowing through the trees and birds chirping. The sound of running water. It was so peaceful here. Running water? Yes, a stream or a river. The sound was coming from just up ahead.

She climbed over the trees and started to run. Several yards down the overgrown road it widened into a grassy clearing. She stopped when she reached the clearing and just stared at the wide river. There was nothing but trees visible on the other side. She looked in both directions. Nothing. Her legs suddenly became weak and buckled. Collapsing in the grass, she started to cry.

\* \* \*

**Tuesday, May 9, 5:00 p.m.**

"That's it," said Jason. "You have the formula. I've shown you it works. Now, will you let me go?"

"First we have to see someone," said Bowerman. He glanced at Lockner. "There's rope in the barn. Take him out there and tie him up while I make a call."

"Is that really necessary?"

"Sorry, but we don't want you taking any walks while we're gone."

Jason's hands were already tied behind him. Bowerman took him by the arm and guided him up the wooden basement stairs to the kitchen. Jason quickly took in everything, the kitchen cabinets, a stove, a door, and the phone on the wall next to the door.

There was a small room off the kitchen. As they passed through it, he saw a washer and dryer and an ironing board propped against a wall, nothing else. He wondered where the people were that must live here. Had they been killed?

Jason almost fell going down the three steps to the dirt walk. His leg was throbbing. It was hurting like hell and had started to bleed through the bandages. He leaned against the handrail, taking the weight off the injured leg.

"I can't make it," he said.

"What's wrong?"

"My leg. Look at it."

Bowerman examined it briefly. "You can make it," he said, and gripping Jason's arm, pulled him along.

"Wait," Jason resisted. "Just give me a few seconds."

Bowerman looked around the deserted yard. "A couple of minutes," he said impatiently.

Jason sat on the second step and looked around. Three big oak trees stood between the house and the barn. A dirt driveway circled around the trees, the wooden frame farmhouse, and paralleled a white wooden fence over the hill and out of sight. The farmhouse had two floors. It was white with red shutters, not a very big house.

"That's it." Bowerman pulled him to his feet. "Time to go."

Bowerman half supported him the rest of the way to the barn. Inside, he shoved him against a large beam in the center of the barn. The inside of the barn smelled of stale hay but nothing else. It evidently hadn't been used for some time.

Jason couldn't bare the weight on his leg any longer. He slid down to a sitting position. Bowerman started to pull him up.

"I can't stand any more," insisted Jason.

Bowerman shrugged, "Suit yourself." He wrapped the rope around him and the beam and tied it securely. He then tied Jason's feet together.

"Is all this really necessary?" Jason asked.

Bowerman laughed, "Probably not."

"You have the formula. Why don't you let me go?"

"Not yet. Tell you what. We'll talk about it when we get back."

"You have no intentions of letting me go, do you?"

Bowerman hesitated and Jason knew the answer.

"I didn't think so."

Bowerman knelt and checked the ropes.

"If you let me go I swear I won't say anything."

Bowerman just laughed. "That's what they all say."

"I mean it. Look at me. I'm not in any shape to go running off anywhere. By the time I find my way out of here you two will be long gone."

"Who says we're planning to go anywhere?"

"I just figured. Look, you don't have to kill me. I won't say anything. I swear"

"Sure. But who said anything about killing you?"

"That's what you're planning on doing, isn't it? I mean, after you make sure I've really given you the formula, of course."

Bowerman didn't answer. He checked the ropes one last time, stood and went to the doors.

"Don't go anywhere, now," he said just before closing the barn doors.

Jason tugged on the ropes and worked his wrists back and forth. With every movement the ropes seemed to tighten more.

"This is a fine mess you've gotten yourself into," he said to himself. "Even if they don't intend to kill you, they sure as hell will when they discover the formula is a fake." Then he remembered Daren said it would be ten hours before the formula broke down.

He thought about Patricia. Where was she? Had they really let her go like they said? He wanted to believe it, but he didn't trust them. Had they ever had any intentions of letting either of them go?

* * *

### Tuesday, May 9, 5:15 p.m.

They met at an abandoned stone quarry in Gainesville, Virginia, just ten miles from the farmhouse.

A big black man opened the rear door of the black Limousine and motioned for Bowerman and Lockner to get in. They looked around, checked out the two beefy black men standing guard, then got into the back of the car.

"Good evening," said Talmadge Hollister.

"Soon to be even better," smiled Bowerman, handing over the disk containing the formula."

Talmadge was wearing an expensive charcoal gray suit and dark glasses.

"This is it? This is all you've brought me?" He took the disk and studied it.

"What did you expect? A book?"

"I expected more than a piece of plastic."

"Don't worry," assured Bowerman. "The formula is on the disk. We've seen it."

"Yeah," added Lockner. "We even had Harding brew up a sample to test." He handed Talmadge the quart container that was three quarters full of blue liquid.

"How do I know this is the real formula? It just looks like colored water to me."

"Give us some credit, Talmadge. We tested this shit. It works."

Lockner asked, "Do we get our money now?"

Talmadge was sitting in the seat opposite them. He studied Lockner for a minute without answering. To Bowerman he said, "So show me."

"That's exactly why we brought the bottle. So you can see for yourself," said Bowerman.

Talmadge was still studying Lockner. "Is this the man you told me about?"

"My partner. Yes."

"Evan Lockner," said Lockner. "And I already know who you are."

"Oh?"

"Yeah. I saw you on television. You're that senator that's been on the news lately. You've been trying to shut down the EPA."

Talmadge laughed. "That's not completely true. The EPA does some wonderful things. They are just a little too free with the taxpayers' money. I think it's time to pull in the reins a little."

"Whatever," said Lockner.

"This formula Harding has been working on ..." Talmadge held the jar up and studied the blue liquid. "I don't have as much faith in it as the EPA."

This time Lockner laughed. "That's bullshit. You're paying us a million bucks each to steal it for you. That sounds like a lot of fucking faith to me."

"Let it go, Evan. It's none of our business." To Talmadge, he said, "Personally I don't give a flying fuck what you do with the formula. I just want the money."

"Well, I care." Lockner didn't want to let it drop. "I killed a man to get this formula. So I'd like to know why the senator wants it so much."

"It doesn't matter, Evan. It doesn't concern us."

"Like shit it doesn't."

"Bowerman's right," said Talmadge. "Why I want the formula and what

I plan to do with it doesn't concern either of you. Now, let's discuss the fate of Jason Harding."

"What do you mean?" asked Lockner.

"Don't worry about Harding," answered Bowerman. "We'll take care of him."

"I do worry about Harding. You *do* remember our deal?"

"Of course I do," Chad said.

"What deal?" Lockner looked at Talmadge and then at Bowerman.

"Mr. Hollister offered us a bonus to remove Harding."

"Why? We have the formula. Isn't that enough? Haven't we killed enough people?"

Talmadge shook his head slightly. "As long as Harding is alive, the formula can still be reproduced and distributed. Harding must be eliminated. Call it insurance. I must be assured this is the only copy of the formula."

"I don't like it, Bowerman." Lockner shook his head. "I don't like all this killing. You never said we'd have to kill anyone."

"Shit happens," shrugged Bowerman. "We've both killed before. It's nothing new to either of us."

"But those were the bad guys."

Talmadge smiled. "What makes you think Harding isn't one of the bad guys?"

"Bullshit. The guy is honest as a Sunday school teacher."

"Trust me. You have no idea."

"Trust you? Why should I trust you? You're a politician, for Chris-sake."

"Enough of this talk," said Talmadge. It was clear he was getting irritated and losing what patience he had. He opened a portable computer that was lying on the seat next to him and turned it on. He slid the disk into the drive and asked, "How do I access this disk?"

"Harding said he wrote it in something called Word Perfect."

"That's a word processor." He loaded the program and brought up the file. "I don't understand any of this. I suppose it looks legitimate. I think I would like to see a test, though." He motioned to the door. "Gentlemen." He set the computer aside and opened the door on his side of the car.

"Sure," said Bowerman.

Bowerman and Lockner got out and came around the car. Talmadge looked around. There was a puddle of muddy, stagnant water in a ditch near the car.

"Will it work on that?" he asked.

"It's supposed to," answered Bowerman.

"How much?"

"Harding never said. I guess it doesn't matter."

"Let's hope not." He poured a quarter of the liquid into the murky water.

The three men watched and waited. It took only a few seconds before it started to change.

"Very good."

"So where's the money?" Lockner asked impatiently.

Talmadge laughed. "Come back to the car."

Inside the car, Talmadge accessed the Swiss bank where the majority of his fortune was located. He entered his password and account numbers. A minute later he looked up at them and smiled. "You have just become very wealthy men. Now, about Harding."

"He'll be taken care of," said Bowerman.

"When I know he is dead, an additional two hundred and fifty thousand dollars will be wired to each of your accounts."

"I still don't understand why Harding has to die," said Lockner.

"It doesn't really concern you, but I will tell you anyway. When I was just a teenager, a white man saved my life. The KKK had a rope around my neck and they were going to hang me. This man kept them from doing it and got himself killed in the process. Before he died, he told me about the formula. I owe that man my life. I made him a promise that night, and I always keep my promises."

"You don't have to explain. Just consider it done," said Bowerman. "You have my word on it."

Talmadge laughed. He laughed hard. "I have your word. Okay. I want Harding dead by tomorrow morning."

"You got it."

"Good. Now, let's conclude this business," Talmadge smiled. "My client is going to be most pleased with your work. This formula is worth more than all the oil in his country."

"You said it was worthless," said Bowerman.

"I said something is wrong with the formula. I never said it was worthless. To you, it's worth two and a half million. That's all that should concern you."

* * *

### Tuesday, May 9, 6:15 p.m.

"I'm glad that's over," said Lockner.

"Yeah, but you did your best to screw it up."

They were on their way back to the farmhouse.

"We're not really going to kill Harding, are we?"

"I gave my word," said Bowerman. "Don't you want the extra two hundred and fifty thousand bucks?"

"The million is okay by me. Let's just get out of here."

"You don't understand, Evan. I gave my word. Harding dies, and then we leave the country. I didn't kill the woman, but Harding has to go."

"I don't like it. I don't like all this killing."

"So you said. It was you who killed Robert Williams. Or don't you remember?"

"That was an accident. I didn't mean to kill him."

"Like I didn't mean to kill those FBI agents."

"Bullshit. We chloroformed them. They were asleep. You know you didn't have to kill them."

"Yeah, I know, but it was easy as shit, wasn't it?"

"You're really enjoying this, aren't you?"

"The killing was what I liked best about my job," he answered. "When I was with the FBI, there just wasn't enough of it."

"I still don't like it."

"I tell you what. We'll wait until tomorrow. In the morning we'll go back to that farmhouse, kill Harding, and burn the place. Then we get out of the country. You can send for Marge and the kids after you get settled in--if you still want them."

"What's that supposed to mean?"

"You're a millionaire, old buddy. Things change when you got money."

\* \* \*

**Tuesday, May 9, 11:00 p.m.**

Talmadge Hollister sat behind the big cherrywood desk in the library of his Middleburg, Virginia country estate. The big house was quiet; the vastness of it seemed to swallow up sounds. He didn't need this big place any more and often contemplated selling it, but then he would remember how much Amanda, his wife, had loved it. He knew he could never sell. Her memory was still alive here. Her spirit walked the halls and her scent filled the interior. She had died in her sleep in the master bedroom and was buried in the family cemetery near her sister and mother. No. He could never abandon her.

"What should I do, Amanda? Do I give Omar the formula? I know what you would say. You would tell me to listen to my conscience. Well, I don't think I have a conscience any more. I sold that along with my soul a long time ago."

Talmadge got up from the desk and went to the bar where he poured a glass of seven-year-old scotch. He downed it all at once and started to pour another but changed his mind. He turned back to the desk. The half-full bottle of blue liquid and the disk were sitting there. For a brief moment, he thought he saw Amanda's reflection in the big window behind the desk. He must have imagined it. Amanda was dead. She had been dead for almost eight years now. It was about the same time, or shortly thereafter that he had sold his soul to Omar Amah.

He went back to the desk, sat in the plush chair, and stared at the two objects. Did he have a choice? He had already accepted Omar's money. What would happen if he refused to deliver the formula? Men had been killed for a lot less. No, he had to give him the formula.

Did he really believe what Howard Levi had said nearly forty years ago? Maybe he hadn't heard correctly, or maybe the man was a psycho. After all, people couldn't really travel through time. It was just impossible. Still, he had known about Jason Harding and the formula. How else could that be possible? Could he have been right about other things also? Maybe it was all just bullshit? He probably imagined it all? Maybe it had even been a dream that had taken on a degree of reality over the years.

If it was real, perhaps he hadn't heard correctly. Maybe it was the man, not the formula. Maybe the formula was okay. Didn't he owe it to the human race? The formula would end pollution for all time. How could he destroy something like that? Who was he kidding? He was doing it for the money. More importantly, he was doing it because he was afraid of Omar Amah.

Talmadge loosened his collar. Since that night so long ago he had never been able to have anything tight around his neck. Sometimes he could still feel the rope choking him. And he always remembered that mysterious man who claimed to be from the future. The memories were too vivid not to be true.

Talmadge leaned forward and looked closely at the blue liquid. If this worked, and evidently it did, then it was worth a fortune. Could he destroy it to keep a promise he had made all those years ago? Was it really as dangerous as Levi had said?

Omar Amah was responsible for his accumulated wealth. His fortune was a result of some shrewd and maybe not so legal land investments. Omar Amah also contributed generously to his election campaign and was a close friend. Without him, he would never have amassed such a net worth. How could he refuse this request? Omar had already paid him fifty million dollars to secure the formula. Did he dare to turn him down and just throw that kind of money away all to keep a promise made nearly forty years ago? There was only one answer.

For better or worse, there was only one answer. He turned the desktop computer on, dialed a secure number, and transmitted the formula.

# Chapter Twenty-Four

**Wednesday, May 10, 8:30 a.m.**

Patricia awoke suddenly, sat up and looked around. Had it been a dream? She wasn't sure. She searched the trees and brush but saw nothing. The river was calm and there were geese flying overhead. She had spent a restless night by the river. She had tried to stay awake, but sometime during the night she had fallen asleep.

Something had happened to Jason. She couldn't explain what she was feeling, but she knew something had happened to him. She felt it.

Pushing herself up, she stood and stretched. There wasn't a part of her body that didn't hurt. She was about to start back down the dirt path when she heard the sound of a motorboat.

* * *

**Wednesday, May 10, 8:45 a.m.**

Dan found Lauren out on the deck. She was leaning against the railing and watching the ducks in the small pond below. She was wearing a thin nightshirt and nothing else.

"What are you thinking?" He put his arms around her from behind and kissed her neck.

She turned around in his embrace and put her arms around his neck and kissed him.

"Nothing," she said.

"Don't want to tell me, huh?"

"No. Really. I wasn't thinking about anything."

"Well, I've been thinking. What do you say we run off to the mountains for the day?"

"You know I can't, Dan."

"We have all day. Why not? You're not meeting your friends until six."

"Why don't we just wander around the city? I'd love to see what Washington was really like."

"That's what you really want to do?"

She smiled and kissed him again. "There's something else."

"What's that?"

"I'd like to go back to bed and have the same kind of sex we had in Florida."

209

"That I can handle," he grinned.

"Are you sure?" she smiled mischievously.

"I can only try."

Dan took her hand and they started back inside. Lauren stumbled as they were crossing the threshold and fell. Dan caught her just in time to prevent her from hitting her head on the doorjamb. He pulled her up and embraced her, hugging her close to his chest.

"What's wrong?"

"I don't know. I felt dizzy, strange," she said, and suddenly pushed herself out of his arms. Her expression seemed to change. "Who are you?"

"I'm Dan, Lauren."

"Lauren?" She looked around, confused. "Something has happened, Dan. No," she shook her head. "I don't know you. This is my apartment. How did I get here?" She looked at Dan's face again, studying his face. She seemed to recognize him. "I know you."

Dan grinned. "Thank God. You had me worried for a minute."

"You're passenger 21A. Where's Hilary?"

"I'm Dan, Lauren. Dan Sanderson. What's wrong?"

"I'm not Lauren. My name is Susan Hensley, and I'm supposed to be in a plane bound for Tampa. You better start explaining or I'm calling the police."

Dan suddenly realized what was happening. Lauren was disappearing--or had already gone. Somehow Susan had managed to reclaim her body.

Susan looked up at him with those same beautiful eyes, but he realized Lauren was no longer there. Susan was back, and she had no idea who he was and how much he loved her.

\* \* \*

### Wednesday, May 10, 8:45 a.m.

Phil was walking in the meadow when Diane caught up to him.

"I was looking everywhere for you. You've been avoiding me."

Phil didn't look at her. He kept walking.

"I was restless. I couldn't sleep. I've been out here since before daylight, just walking around."

"I need to talk to you."

He was walking fast, and she was trying to keep up.

"About what?"

"Will you stop? I can't keep up with you."

He stopped abruptly and faced her.

"Look, Diane. I'm sorry. I should never have kissed you like that. I don't know what happened."

"I think I do. I've been thinking about what you were saying."

"I said a lot of things I shouldn't have."

"No." She took his hand. "You made me open my eyes. You made me realize I don't love Josh, and I don't think he ever loved me."

"You said you hated me."

She shook her head. "I also told you I love you."

"Don't say that, Diane. I'm going to be gone soon, and you'll have Josh back."

"You don't understand. I don't want him back." She put her arms around his neck and kissed him. "It's you I want. I don't want you to go."

Phil felt her tears on his face. He embraced her so tightly he could feel the beating of her heart.

"I have to tell you something," he said. "I don't know when it happened, but I fell in love with you. It's the best thing I've ever felt. For this, I'll be eternally grateful."

"I love you, Phil. I'll always love you."

"I've been thinking. I don't believe we're just going to cease to exist. We're not going to die, either."

"I don't understand."

He laughed. "I think I'll still be born. If the world changes I believe there's still going to be a place in it for me."

"I hope you're right."

"I wonder what it will be like. The world is going to be totally different. There are just so many questions I can't answer, but I seriously believe there's still going to be a place in it for us."

"Do you remember when we were outside at Denny's last Saturday morning? God! That seems like a lifetime ago, doesn't it?"

"I was pleading with you to stay, and you finally agreed."

"I told you I was staying for Josh. Well, that wasn't completely true."

"I don't understand."

"I didn't either, at the time. It's just that I thought I loved him. Now, I know different."

He put his arms around her again, and she laid her head against his chest. She was listening to the wonderful sound of his beating heart, Josh's heart, when something happened. His heart seemed to skip a beat. She jerked and backed out of his arms and stared at him.

"Diane? Jason is dead."

"No." She shook her head. "No!" she cried.

211

Josh looked at her and at his surroundings.

"Diane? Where are we? How did we get here?"

Diane didn't answer right away. She just stared at him for a long time. Josh reached out for her, but she backed away.

"We came here to say goodbye, Josh. It's over."

"Over? I don't understand. Where is here?"

She wiped the tears from her eyes, turned her back to him.

"I don't love you any more, and I don't believe you ever loved me."

"That's not true."

"I think it is. Goodbye, Josh." She walked away without looking back.

"Wait, Diane!"

* * *

Daren was watching the news when a special bulletin interrupted. "Jason Harding, a scientist with the Environmental Protection Agency, was found at a deserted farmhouse early this morning. He was lying unconscious outside a burning barn and had been shot twice. Incredibly, Mr. Harding was still alive when he was discovered by a caretaker, and he was airlifted by medivac to Baltimore Trauma Center."

The announcer paused, putting his finger to his ear.

"We have just learned that Mr. Harding-"

Daren got up and ran to the door. He saw Diane running up the hill. She looked like she was crying.

"Phil!" he called. "Jason is d-" He never finished.

Bill stumbled and fell through the open door. He sat up and looked around, confused. What was happening? A second ago he was walking down a busy sidewalk in Arlington. How did he get here?

* * *

Albert Fenwick drove to Warrenton after receiving the call from the Virginia State Police. A local fisherman on the bank of the Rappahannock River had found Patricia. She was bruised and cut and hadn't eaten for over two days. Her clothes were dirty and torn, but she still smiled when she saw him come through the door.

She stood as he approached, and he hugged her tightly.

"My dear. My dear. We all thought you were dead."

"Where's Jason?" she asked. "I told them to call Jason."

Albert bowed his head. "I'm sorry, Patricia. Jason's not coming."

212

"Why not? What's happened, Albert? What's wrong with Jason?"

He embraced her again. "I'm truly sorry, Patricia."

She pulled out of his arms and just stared at him.

"They found him at a deserted farm near a little town called Catlick. He was unconscious and lying in the dirt outside of a burning barn. He had been shot twice. A medivac was called in, and he was flown to the Baltimore Trauma Center."

"But he's going to be okay, right? I've got to go to him, Albert. Can you arrange it?"

"He never regained consciousness, Patricia. He died at 8:47 this morning."

"No. He's not dead!" she cried. "Take me to him, Albert. I have to see him. I have to tell him!"

"Tell him what?"

"That I'm pregnant. That I'm going to have his baby."

\* \* \*

One week later, in a palace in Saudi Arabia, Omar Amah discovered the formula he had purchased from his close and trusted friend, Senator Talmadge Hollister, was a fake.

Three days later, a body was found washed up on a beach on the Dutch side of Saint Martin. It was eventually identified as that of Chadwick Bowerman, a former FBI agent.

About the same time that Bowerman's body was washing up on the beach, a maid discovered Evan Lockner in a hotel room in the Grand Caymans. He had apparently put a gun to his head and killed himself. There was an unfinished note to his wife on the desk.

The two incidents appeared to be unrelated.

Senator Talmadge Hollister's body was discovered floating face down in the Potomac on June Third. He had just celebrated his fifty-eighth birthday.

On June Twenty-seventh, members of the EPA team discovered Daren's gift to Jason, on the computer in Jason's townhouse. It was the formula that would end pollution for all time.

On July Fourth, the formula was introduced into a small creek near Berkeley Springs, West Virginia.

# Chapter Twenty-Five

**February 1, 1995, Washington, DC**

Jerrell Hardman stared at the gun in his left hand and the plastic bag in his right. His hands were dark brown, too brown for a tan, and the plastic bag was filled with a white substance. Looking around, he saw that he was in what appeared to be some sort of abandoned warehouse. There were six men surrounding him. They were all dark skinned and pointing antique guns at him.

Hardman looked at the gun he was holding and the bag in his other hand. What did it mean?

"Don't make this difficult, Sourers," said one of the men. He had a gold ring in his left eyebrow and also one piercing the right side of his nose. He had big lips and uneven teeth.

"This is a mistake," said Hardman. He was surprised at the scratchy sound of the voice than came from his throat. He seemed to have been transported into the body of a sorry specimen of a human. He tried it again. "I said, this is a mistake. I'm not who you think I am."

"There's been a mistake, all right." One of the men took a step forward, the only one that wasn't holding a gun. "But you're the one who made it."

A smaller man came up and said, "I say we waste him, Benny. We take the coke he has left and dump his sorry ass body in the river."

Hardman dropped the gun and the bag and held up his hands. "Listen to me, damn you. I said this is a mistake. My name is Jerrell Hardman."

"The only mistake is you," said Benny.

"I am not Sourers," Hardman said in the strongest voice that he could force out of this little man's throat. The sound still came out weak, scratchy, and pathetic. "I didn't do anything."

Benny laughed. They all laughed.

"Whatever this man did, I had nothing to do with it."

"You fucked me, Sourers. You fucked us all. You know what that means?"

Hardman didn't say anything. It was useless arguing with these ignorant men. They were obviously men of little intelligence.

"First let me say I liked you, Sourers. I trusted you. But you fucked me. You fucked me good. No one fucks Benny and lives to brag about it. You know that?"

Hardman still didn't say anything. What could he say? Anything he said was probably just going to make things that much worse. His mind was racing. There had to be a way out of this. He briefly wondered if things could get any worse.

"I'm going to kill you. I know you know that, cause you ain't that stupid, but first I want to know what you did with the money."

"I don't know anything about your damn money."

Benny grinned. He moved to within a foot of Sourers. He put his face so close to Hardman's that he could smell the man's breath. It reeked of sweet-smelling spices and garlic.

"I think you do. The cops don't have it, so you must have stashed it someplace. Tell us where it is, and I'll make this easy. I'm still going to kill you, but I'll make it quick. Don't tell me, and I promise it will take you a long time to die."

"I don't know what you're talking about! I told you. I'm not Sourers. My name is Jerrell Hardman."

This time Benny laughed. He gripped Sourers' jacket with both hands and lifted him until his feet barely touched the floor. He suddenly tossed him across the room. Hardman hit the wall and indescribable pain shot through his body.

He was angry more than afraid. This weak little pathetic body didn't have the strength he needed to fight these men. It was time to use his brain.

"Do you think I'm that stupid, Sourers? Is that what you think?"

Hardman shook his head. There had to be a way out of this. Think, he told himself. Think.

"Forget about the money." Benny took the .45 from the man next to him and pointed it at Sourers.

"Wait." Jerrell held up his hands. "We need to talk about this! I have an idea."

"The waiting is over, Sourers."

Hardman closed his eyes and heard the gun explode. He jerked and clutched his chest. The bullet had missed. He was still alive. Was he immortal, after all?

There was more gunfire.

Hardman opened his eyes and saw Benny stumbling toward him. The gun was still in his hand, but there was an enlarging red spot on his chest. He fell to his knees.

There were more shots. Hardman heard sirens and thought how the sound hadn't changed much down through the centuries. Rescued by the police, he thought. He almost laughed. Jerrell Hardman or Sourers, or whoever he was would live to see another day.

With extreme effort, Benny lifted his hand and aimed the gun at Sourers. "Drop the gun, Edmonds."

Hardman saw two men standing in the large open doorway, the sun silhouetting their shapes.

"Your boys are dead, Edmonds. Give it up! Make this easy on yourself!"

"Screw you," he said so softly that only Hardman could hear. He looked at Hardman and said, "You're going with me, Sourers. I'll see you in Hell."

Benny pointed the gun and squeezed the trigger. A shot exploded and for the second time in less than five minutes, Jerrell thought he was dead. Suddenly, Benny's body fell forward across his legs. He didn't move. Hardman shoved and kicked the massive body away and pushed himself up.

The two men stepped out of the sunlight and moved across the room. Hardman saw there were at least four bodies littering the dirty floor. The two men kicked the weapons away from the bodies and nudged them with the toes of their shoes. None of the shapes moved.

One of the men put handcuffs on Hardman's wrists and said softly against his ear, "I hope I'm there to see you fry, you sorry bastard."

"Billy Ray Sourers," The other policeman said. "I arrest you for the murder of officer Charles Gibbs. You have the right to remain silent. You have the right to a lawyer . . ." He proceeded to read him the Miranda rights, something Hardman had forgotten existed.

This was what he came back for? To spend the rest of his life in jail?

"You're making a mistake!" he said as the two men were guiding him through the big open doorway. "I tried to tell them. I'm not Sourers."

One of the men laughed.

Hardman heard a gunshot. It could have been a vehicle backfiring, but it wasn't. Hardman felt the bullet slam into his chest a fraction of a second later, and he went limp in the two men's hands. They knelt beside him, drawing their guns, but there wasn't anyone to fire at.

Jerrell Hardman struggled with the words. "I'm not Sourers," he insisted. "This was a mistake."

"What was that, Sourers? You say this is a mistake?"

Hardman looked at the two men, and his expression changed. He looked confused. He held up his cuffed hands and then felt his chest. He looked at the blood on his hands.

"I'm shot?" Sourers said with his last breath.

"No shit," one of the policemen laughed.

Jerrell Hardman vanished and Billy Ray Sourers died. They both left this world in the way they had lived it. They both had lived by the gun and at least one of them had died by it.

217

# Epilogue

After a long hot and dry summer, August was showing little indication of change. The rainfall for Morgan County, West Virginia, was two inches below normal for July, and with no rain in the forecast, the Cacapon Creek was at least a foot below normal. The shallow river flowed peacefully within its high banks, making it a perfect day for a relaxing canoe ride down the scenic stream.

Phillip slipped the oar smoothly through the water as the canoe glided along the still surface. Margaret, his wife of seven years, was sitting in the front of the canoe, and their two children, Samantha and Jaime, sat between them. Today was Samantha's birthday. She was six. Her birthday just happened to be their anniversary. She had been born exactly one year after they were married. Jaime was a year and four months younger.

This river held a lot of memories for him. Some of those memories were good and some were unbearably sad. He and Margaret had been married just a little ways downstream in the very park where it all began. The place was now called the Jason Harding Memorial National Park. His father was murdered for the formula that ended pollution for all time, the same formula that was poured into the polluted water of the Cacapon Creek on July Fourth, 1995. When he was five his mother, Patricia, died in a hit and run car accident less than five miles from here. They never caught the person that hit her. His godmother Diane Kimball, a freelance photographer for National Geographic, raised him. The two of them had traveled around the world more than once before he even turned sixteen. He hadn't seen her for over two years. The last he heard she was someplace in the Australian Outback. She was over sixty and still riding horses and sleeping in tents.

Phillip leaned forward and whispered in Samantha's ear, "Look honey. Do you see the family of beavers?" He pointed across the water to the other side of the narrow river.

Samantha nodded eagerly. "I see them. I see them. Oh, Daddy! They're so beautiful."

Phillip laughed.

Momma beaver sat up when she heard Samantha laughing and looked around. She seemed to notice the four humans in the boat for the first time and quickly gathered her offspring and disappeared into the water.

"What beavers?" Jaime asked. "I didn't see any beavers."

Jaime tried to stand up, but Margaret grabbed him.

"Sit down, Jaime. You're rocking the boat."

"Be quiet, Jaime," Samantha said. "Maybe they'll come back."

"I tell you what. How would you like to go play in the park?" Phillip suggested.

"Oh, can we, Daddy? Can we?"

"I want to play in the park." Jaime said. "I want to play in the park too."

Phillip laughed, guiding the canoe to a ramp where several small boats were moored. He and Margaret helped the children out of the canoe. Then he pulled the canoe to the shore and up onto the bank.

The two children ran up the grassy bank with Margaret close behind. They were all laughing, and he knew he had made the right decision to come here today. What better place could there be for his family to be together than where it all began?

Philip smiled at the sound of their laughter.

When he came up the bank, Margaret put her arms around his waist.

"Thank you."

"For what? I don't remember doing anything."

"For just being you."

Samantha and Jaime had found the swings.

There were a few cars in the parking lot, but Phillip didn't see any other people. It looked like they pretty much had the park to themselves.

"Do you mind if we go over to the monument?" he asked.

"Of course not. It's been a while since we've been up here."

They held hands and walked to the larger-than-life bronze statue of his father. It had been erected here on the first anniversary; one year after his father was killed.

Margaret was staring at the bronze face that gazed out across the river.

"I wish I had known him," she said. "He must have been a really great man."

"I don't know. I suppose he was. My Godmother used to tell me about him and the man I was named after. Sometimes I have the strangest dreams. It's like I am with him... like I'm that man she was always talking about. She loved him, you know."

"Loved who?"

"The man I was named after. His name was Phillip Rollins. She said he came from the future." He laughed. "Sounds like she might be a little crazy, doesn't it?"

"Why do you say that?"

"From the future? Come on. That sounds crazy even to me. One thing though. She never married. Whoever this man Phillip Rollins was she loved him. I mean she really loved him."

He kissed her on the lips. "Do you ever wonder what this place was like before?"

"Before what?"

"You know. Way back in 1995."

"Oh. You mean before your father's formula was poured into the water."

"Yeah. Do you realize because of him there is no more pollution. He got rid of it all."

"He did a wonderful thing," she said.

"And was killed because of it."

Philip Harding read the words on the bronze plate at the base of the statue again. He knew them by heart and understood them even less.

"I've read these words a thousand times or more, and I still don't understand what Mother was trying to say. She must have really loved Dad. I feel cheated because I never really knew either of them."

He read the words again.

*Out of the future,*
*There is hope;*
*Out of the dusk a shadow,*
*There is a spark;*
*Out of the clouds a silence,*
*Then a lark;*
*Out of the heart a rapture,*
*Then a pain;*
*Out of the dead, cold ashes,*
*There is life again;*
*Out of the past,*
*There is Tomorrow's Child.*

In memory of Jason Harding
October 7, 1960 to May 10, 1995

Printed in the United States
1154700005B/1-24